A voice began howling in protest at the back of the chapel . . .

All heads turned to espy an outraged Snow prancing down the aisle, waving his tail like a flag.

His destination appeared to be the earl. Lord Hadley stepped hastily forward to shoo away the animal, dropping the wedding ring in the process. While Jerry retrieved it, David scooped up the hissing cat and told his uncle to proceed.

As the point had arrived to place the ring on Paige's finger, David handed the startled bishop the cat while he carried out this action. Paige was barely concealing her mirth, and to Kit and Cornelia's horror, burst out laughing at the sight of Snow clawing the clerical vestments. Throughout the rest of the ceremony, Snow looked on, purring contentedly, from the comfortable position in the crook of his mistress' arm.

As the final words were said, David kissed his wife full on the lips. The sensation was so pleasurable that the length of the kiss exceeded what was called for. Paige stepped back, breathless, looking at him in confusion, and encountered a gaze that was no more steady than her own . . .

D0378560

Temporary Wife

Samantha Holder

WARNER BOOKS

A Warner Communications Company

WARNER BOOKS EDITION

Copyright © 1985 by Carol Burns and Deborah Jones

Warner Books, Inc.
666 Fifth Avenue
New York, N.Y. 10103

 A Warner Communications Company

Printed in the United States of America

First Printing: April, 1985

10 9 8 7 6 5 4 3 2 1

To the memory of Georgette Heyer

Chapter I

THE sudden lurching of the coach prompted the smaller of the two ladies occupying it to glance uneasily at her companion and exclaim, "Miss Paige, I am frightfully worried about this snow. We have this day been stuck in two snowdrifts, and I am afraid even your remarkable Jack Coachman will not be able to extract us from the next one."

Her elegantly dressed traveling companion narrowed her exceptional green eyes and expostulated, "Kit! Stop being such a goosecap! *Miss* Paige, indeed! As I was 'Paige' to you when we romped together in the woods of Waverly, I am 'Paige' to you still."

Then, seeing the look of consternation on her friend's pleasant, freckled countenance, she softened and said more gently, "Your calling me 'Paige' would please me; indeed it would."

Kit smiled at her and replied, "You know I could not refuse to please you, my dear Paige."

These words served to further vex the strong-willed Miss Paige Undershaw, who had hoped that her friend's financially straitened circumstances would not alter their easy, confiding relationship. At least that was what Paige had hoped when two years ago, on the death of Kit's profligate father, she had asked Kit to reside as her

1

companion at Waverly. Unfortunately, Kit's arrival coincided with Paige's decision to dismiss, and not replace, her tale-carrying abigail. Kit immediately took it into her head that *she* was to fill that bothersome woman's position. Explain as she might, Paige was unable to convince her childhood friend that what she wanted was an intelligent, convivial equal—not a fawning servant.

Suppressing her annoyance, Miss Undershaw decided to apply her considerable understanding to their present predicament. They had left Surrey nine hours ago and by now should have been sipping tea in front of a cozy fire in Park Place with their bosom-bow, Cornelia. Instead, an unprecedented blizzard had them inching their way along the London road only halfway to their destination, and what little daylight there had been was fading rapidly. As she shifted her feet for warmth, she encountered the bricks that hours ago had helped reduce the chill—but now only added to her discomfort and annoyance. She sighed as she resigned herself to putting up for the night at the next coaching inn. What a disagreeable thought! Most probably the fireplace would smoke and the sheets need airing.

Never one to let herself sink into the dismals, Paige recollected that a discussion of anticipated delights usually revived her spirits; so she turned the conversation to the object of their journey. As she leaned over to tuck the fur-lined traveling rug around Kit's skirts, she patted her companion's plump hand and asked, "Will it not be wonderful to see our dear Cornelia again? It has been over three years since we were last together at her nuptial celebration." Observing the tears that suddenly sparkled in her sensitive friend's large hazel eyes, Paige remembered that the purpose for their visit was not a happy one. Lord Bragdon, dead! It was still inconceivable that such a notable whip could have had his life snuffed out in a carriage accident, leaving Cornelia a childless widow at six and twenty.

"Dearest Cornelia! How *can* she be managing?" Kit

asked in a trembling voice, as the vision of that beautiful lady, resplendent in her wedding finery, swam before her brimming eyes.

"*That* we shall soon know, but I should think she manages quite well," Paige replied thoughtfully. "Though," she reflected, "her missive conveyed that she deeply felt the loss of her 'dear Tracy'—and yet her desire for us to join her seemed to originate more from a wish for cheerful affection than from a need for solace. I collect that what she most requires is a buffer to counteract the morbid moanings of her in-laws."

With her customary candor, Paige continued, "The dowager Lady Bragdon, silly gudgeon that she is, was never adequately perceptive to comprehend that the wife of her favorite son brought to the match an excellent portion, great affection, and friendship—but not a heart fully engaged."

"Whatever can you mean?" gasped a shocked Kit. "Surely Cornelia—that is, Lady Bragdon—felt all that a wife should properly feel!" As often occurred with Paige in completely inappropriate situations, laughter sprang to her expressive eyes. She asked, with barely concealed amusement, "My dear, whatever can we spinsters know of the proper feelings of a wife?" Paige contrived to be in earnest and very much hoped that her twitching lower lip would not betray her in the dim, snowy twilight.

"Oh!" choked Kit. "You cannot compare *our* situations, Miss Paige—oh, I beg your pardon—*Paige;* no one can regard *you* as being on the shelf. I care not for *Dorcas's* perception! What with three eligible offers in your first Season, and one each year since . . ." To support this undeniable observation, Kit continued, "Why, only within this last fortnight! Did I not walk in, untimely, to the withdrawing room (and I had not the least notion of what I would observe, or I never should have done so) to find Squire Singleton on his very knee before you?"

As the memory of the denouement of this unwelcome

suit presented itself in such vivid recollection to Paige, she could no longer contain her mirth and briefly covered her bow-shaped lips with the green velvet muff that exactly matched her eyes. Barely in command of herself, she clasped Kit's hand in merriment and said, "I apprehend that I have not thanked you adequately for your welcome intervention. I fear I would have gone beyond all limits of propriety by laughing outright at Squire Singleton's portly, pink face. Verily, my thought at the moment of his declaration was of my envy of his complexion."

"I collect that your sister-in-law was vexed that the suit did not prosper," Kit mused, having a more serious view of the importance of making an eligible connection.

Paige, though charitable, could not take exception to this observation. "Ah, yes," she reflected. "Dorcas would fancy seeing me away from Waverly, so poor Richard would be more submissive to her every selfish whim. I daresay I have enjoyed confounding her schemes to alter my brother's situation—and my own."

"Damn it!" shouted a raspy voice (male, they apprehended), as the coach lumbered to a halt. "We're for it now!" Jack Coachman's abbreviated speech continued, barely audible to the coach's occupants. "Big drift . . . coach stuck. . . . Nags done in. . . ."

The coach's door was clumsily opened, and its tenants were greeted with the advice that they were to undertake a personal inconvenience: "Inn straight ahead. . . . Walk . . . Jemmy and me bring trunks. Best you walk on, now. . . ."

Paige, who was the first to exit, found her fashionable bonnet blown back from her glossy brown mane of hair by a sudden gust of wind. Icy snowflakes stung her face and heightened the color of her already rosy cheeks. "This is going to be rough," she muttered to herself as she surveyed the deep white blanket of snow separating them from the welcoming lights of the inn. "Especially for Kit, whose inches are even fewer than mine."

Knowing that her companion would deem it unfitting for her "mistress" to help her through the drifts, Paige resigned herself to subterfuge and, in an uncharacteristically tremulous voice, requested Kit's arm for support on their journey.

The prospect of at last being of service to her normally self-sufficient friend caused Kit to forget the fears that had risen in her bosom when the coach halted and to step boldly out of the carriage.

Three-quarters of an hour later, the innkeeper's stout wife was surprised to find two very wet and cold ladies at the front door. Although their bonnets were askew and they had no trunks or attendants, that astute woman recognized Quality when she encountered it—which was not very often. Modish coaches usually stopped at the George, two miles farther along the road, where the *ton* could be assured of the cosseting of both themselves and their prime cattle.

Eyeing their sodden half-boots and pelisses, she cried, "Oh, ye poor dears, come in! We've a comfy fire burnin' in the parlor and a pot of my special rabbit stew ready for servin'."

This cheery greeting and the fragrance of freshly baked bread emanating from the kitchen melted the apprehension Paige had developed upon espying the unimpressive exterior of the place. "Mrs. . . ?"

"Stubbins, miss," replied that worthy, dropping a small curtsy.

"Mrs. Stubbins," continued Paige, "our carriage is stuck in a drift about half a mile down the road, so we shall require accommodations for ourselves and our groom and coachman, who will be along shortly with our portmanteaux."

"Ye're in luck. We've only two bedchambers—this bein' a simple place—but they're available, seein' as how we haven't had much traffic on the road today on account of this dreadful storm. They're not fancy, mind, but ye'll find 'em clean and comfortable. Yer servants can share my son's room.''

Then, observing Kit's blue lips, she hustled them out of the drafty hallway into the parlor, where the aforementioned fire was blazing. ''While ye be waitin' for yer belongin's, I'll lay a table by the fire, and ye can warm yer innards with some stew—an' something stronger, if ye'd like.''

Following this sensible advice, the ladies enjoyed a deliciously simple repast, which ended with the welcome sound of Jack Coachman's gruff voice in the hallway, signaling the arrival of their trunks. Longing to get into something drier, Paige suggested they go up to their rooms to change and have tea sent up.

''Oh, yes.'' Kit sighed, relief showing on her abnormally pale countenance. ''I've been worried about your catching a chill in those damp clothes, dear Paige.''

''Stuff and nonsense!'' came the predictable reply. ''If anyone is destined to catch a chill, it is you. Unladylike as it may seem, I have the constitution of an ox.''

Kit, finding it difficult to disagree with this statement, arose, ostensibly to locate Mrs. Stubbins and bespeak the tea—but also to ensure that her own belongings were placed in the smaller of the two bedchambers.

Settling into their rooms, Kit called through the door connecting the two chambers, ''Is this not convenient? I will be able to hear you if you want for anything during the night.''

Since this statement was concluded with a sneeze, Paige replied, ''It seems more likely that it will be *you* wanting *me*, as I detect it is you who have—as I predicted—caught the chill.'' As her sniffling friend appeared in the doorway, prepared, no doubt, to help Paige unpack, Paige sternly ordered her to bed.

''Dearest Kit, we cannot have you coming down with that wretched influenza that is about. I'll bring the tea when it arrives, and tuck you up. Then we can have a nice coze and forget about this nasty storm.''

Firmly shutting the door between their rooms, Paige finally prepared to divest herself of her damp traveling attire. As she pulled from her trunk the beruffled red dressing gown purchased especially for her sojourn in London, she smiled at the memory of her dressmaker's undiplomatic protestations that such a style was much too frivolous for one with Miss Undershaw's looks and figure. Years ago, Paige had realistically assessed her physical attributes, acknowledging that her flyaway hair (which resisted the influence of the curling iron) and her trim, athletic build were not *à la mode;* but she felt very feminine and cherished a fondness for privately dressing in the frills and furbelows she eschewed in public.

Impatient now to wrap that soft, luxurious garment around her, Paige hurried to extract herself from her ruined merino traveling dress. So intent was she on this awkward task that she failed to hear the sounds of approaching footsteps until the door was flung open. Annoyed at the intrusion, but thinking that the skirts covering her head had muffled Mrs. Stubbins's knock, she called out for the tea to be placed on the table by the fireplace. She was more than a little surprised to hear a deep masculine chuckle in response. While she wrestled to free herself from the confines of her skirts, the voice continued in cultured accents, ''You seem to need some help. May I offer my services?''

Quickly dismissing the only two alternatives that were available to her as a properly bred young lady—falling into the vapors or shrieking to be rescued—she calmly answered, ''Being at a disadvantage, and presuming that you don't intend to ravish me or boast of this to your friends, I could use some help.''

''You have my word,'' said the amused voice, as deft fingers quickly released the strands of her hair from the hook around which they were tangled. She soon found herself looking up into the twinkling gray eyes of a military gentleman.

As though men barging into her chamber were an everyday occurrence (and it *had* been at Waverly, for her brother had been used to visit her rooms frequently), she offered the mud-spattered stranger a chair as she slipped into her dressing gown. Then, looking him directly in the eye, she inquired in a tone any Bow Street runner would have admired, "What are you doing in possession of a key to my room? I distinctly remember locking the door after me."

Determined to keep his countenance in this unprecedented situation, the gray-templed intruder contemplated the vision before him. The petite young woman with the disheveled brown locks was not beautiful, but her arresting emerald eyes and air of self-possession were out of the ordinary. Resisting an impulse to raise his quizzing glass, he reached instead for his Sèvres snuff box and opened it with a practiced one-handed motion. Taking a pinch of his personal blend, he drawled, "How droll of Mr. Stubbins to have sent me to occupied rooms; yet I was assured that there were only these two chambers to let, owing to the storm."

Paige's eyes danced mirthfully. "Oh, I daresay I comprehend the situation! The good Mrs. Stubbins cannot have conveyed to her husband that these rooms were bespoken. I collect that it was an innocent omission—and how vexed they will be to discover it!"

"Oh, pray not another commotion!" he exclaimed. "Three years of war in the Peninsula cannot rival the calamities that have beset me since I left Wales—can it only be four days ago? Seems like a se'nnight!" With a sigh, he pressed his hand to his temple.

"You do appear the worse for wear," Paige said kindly, taking in his torn, stained uniform and bloodshot eyes. "I need a moment to conceive what's to be done. I can usually contrive something," she affirmed with a determined look.

"No doubt," he interjected, finding himself bemused by her air of consequence and reflecting that he wished he had more such resolute persons under his command.

"There won't be accommodation for you in the Stubbins boy's room, as my own servants are to bed down there," Paige considered with furrowed brows. "It will have to be Kit's room, then."

"Kit?"

"My traveling companion."

"And who is *her* traveling companion?"

Momentarily at a loss, Paige replied, "Why, *I* am, of course. . . . Oh! I see; we have not introduced ourselves. I am Miss Undershaw of Waverly. And you, sir?"

"Captain Owens, of the Seventh Hussars," he explained, leaping painfully to his feet. "On my way to rejoin my regiment on the Continent."

"Now that the formalities have been dispensed with, we must post-haste decide upon the room arrangements, for Mrs. Stubbins will be here directly with our tea—and the commotion you so wish to avoid will occur," Paige reminded him.

Recalled to his senses of gallantry and propriety, Captain Owens protested, "It really is no concern of yours, ma'am. I can see that these rooms are in your possession, and I will take myself off to consider alternative arrangements."

"Fudge! There *are* no alternative arrangements, unless you have a remarkable carriage that can convey you through these drifts the two miles to the George."

"Alas, for all intents and purposes I have no carriage. That blasted—beg pardon—conveyance is a mile down the road, overturned, with a broken axle—and quite beyond repair."

"Well, that settles it. You and your man will put up in Kit's room, and she will bed with me. There are truckle beds in both chambers, so no one need be inconvenienced."

Moving toward the connecting door to Kit's room, Paige airily commanded, "Sir, get you downstairs and explain to Mr. Stubbins, and I shall make all right with Kit."

"If that is the door to the other chamber, I am persuaded it is a most unsuitable arrangement," he remonstrated.

With her hands on her hips, Paige said arctically, "For a military man, you are shockingly hen-hearted! It will be wonderful if we do not get news that Boney's captured London within a fortnight, if you are a sample of our fighting spirit. . . ."

"For the sake of the reputation of Wellington's forces," he replied, chuckling, "I'll do as you bid." More severely, he added, "But I cannot like it above half."

"Fustian! Now take yourself off!"

Kit was more easily convinced of this program than had been the captain, as she was weakened by her chill and ignorant of the events that had taken place in the adjoining room. She was allowing Paige to tuck her up in the large bed when Mrs. Stubbins arrived with the tea. As she set the tray by the fire, she commented, "Aye, I figgered ye for Quality when I first clapped eyes on ye. That was a might' generous thing ye did, miss, giving that nice soldier yer other room, he being all done-up, what with his recent bereavement 'n' all, and this God-awful blizzard."

"I don't know about *that*," Paige protested. "Any Christian would have done the same."

Mrs. Stubbins clucked knowingly. "Ye'd be surprised at the tales I could tell about so-called Christians!"

Not wishing to hear them, Paige thanked Mrs. Stubbins for the tea and dismissed her gently.

In a short while, warmed by the comforting brew, Kit began to drowse, while Paige silently mulled over the extraordinary events of the day. Her face flushed as she realized the impropriety of entertaining a strange gentleman in a state of deshabille. And in her bedchamber! Whatever could she have been thinking of?!

Considering further, she decided that something about

Captain Owens had reminded her of her dear brother, Richard, though there was little *physical* resemblance. Blond, blue-eyed Richard was in sharp contrast to the dark, gray-eyed captain. The similarity must, then, have been something in his manner and address. Both men had a distinctive air of breeding and an appreciation for the absurd.

This thought saddened Paige, as she realized that Richard had not displayed the latter trait since his marriage to Dorcas. What a shock that had been! Paige had always expected that Richard would make a match with someone like Cornelia. . . .

Suddenly she was bestirred from her reveries by the sound of something metallic grating on the floorboards across the room. Arising with her candle, she walked toward the connecting door and discovered that the key to that door had been pushed under from the other side. Yes, Paige thought, smiling. Captain Owens is very like Richard—a man of honor. She wished the captain a better fate than had befallen Richard.

Chapter II

NEVER one to allow worrying circumstances to intrude upon her slumber, Paige awoke the next morning feeling refreshed and ready to cope with whatever the day offered. Her first thought was of Kit; and, as she glanced anxiously at the bed, she saw that her friend was beginning to stir.

"You look a good deal better for your rest, dear Kit. How are you feeling?"

"I will own being as yet indisposed, but I am convinced that I shall be right as a trivet by teatime," she responded softly. "Do not bother yourself on my account."

Her companion smiled tenderly as she plumped up the pillows and smoothed the bedclothes. "I'll speak with Mrs. Stubbins about preparing something restoring for your breakfast. Is there anything special you desire? As for me, I'm famished, and will partake of my breakfast in the parlor, where I will have the opportunity to further study our surroundings."

A few moments later, as she descended the stairs in her burgundy merino morning dress, Miss Undershaw espied the back of a broad-shouldered, green-coated gentleman entering the private parlor. Damn! she expostulated silently. He has beat me to the sole private parlor! The dictates of society would have me return to my bedchamber, rather than intrude upon his privacy; but as it has never been in my style to adhere blindly to such precepts, I shall ask him if he objects to my joining him.

Chuckling to herself, she realized that as a gentleman he could scarcely refuse, especially in view of her kindness of the previous evening. Mentally tasting ham and baked eggs, she licked her lips in an unladylike fashion and lightheartedly strode toward the parlor door.

Hearing a tap at the door, Captain David Owens looked up from his plate of kidneys and toast to discover an elegantly turned out woman of fashion who bore a striking resemblance to the tousled charmer of last evening.

With dancing eyes, Paige inquired, ''I trust our tossing and turning did not keep you awake last night, Captain Owens?'' Without waiting for his reply, she resumed, ''Ah, I see it cannot have done, for you are enjoying a hearty repast. I'm glad to see the breakfast here looks so good; I only wonder where *I* might partake of some, as it would be insupportable to subject Kit (in her weakened condition) to the sight of me sating my ravenous appetite.''

His eyes twinkled at this challenge as he replied in dulcet accents, ''But I have it on good authority—your *own*, ma'am—that if given a moment, you can contrive a solution to any vexatious problem.'' He then turned zestfully back to his meal.

''Odious beast! Ask me to join you at once,'' she gurgled, stamping her dainty foot in mock petulance.

Clapping his hand to his forehead, as if the thought had never occurred to him, Captain Owens leaped apologetically to his feet. ''How shatter-brained of me not to have seen that as the obvious solution! I hope you will not report my stupidity to Wellington.''

Making an exaggeratedly sweeping gesture toward the chair opposite him, he gallantly invited her to join him. ''May I have the honor of your company for breakfast...um, it *is* Miss Undershaw, is it not? I scarcely recognized you with your, um...hair up,'' he said mischievously.

Alternating between a burning desire to give him a severe set-down and a burning desire to get at the kidneys and toast, Paige opted for the latter, realizing that there would be ample opportunity during the day to deliver the set-down. As she accepted the proffered seat in what she hoped was icy silence, Captain Owens bade his man, Dickson, summon Mrs. Stubbins to bring more victuals.

"And do ask her to take tea and toast up to Miss Roche," added Miss Undershaw, momentarily guilty that her own gluttony had caused her to forget her duty to her friend.

When Mrs. Stubbins returned with a heaping platter of eggs and more kidneys, Paige requested a moratorium on conversation until she had eaten her fill—a process she applied herself to with alacrity.

Leaning back in his chair and surveying his companion, David could not help but contrast her with other females of his acquaintance. Most were dead bores. Having been raised to have no thoughts of their own, they resorted to simpering and having fits of the vapors whenever anything untoward occurred. Obviously, Miss Undershaw did not fit this mold, though there could be no doubt that her family was of the first consequence. Sir Richard Undershaw, if the captain's recollection served him well, was the feisty gentleman he had narrowly defeated in a sparring match at Jackson's a year ago. At that time, David had hoped to further his acquaintance with his worthy opponent but was informed when he had gone to seek him out that Sir Richard had returned to his country home to be wed. Estimating that Mr. Undershaw was about his own age, two and thirty, Captain Owens surmised that Miss Undershaw was likely the younger sister he had mentioned.

Shifting his position and flicking an imaginary mote of dust from his highly polished hessians, he continued his comparison. She certainly was not a diamond of the first water but would have been able to hold her own among the beauties at Almack's. She had a distinctive air about her and carried her slight form in such a way as to lead one to suppose she were more statuesque. The corners of her wide, bow-shaped mouth seemed perpetually curved upward in a manner that gave her face a mysteriously impish aspect; she appeared continuously happy. What a breath of fresh air she must be at the assemblies! He must remember when he reached London to suggest to Jerry that he make her acquaintance.

Her hair now appeared a bit too severe. He thought that the way it had lain upon the shoulders of her dressing gown last night was a far more attractive style for her tiny face.

Suddenly he realized that he was being addressed by the object of his scrutiny and apologized. "Forgive me. I was woolgathering. What was it that you said, ma'am?" Noticing her spanking-clean plate, he added, "Perhaps you'd like more kidneys sent in?"

"I was inquiring whether you'd be able to depart this day, and do you stop at London on your way to the coast?"

"In answer to your first query, ill fortune continues to dog me. Dickson reports that I cannot continue my journey until I can hire another coach—and the prospects for doing that appear dim, as this snowfall is greater than any I have ever seen in England."

Before he got to the second question, Paige interjected, "Oh, dear! It appears, then, that we, too, will be unable to continue to London today." This speculation was soon to be confirmed by Jack Coachman, whom she heard inquiring after her in the hallway. "Excuse me, sir, but I must attend to my coachman," she apologized as she quit her chair.

As expected, the news was not good, though Jack did think that he would be able to extract the coach early on the morrow, and they could set out then. Since *that* was cheery news, Paige rushed upstairs to convey these tidings to Kit, hoping very much to find her friend looking more the thing.

She surprised her patient reading one of Miss Austen's novels, of which she was extremely fond, and seemingly much improved. "Feel you stout enough to resume our journey tomorrow morning?" Paige inquired.

Kit, startled by Paige's unexpected entrance, guiltily shut her book and began apologizing for being poor company. "It is so stupid of me to have contracted this silly ailment, and so improper to require attention from *you*." Pushing back the bedclothes, she made as if to get up, wheezing, "I will be up at once and join you in the parlor—and you will see for yourself that I am perfectly well enough to leave tomorrow."

"Nonsense! Your illness is not discommoding me in the least. I am finding my conversations with Captain Owens most diverting, and think you must not risk exacerbating your condition by leaving your bed. I *had* worried about leaving you alone, but I see that you are being entertained by the escapades of the Bennet family," Paige said mischievously, glancing at the cast-aside book.

"Paige, you are not sitting with him unchaperoned in the parlor, are you?" Kit inquired, fearing that she already knew the answer.

With mock solemnity Paige responded, "Kit, what do you take me for? His man, Dickson, is with us." (If she were perfectly honest, she ought to have added, "From time to time.")

Throwing up her hands, Kit said, "Paige, you know full well that a valet is not an acceptable chaperone for a young lady."

"I am not a *young* lady! Why, I've been on the shelf for years! Oh, it galls me that because I am not married I must needs live a sheltered, restricted life. If this continues much longer, I shall wither and die, as a plant does when it is deprived of sufficient space in which to grow," Paige concluded dramatically.

Taken aback by the unexpected vehemence in Paige's voice, Kit ventured, "It is not my place to criticize you, but I would be remiss in my duty if I were not to recall you to your sense of propriety. If you continue in these hoydenish ways, you will ruin all chances of contracting an eligible marriage."

Sitting herself down on the bed, Paige looked earnestly into Kit's worried face and said, "It is hard for you to understand me. At times it is hard for me to understand myself. I know you would like nothing better than to be mistress of your own house, and to dote on a husband and children—and that life is right for you. But at present it does not feel right for me. Married women, although society allows them more freedom, seem to lose their individuality. They become 'worthy matrons,' talking incessantly of household matters and the illnesses of their offspring, or spreading the latest *on-dits*. *I'd* rather be the one gossiped about than the one who does the gossiping."

Kit, with a sense evolved from long experience, knew that Paige was not finished, so did not speak.

"Moreover," Paige reflected, "I have not met a man who stirs my senses, and yet I feel I am not coldhearted. Whenever I feel I may be beginning to develop a *tendre*, the gentleman in question assumes a proprietary air, and begins to treat me as one of his prized possessions. Such behavior acts on my heart as a rain shower on a newly kindled fire."

Much touched by this confiding soliloquy, Kit abandoned her customary servile mien and began to speak as one woman to another. "Oh, Paige, when I have contrasted myself with you, I have always felt that you had all the advantages—countenance, financial means, and spirit. I now see that I have one advantage over you: a calmness born of the certainty of knowing the future I want." Feeling a need to lighten the effect of her comment, Kit added, "Methinks *you*, rather than I, should have the red hair."

Paige, appreciating her friend's attempt to adopt a less serious tone, leapt from the bed, twirled around, and said, "I think you are right! I understand red hair and green eyes are all the crack in London. I'll leave you now to ponder how we can effect the transformation, as I wish to confer with Jack."

Paige actually had no intention of doing so and blushed to think that she had lied to her friend in order to escape the confines of the stuffy room. To make amends, once downstairs she requested that more tea be sent up to Kit, then reentered the parlor.

Finding it empty, Paige felt an unfamiliar sensation; reflecting on this, she decided that what she felt was disappointment. She had been favorably anticipating more verbal fencing with the captain.

Exploring the cozy room in the hope of discovering some diversion, she found a chessboard and pieces in the drawer of a writing table. Since the drawer also contained stationery, and playing chess by oneself was not very entertaining, Paige decided to pen a line to Richard. She knew she was a lively and diverting correspondent and felt her account of their plight and her chance meeting with Captain Owens would reassure Richard of their safety while providing some levity to his henpecked existence.

While she was engaged in a colorfully exaggerated, if not mendacious, account of the life-threatening obstacles she and Kit had encountered on their trek from the carriage to the inn, Captain Owens strode into the room. Imagining that he could detect her prevarications from where he stood, Paige reddened to the roots of her stylishly plaited hair.

"You surprise me, ma'am. I had not thought you capable of blushing—since you seemed not the slightest unsettled when caught last night in your petticoats. I can only imagine, therefore, the worst—that I have interrupted you making arrangements for a tryst."

Chagrined at the missishness her heightened color implied,

she adopted a shocking air of worldliness and replied saucily, as she turned back to her letter, "But you have not interrupted me at *all*, sir! I shall proceed to make my plans."

"Your point," he conceded, allowing an appreciative guffaw to escape his control. "Among my comrades, I am known to have a romantic sensibility. Is there anything I can do to assist you?"

"No; all I'm wanting is a frank, and *you* cannot help me there."

"Ah, but I can, ma'am," he confessed after a moment's hesitation, painfully remembering that the recent death of his beloved brother had left him Earl of Penllyn.

"Do not be foolish! Only peers can frank letters. Just find something to occupy yourself until I have finished this *billet-doux*, and then we can play chess," she snapped imperiously.

"By all means," he responded in mock meekness, deciding to adopt an air of mystery equal to hers and not to inform her of his elevated station. Restlessly moving about the room, he replenished the fire and settled himself into a comfortable, if shabby, chair near it. He had been hoping that there would be no time to think about the distressing events of the last two months. How he missed Evan! He could still scarcely credit that his stalwart elder brother could have been carried off, along with his cherished lady, by the raging influenza epidemic. Evan had been the perfect firstborn son, as he was temperamentally inclined for all the onerous duties expected of an earl. David had always been the one to lead them into scrapes, and Evan the one to extract them.

But that is all past, he reflected grimly. Now the cloak of responsibility lay on his own shoulders, not only for the management of their large landholdings in England and Wales, but for the care and upbringing of the infant Pamela, just six months old. The latter concern would have been easily assuaged if his mother, the Lady Susan,

had been well, but she had been so weakened by her own
bout with the influenza that he feared for her health. He
wished, in fact, that he need not leave Penllyn just now,
but Boney's escape from Elba made it imperative that he
rejoin his regiment at once. From the dispatches, he
understood that a showdown was imminent, and he must
be there to lead his men.

He was sure he could entrust his business dealings to the
capable solicitor Mr. Oakes, but he lacked a caring guardian and protector for his mother and niece. A frown
furrowed his brow as he recollected his cousin Sylvester,
who ought to have filled this role. But to leave the affairs
of his loved ones in the hands of such a rake and scoundrel
would be the grossest dereliction of David's duties. Yet he
could see no other avenue; after all, Sylvester was next in
line to the earldom, and there was a good chance that
David might not survive the hostilities.

Suddenly he was recalled to his present situation by a
gentle touch on his shoulder. Glancing up quickly, he was
disconcerted by an uncharacteristic look of concern in
Miss Undershaw's expressive eyes.

"What troubles you, sir? I have spoken your name
several times and you have not responded. You may
censure me if I am being forward by asking, but are you
perhaps preoccupied with thoughts of the 'recent bereavement'
Mrs. Stubbins alluded to?"

"You have fine sensibilities, ma'am; that is exactly what
troubles me, and I would appreciate your helping to divert
me from such thoughts, for I fear becoming lachrymose—
and *that* would make me a poor companion indeed."

Respecting his right to privacy, she suggested, "I think
a game of chess will answer. We have just time for one
before nuncheon, I believe."

David was not surprised to find his mind fully engaged
in thwarting the aggressive attempts of Miss Undershaw to
capture his king. Eventually he did succeed in this task but
was moved to comment that he was not accustomed to

playing with females who made him exert all his powers of understanding to extract a thin victory.

"I shall take that as a compliment, Captain Owens—the first I've received from you since I met you, though I *had* thought military men to be always gallant. It is something else about you I should report to Wellington," she twinkled.

"I'm undone again! I intended a set-down, Miss Undershaw, not a compliment. Can no one have told you that a woman's role is to make a man feel superior?" he queried playfully.

He immediately recognized that this was not a subject for cheerful banter with Miss Undershaw when she grimaced and rose from her chair, saying glacially, "You are not original, sir! I have been told this more than once, but my good sense cannot support that concept—nor can my behavior. Knowing that, do you have objections to continuing to share *your* parlor with me? I can always take my nuncheon in the coffee-room."

"Oh, do not get on your high horse. I was just bamming you. By all means let us share a cold nuncheon here together."

Somewhat mollified, Paige agreed to this and left to seek out Mrs. Stubbins to order a nuncheon for them—and to quickly inquire of Kit's preferences for her own repast.

These tasks completed, she returned to the parlor for a preprandial sherry. As David handed a glass to her, he ventured politely, "The name 'Undershaw' is not completely unknown to me. Can it be that you are related to Sir Richard Undershaw, whose acquaintance I made at Gentleman Jackson's about a twelvemonth ago?"

Brightening at this mention of her brother, she nodded vigorously, then laughingly confessed, "It was in fact he to whom my '*billet-doux*' was addressed; but he is my brother, not my beau."

"How relieved I am to hear that!" Then, not giving her time to respond to this puzzling sentiment, he asked, "I understand he has been wed since I last saw him: how is married life agreeing with him?''

Unwittingly, Paige rolled her eyes mournfully, wondering whether or not to confide her concerns. To unburden herself to a disinterested gentleman was a luxury she longed for, but she was too well bred to yield to this temptation. Airing family linen to a chance acquaintance was just not done. Happily for her, nuncheon arrived just then, and she merely replied, ''He enjoys his customary good health, sir.''

Noticing that her response was uncharacteristically bland and the normally sunny look had vanished from her face, Captain Owens assumed all was not well with the newlyweds—but he was too well bred to pursue his hunch. ''I am glad to hear it. I hope you will send him my greetings.'' She nodded, and they turned to inspect their fare. They confronted a cold nuncheon of ham, pickled tongue, cabbage, beetroot, freshly baked bread, and butter. Captain Owens found himself distracted from his meal by trying to reconcile Miss Undershaw's trim figure with her zestful eating habits. She attacked her food with a ferocity that he had not seen equaled since his regiment had come upon a citrus orchard after a two-day trek through the Pyrenees with inadequate supplies of food and drink. Again he was struck by how delightfully unusual a woman she was. Ordinarily he was at a loss for words with attractive members of the opposite sex, since he was not an accomplished flirt. However, with Miss Undershaw he was very much at his ease; he related to her as he would a comrade, though he was never unaware of the fact that she was a woman.

Feeling his eyes upon her, Paige asked if he were not enjoying his meal. Continuing to gaze at her, he replied without touching his food, ''But I *am* enjoying it.''

Pondering for a moment the meaning behind his words, a flash of disappointment flickered across her features. ''I hope you do not flirt with me, sir! That would ruin everything! I wish men would spend more time building friendships with women than making love to them. I had hoped we had made a start in that direction," she concluded, savagely buttering a slice of bread.

"Again you mistake my meaning, Miss Undershaw," he retorted in exasperation. "My motive for making that statement sprang from a desire to tell you honestly how much I am enjoying your society." Sensing that she still did not believe him, he went on to say, "I agree that men should spend more time building friendships; but how *can* we when women see every attempt to do so as trifling with their affections? Believe me, ma'am, insincere compliments are not in my line."

Struck by the genuine emotion in his voice and the kernel of truth in his words, Paige paused, and then, as though thinking out loud, said, "You are right, sir. It is a lowering reflection to discover my contradictions—on the one hand I pride myself on my powers of understanding, and on the other I am quick to leap to conclusions which, upon reflection, prove unsound." Placing her elbows on the table and resting her delightfully dimpled chin in her hands, she gazed intently at him and admitted that their acquaintance was of too short a duration for her to be taking the liberty of judging him.

Surprised by her abrupt mood change, and suspecting that he might still be on thin ice, Captain Owens found himself struggling with a suitable reply. As her candor had taken him off his guard, he finally decided that his best tactic at this point was to change the subject, which he did by suggesting another game of chess.

She demurred, suddenly remembering that she had not looked in on her friend for the past two hours. Pushing back a perpetually straying lock of hair, she rose gracefully and proposed that the rematch be held in an hour—adding that he best spend the intervening time practicing his moves, since she had no intention of letting him win a second time. Smiling teasingly, she exited from the room. Behind her she heard an appreciative laugh.

Paige found Kit sitting before the fire in their room, looking much improved and laboring over her needlework. "Ah, Kit," Paige twinkled, "you have exceeded your prognostications. It wants several hours 'til teatime, and you are out of your bed. I am so glad." Pulling another chair up to the fire, Paige inquired as to the fate of the Bennet sisters. Kit launched into an enthusiastic précis which at times would have been difficult to follow had not Paige already read *Pride and Prejudice*.

Kit interrupted her own narrative, clapping her hands with sudden inspiration. "Oh, Paige, would it not be marvelous if you could meet a Mr. Darcy in London? You remind me so of Elizabeth Bennet!" she beamed.

"You mean sharp-tongued?" questioned Paige playfully.

"That, of course," Kit replied undiplomatically, then ameliorated it by continuing, "And that rare combination of intelligence, beauty, and deep family affection."

Touched and complimented by her friend's comparison to Paige's own favorite literary heroine, she averted her eyes and protested weakly, "Don't be silly, Kit! Your imagination runs away with you."

"No, really, Paige," insisted Kit, "you are just like her. You so often develop prejudices about the most eligible men."

Paige stifled a ready retort as she recognized how similar this observation was to her recent musings in the parlor. Vowing to reflect further on this at a more convenient time, Paige switched the conversation to their plans for the future in London. "Kit, since we will be arriving in London tomorrow, I think it best that we make final arrangements so we can inform Cornelia straightaway. Now, my plan was that we would stay with Cornelia for a fortnight, during which time we would search for an appropriate townhouse to let for the Season. At the end of the Season we will remove to Bath."

"Yes, that is what we discussed, Paige, but I cannot be comfortable with it. Whatever will Richard and Dorcas say when they find you have no intention of returning to Waverly?"

"You know I care nought for Dorcas's opinion, though I am saddened at distressing Richard. But I fear I would cause him more unhappiness if I were to return to Waverly and resume my skirmishes with his wife. And it is no use telling me not to brangle with her, for I cannot help myself. She raises my hackles, and I cannot forgive her for entrapping my trusting brother into marriage."

Becoming agitated, as she usually did whenever the subject of Richard's marriage was brought up, Paige began to pace around the small room. Turning suddenly, she said emphatically, "So my mind is set on establishing my own household. That is final!" she added fiercely, as Kit began to object again.

"What part of Town do you fancy, Kit?" Paige ventured after taking a moment to compose herself.

In measured tones, Kit replied, "Let us rely on Cornelia's judgment. She is more familiar with the suitable locations," silently pinning her hopes on Cornelia's ability to dissuade Paige from her indecorous proposal.

"By all means," Paige responded blithely.

Stifling a yawn, Kit said, relieved, "I am glad to hear it."

Paige, noticing her friend's weary countenance, said softly, "How inconsiderate of me to be prattling away when you are obviously in need of further rest! You know my feelings on this: pills, potions, and cordials are not half as efficacious as allowing the body to heal itself through sleep. Allow me to assist you back to bed, where you can doze until teatime. Then perhaps you'll be well enough to join us downstairs," she concluded cheerfully.

When Kit was comfortably established, Paige rejoined the captain, who had the chessboard ready and seemed to be planning his opening gambit.

"Ah, I see you have been taking my advice," she remarked pertly.

Ignoring her comment, he asked how Miss Roche fared. "So well that she may be able to join us for tea," Paige said brightly. He responded appropriately, but with a noticeable lack of enthusiasm.

Withdrawing his snuff box from his pocket, he offered it to Paige. She declined quickly, declaring that the practice was unnatural and unhealthy, besides being messy. "I was forever having to brush snuff off my father's waistcoat."

He gently inquired if this parent still resided at Waverly. She smiled at the memory of her father and said, "He is dead these six years—and I do miss him. He was the best of fathers! He displayed no preference for either one of his offspring, treating Richard and me as though there were no distinction in our genders. Although others often criticize me for my lack of proper conduct, there has never been a day when I have not been grateful to him for insisting that I have a mind of my own, and challenging me to make use of it. Indeed, I shall make use of it forthwith!" she crowed, moving her pawn. "I have talked of both Richard and my father. What of *your* family, sir?"

Steering clear of more recent events, he began to talk of his own parents. "My father, the sixth Earl of Penllyn, was a distant man, more comfortable around his horses and hounds than with his sons. He died in a fall when his horse balked at a hedge. Since I was then just out of leading-strings, I scarcely knew him, and cannot miss him. . . . My mother, though, is a great gun, and was more than capable of handling both parental roles. My brother and I could rarely gammon her, and I've never seen her have need of hartshorn or vinaigrette," he chortled. Immediately sobering, he reflected, "At this moment she is not enjoying her customary good health, and I worry about leaving her alone in Wales while I am on the Continent. But"—he sighed—"it is not to be helped."

Taking his bishop, Paige speculated, "Surely your brother will see that all is well with her."

"My brother, ma'am, is recently deceased," he intoned in an abnormally flat voice.

"Methinks I have inadvertently strayed onto that subject you wish not to discuss. I am so sorry," she said gravely. "I *would* like to know more of Wales, if that is an agreeable topic. I always thought Welshmen were dark, short, and spoke in an unintelligible tongue composed exclusively of consonants."

Gratefully, he said something incomprehensible in the Welsh tongue, with an interrogative intonation.

Laughing approvingly, she said, "Just so!" and took another of his pawns.

"I'm beginning to suspect, ma'am, that your strategy is to distract me—but I do so love talking about my home that I will do it, and risk losing to a woman." Not wishing to tamper with his restored spirits, Paige refrained from comment.

David had not expected one and went on to explain that he owed his above-average height to his English ancestors and his dark hair to his Welsh. Legend had it that his ancestors had fought with Llewelyn, and David was clearly captivated with this thought. He then went on to describe at length and with vigor the issues facing Wales on his most recent visit. Paige listened attentively and was struck by certain phrases in his narrative:

"Ah, it's a beautiful land, but a deuced sad place at this time. . . ."

"There is a lack of understanding between the English and Welsh, which I, given my dual ancestry, hope to reconcile should I return. . . ."

"I do think *you* would like it there. The people are so individualistic. They have been under English rule for so long, and yet they have not changed their ways or absorbed those of England. . . . I do not know you well, but—this is not a criticism—I detect a bent toward stubbornness in you, which is very like the Welsh. . . ."

Finding herself caught up in this fascinating narrative, Paige began to lose her concentration and was soon struggling to protect her queen. Oddly, the prospect of losing no longer seemed of import, as she was enjoying the stimulation of broadening her understanding of the world outside Surrey. Fortuitously, David made a grievous error and Paige took full advantage, triumphantly checkmating him.

Not being one to gloat, Paige acknowledged his congratulations pleasantly and remarked with surprise on the lateness of the hour. Deciding to ascertain the conditions of the road, she went to the window.

In the dusk, at first all she saw was a series of undulating mounds of thick, wet snow. Suddenly one of the smaller mounds seemed to move. Blinking her eyes to focus them, Paige realized that what moved was a living creature. Pressing her aristocratic nose to the glass to get a better view, she cried out, "Oh! It is a kitten, a dear little kitten! He'll freeze to death!

"We must save him," she ejaculated, rushing to David's side and pulling at his coat.

"I must indeed be a slow-top, for I cannot collect your meaning," the recipient of this mauling said reasonably.

Not pausing to clarify, Paige pulled him into the hallway and, gathering her cashmere shawl more closely around her shoulders, wrenched open the formidable oak door. Heedless of her long skirts and the reluctance of her companion, she plunged out into the snow and soon held a shivering ball of white fur in her arms. Wondering what *his* role was supposed to be in this rescue, David reminded Miss Undershaw of the possibility of frostbite and ushered her indoors.

"Build up the fire!" Paige commanded him, crooning in silken tones to the beneficiary of her ministrations. Raising her head from the icy fur in remembrance of another requirement, she added, "And tell Mrs. Stubbins to bring some warm—not hot, mind—milk along with our tea.''

While the captain went off to implement these instructions, Paige inspected her find. The kitten was neither a newborn nor a grown cat and seemed to be no worse for its adventure, since it was purring lustily as it rubbed its head against Paige's hand. The cat's green eyes, surveying her devotedly, stood out strikingly against its pure white coat.

Captain Owens returned to find a charmingly domestic scene: Paige was settled on the hearth, stroking the cat. As he had suspected, this independent sprite was also possessed of a soft heart.

He surprised Paige by leaning down to set the saucer of milk (at just the right temperature) within the kitten's reach, and soothingly stroked its head. Her experience of men was that the only interest they had in cats was in drowning them or, more likely, ordering some poor kitchen maid to do so. ''Thank you for the milk, sir,'' Paige murmured gratefully. ''When will tea be served? I must go up to Kit, but I know I leave the cat in good hands. Perhaps you could occupy yourself in finding a suitable name for this dear stray until I return,'' she suggested helpfully.

Her return was a quick one, as she had found Kit sleeping soundly and had not the heart to awaken her, eager though she was to impart the news of the cat's rescue. Rejoining Captain Owens, she was greeted enthusiastically with the one word: ''Snow!''

Confused, and a bit awed by his air of joyful conviction, she agreed that it *was* a most abominable inconvenience. ''No, no, the *cat!*'' he elucidated cheerfully.

Vexed, Paige confessed, ''I'm sorry, sir, but I do not understand your meaning. Perhaps I've become addle-brained, being cooped up here this entire day.''

Slowly he articulated, as if speaking to a child, ''I-have-named-him-'Snow'!'' In normal tones, he resumed, ''I had thought of naming him 'Miss Undershaw' because of his beautiful green eyes, but realized that was rather a large appellation for such a tiny creature—and, besides, I do think it *is* a boy.''

"Just right!'' crowed Paige. "It suits both his coloring and the circumstances under which we found him,'' she confirmed decisively.

As the door swung open to admit Mrs. Stubbins with the tea tray, Captain Owens recalled the possibility of an enlargement to their party. "Will Miss Roche be down soon?'' he queried halfheartedly.

"No, she continues to sleep. Did I not previously inform you of that?'' Not waiting for him to reply, Paige realized, "Of course I cannot have done, or you would not have asked.'' Then, after pausing and glancing impishly at him for approval, she added, "Notice, sir, that I no longer misjudge you.''

"Does this mean, ma'am, that Wellington is not to receive an inventory of my failings?'' he suggested with mock relief.

"Idiot!'' she retorted, emerald eyes sparkling, then turned to pour out their tea. As they eased into their chairs, balancing their cups, an intimate silence settled on the fire-lit room, disturbed only by the sounds of the purring kitten, the settling of a log, and the soft clink of china.

The comfortably languid mood was broken some minutes later by the crunching of wheels on the snow, directly outside. David was the first to satisfy his curiosity by peering out the window and reporting to his companion, "We have a visitor of consequence, for the traveling chaise that has just arrived is elegant—though it has no crest.'' He noted admiringly the beautifully matched high-steppers, the well-sprung body of the coach, and the precision of its lines.

Stepping to his side inquisitively, Paige burst into laughter. "You are indeed perceptive. How flattered I am to hear you speak of me as a person of consequence!'' Satisfied that her words had sufficiently puzzled him, she explained proudly, "That is my own vehicle."

"Minx!" he chided teasingly, adding untruthfully, "I guessed it."

A forceful knock on the door of the parlor saved the captain from hearing the response Paige was preparing. At her welcoming command, a very wet, but proud, Jack entered bashfully and triumphantly announced the coach's readiness for tomorrow's departure.

Having succinctly delivered his tidings and received his mistress's fond commendation, Jack quickly withdrew, relieved to be able to relax in the coffee-room. David was the first to voice his reaction, wistfully confessing, "I know this is selfish of me, but I shall be sorry to see you depart, as *I* will be here at least another day—and with just Snow for company." He nodded in the direction of the cat, who was now methodically cleansing its hind legs, and concluded that he did not suppose he could teach chess to this esteemed feline.

In shocked accents, Miss Undershaw exclaimed feelingly, "But Snow is mine! *I* rescued him and I intend to take him with me. Cornelia will not mind in the least!" Then, dramatically confirming her ownership, she clasped the bewildered cat to her bosom and pressed her nose against his pristine fur, whispering endearments into his ear.

"What?! To be completely and heartlessly abandoned? How shall I get on?" the good captain protested indignantly.

In an impulsive gesture of friendship, Paige handed the cat to him, watching with amusement the several white hairs that clung to his coat as David cradled the furry bundle in his arm. "I am sure you will get on quite well without us, sir; and your valet will be glad to see you part company with Snow! However, upon a moment's reflection— for surely the thought had never occurred to me until this instant—it seems high folly for you to remain here when there is ample room for both you and your man in my carriage—that is, if London is en route to your destination."

David shifted Snow to his other arm, considered her remarks, and admitted, "It _is,_ as I must meet with my solicitor, and if the situation were not so pressing, I would perfunctorily demur, not wanting to discommode you. However, as things stand, I most gratefully accept—but will understand if, after you speak with Miss Roche, you decide to rescind your invitation."

Laughing at his accurate prediction of Kit's probable reaction to this scheme, Paige questioned whether he had sneaked through the connecting bedchamber door to visit with Miss Roche and had thus become familiar with her character.

Captain Owens solemnly responded that though he had not had the pleasure of meeting that lady, he was well acquainted with many worthy female companions and knew their views concerning "encroaching strangers," especially unknown military officers.

Paige loyally, and automatically, sprang to her friend's defense, being the sort of person who would allow criticism of her dear ones to come only from her own lips. She ended by confidently assuring him that the invitation was secure but was secretly contemplating with vague dread the prospect of convincing Kit.

Plucking Snow expertly from the crook of David's arm (with a mild protest from Snow's claws) and politely taking her leave, Miss Undershaw ascended the stairs to confer with the recently awakened Kit, who was still too groggy—and too enchanted by the kitten—to accomplish anything more than a mild and perfunctory protest at the unseemliness of the plan to enlarge tomorrow's party. Relieved that her proposal had been accepted with a minimum of bother, Paige magnanimously suggested that they share their supper in the bedchamber, thus saving Kit the exertion of dressing.

This arrangement having been gratefully agreed to, Paige departed to convey their dining plans to Mrs. Stubbins, who was only too happy to accommodate their wishes, silently observing that members of the Quality were more reasonable and polite in their demands than were her usual clientele.

On her way to the parlor to settle the arrangements for the morrow, Paige encountered Dickson, who agreed to inform his master that she would not be joining him for supper, and that he should be in readiness to depart at eight in the morning.

The two ladies spent their evening in merriment, as Snow, investigating his new surroundings, discovered Kit's needlework and vehemently decided to improve upon it by rearranging the carefully, if not artfully, worked strands of yarn to a design of his own.

Chapter III

THE early morning sun on the snow dazzled Paige as she squinted through the parlor windows while awaiting word from Jack as to the moment of departure. She was glad that Mrs. Stubbins had warmed their bricks, as the air appeared crisp and uninvitingly nippy: in the courtyard the shabbily dressed ostler was rubbing his hands to warm them as he harnessed the snorting, stomping horses to the coach.

Turning from the window, Paige was glad to see that Kit had finished her breakfast, and that the color had returned to her cheeks. "It appears we have just time to take our leave of Mrs. Stubbins, as Captain Owens's trunks are now being tied on," Paige announced genially. By happy coincidence, that embodiment of hospitality bustled in bearing a warm pot of tea and cheerily greeted them, "Me and Mr. Stubbins was saying as how we be sorry to see ye go, for ye be the most courteous and untroublesome guests what ever put up 'ere. We 'opes when ye next travel the Lunnen Road that ye'll stop in 'ere fer some o' my fresh-baked cinnamon buns (an' I've tucked in a bunnel fer yer trip, by the by)." Brightening at the news she was about to impart, she added robustly, "An' ye won't be 'avin' much trouble gettin' to Lunnen today, as the roads be hard-froze—so there'll be no mire to bog ye down."

Impetuously Paige crossed the room and grasped Mrs. Stubbins's reddened hands in her own soft ones. "You have been so kind. I do not know when I have enjoyed an 'inconvenience' more, and I am certain that the George would not provide the genuine warmth and kindness that *you* have shown us." Gesturing toward Kit, she twinkled, "Why, as you can see, Miss Roche has recovered her bloom! Methinks your tasty chicken broth is really a magic potion."

Mrs. Stubbins, unaccustomed to praise, blushed and remonstrated, "Aw, g'wan with ye. 'Tweren't nothin' special. Like ye said, miss, it's what any Christian would o' done."

Kit chimed in approvingly, "And you, Mrs. Stubbins, are one of the finest Christians we have ever met!" Embarrassed, Mrs. Stubbins was relieved that at that instant Captain Owens plunged into the room, blowing on his hands to ease their numbness.

"Excuse me, ladies, but it wants five minutes 'til departure." Attempting to suppress his twitching lips, he confided, glancing meaningfully at Paige, "You are the best judge of this, ma'am, but I collect from Jack's expression that he would prefer to leave with an empty coach rather than be behind in his schedule."

"I again salute your insightfulness, Captain—but Jack's bark is worse than his bite," she exclaimed heroically. Then, more practically, she admitted, "But if we want Jack to be in good humor for our journey, we'd best depart promptly."

A meaningful clearing of Kit's throat reminded Paige that she had not yet presented the captain to her companion. "Excuse my lapse, but I realize that you are not known to each other! Kit, may I present Captain Owens? Sir, this is my dear friend, Miss Roche."

"Your servant, ma'am." The captain bowed elegantly, raising his head to encounter a piercingly thorough surveillance. Kit was favorably impressed by his easy address. Her scrutiny of his person revealed a man of well-formed, slender proportions, and above-average height. She could not decide whether his most striking feature was his raven hair streaked with silver, or his hooded, gray eyes. The overall picture was of a well-bred gentleman. Relieved that her impulsive friend had not jeopardized her virtue by becoming entangled with a fortune-hunting cad, Kit melted perceptibly and thanked the captain for acting as a surrogate companion to Paige while she herself had been indisposed.

Recognizing in Miss Roche a Celtic sensibility akin to his own, David discarded his unfounded apprehension and began looking forward to the hours ahead. Anxious to be off, he inquired if the ladies were ready.

Mrs. Stubbins offered to fetch the pelisses while the party took a last sip of tea and plucked Snow from his position midway up the chintz curtains. Unhappy at being forestalled from completing his challenging climb, that indomitable animal refused to cooperate with his mistress's attempts to place him in a carrying basket provided by the Stubbins boy. Flinging out his limbs in four different directions and stiffening them defiantly, he yowled in protest to Miss Undershaw's importunings to "be a good boy." Since these soft words did not immediately produce the desired results, the captain, reverting to a familiar role, assumed command of the situation. Using a piece of milk-soaked toast, he enticed the kitten from under the chair where he had sought refuge. Then, in what seemed like one quick, continuous motion, David grabbed Snow, thrust him uncompromisingly into the hamper, and slammed shut the lid.

Kit, appreciating his exigencies, sighed admiringly. "It is so comforting to have a man to lean on in an emergency."

Paige, who thought men caused more emergencies than they solved, and who was certain that she would have been equally successful with Snow if given another minute, glowered menacingly at her "dear friend," a vitriolic retort on the tip of her tongue. Just in time, however, Miss Undershaw remembered her manners and turned to politely, if woodenly, thank the captain. Then, hearing Mrs. Stubbins's heavy tred in the hallway, Paige abruptly announced, "Our wraps are here. We need not delay further," and stomped from the parlor, leaving the captain to carry Snow's basket.

The party was soon comfortably settled on the plush velvet squabs. With an unknown male in their company, Kit was relieved that the interior of the Undershaw coach was so roomy. The passengers need not worry about being thrown into contact with one another even during the most severe lurchings.

Paige, still annoyed that the captain had succeeded where she had not, and thoroughly vexed at Kit for magnifying her failure, refused to assume her conversational duties as hostess and simulated an intense preoccupation with the wintry landscape (which must have quickly bored that lively lady, since even the keenest mind would not have been able to distinguish more than varying shades and shapes of whiteness).

Deciding that the trip would be dull indeed if Miss Undershaw persisted in her sulks, Captain Owens resolved to provoke her. Leaning toward Miss Roche in a conspiratory whisper designed to be overheard, he inquired solicitously, "I collect that your friend suffers from the traveling sickness, since she is unusually silent."

A confused and vaguely anxious expression wandered across her freckled face as Kit wondered how to reply. Indeed, she could not account for Paige's uncharacteristic behavior, since her friend had never suffered an indisposition on a journey. "Oh, I am sure it is just that Miss Paige has a great deal on her mind, sir," she eventually responded, nervously hoping that it was nothing she herself had said or done to put her friend out of temper.

"Miss *Paige?* I thought she was Miss Undershaw," quizzed the captain, looking bewildered.

Now she was for it, thought Kit. If Paige had not been

angry at her before, she was sure to be now; and it was not to be hoped that Paige had not heard this exchange, for both she and the captain had been speaking in normal tones. But Paige resisted the impulse to intervene, curious to hear how Kit would explain her confusing nomenclature.

Reluctant to delve into her benefactress's personal history with a stranger, Kit temporized, saying, "Actually, Captain Owens, her Christian name is Babette, and (oh, dear, what a muddle!) I suggest you seek further information from the lady herself."

Before the captain had done so, Paige spontaneously turned from the window, abandoning the role she had decided to adopt all the way to London (one of haughty indifference), and enthusiastically launched into telling a tale she relished.

As a child she had stubbornly refused to wear skirts, for she found they hampered her attempts to keep up with her brother in tree climbing, stalking imaginary enemies, and crawling through hedges. Her indulgent father sided with her against the protestations of her prudish governess; thus Paige could be seen playing in the woods and fields in a blouse and short pants, hair unrestrained by ribands. Once, when she bolted into the drawing room, where her parents were taking their tea, to recount her day's exploits, her father remarked (winking at his fashionably beribboned French wife) that their daughter did not resemble her mother, for whom she had been named. Dandling Paige on his knee and pushing her hair from her eyes, he laughingly told her she looked like a page in a medieval history book. From that point on, he began to call her "my page," then simply "page." When the rest of the family found she delighted in her pet name, they all began to address her similarly—and soon even the servants were calling her "Miss Page."

At this point Kit interrupted the narrative, urging Paige to explain the unconventional spelling of her nickname.

Chuckling at the memory, Paige recalled the day when

she was in her twelfth year and wrote her first letter to Richard, who was up at Oxford. At the end of her scribblings, faced with signing "Page," she had hesitated. Struck by the masculinity of the spelling, but still finding "Babette" unsuitably frilly, she impulsively inserted an "i" between the "a" and the "g" in "Page" and was satisfied with her effort. In fact, she liked it so well that she wrote "Paige" wherever she could—in the margins of her lesson books, in her samplers, and even in the stable yard dust. Later, as a mature woman, she recoiled at signing her given name on formal documents presented by her father's solicitor, for she was not the exotic person "Babette" implied. "Paige" was a much more comfortable appellation; it described the kind of woman she wanted to be—a blend of the best masculine and feminine traits: capable and caring.

"Paige," the captain repeated slowly, drawing the name out as he appraised the suitability of it. "I like it," he concluded. "It is a unique name for an out-of-the-ordinary person."

Appreciative of this sentiment, and struck by the sincerity of its delivery, Paige forgot about the set-down she had been planning for him since leaving the parlor of the Cock 'N' Hen. Instead, she turned pink with pleasure and said, "I am glad you like it, though you are of the minority opinion—as most of my acquaintance think it too earthy a name for a well-bred lady."

Secretly feeling that using the word *earthy* was also unsuitable for a well-bred young lady, Kit turned the conversation in another direction. "Captain, surely you can relieve the tedium of the journey by recounting some tales of your exciting adventures on the Peninsula."

"I am afraid, Miss Roche, that my life has been quite a bit less exciting than you might imagine," he dissembled, shifting his long legs to relieve a cramped muscle. "War is not all heroic deeds; it is dirty, exhausting, horrifying, and often even boring. I would rather regale you with tales of the scrapes my brother and I got into at our home in Penllyn.''

An attractive lopsided grin transformed his features as he recalled his worst childhood offense. He and Evan had been hunting mice in the fragrant hayfield when they'd found a better quarry: a garter snake. David, conceiving a plan to disrupt their science lessons with a genuine specimen, had slipped the harmless snake into his jacket pocket. By the time the boys had finished playing and returned to the house, David had forgotten his reptilian friend, for his goal was Cook's raspberry tarts. Throwing his much abused jacket on a chair in the kitchen, he and Evan had competed to see who could eat the most without getting sick (a contest traditionally won by neither competitor). During this event the snake had crawled out of its prison and slithered across the stone floor, right into the path of Molly, the easily frightened scullery maid. The spectacle of Molly shrieking and hopping about the kitchen would have been great entertainment had she not been carrying a loaded tray of his mother's prized Sèvres china.

At this point David's narrative was interrupted by a horrified gasp from Kit and a shout of merriment from Paige.

"Well you may laugh, Miss Undershaw, but it was only momentarily amusing to *me,* for I was punished by being deprived of a visit to the annual village fair—a fate worse than death for a nine-year-old.''

"Did your brother share in your punishment?'' Kit asked.

"That would have been unjust, for he had tried to dissuade me from taking the snake home. I persuaded my parent that he was not involved.''

Kit praised warmly, "What an honorable act for a boy of only nine years! Where is your brother now, sir?''

With a sharp intake of breath, Paige looked anxiously at the captain, who assured her, with a shake of his head, that it was all right now to discuss this once forbidden subject.

Turning to Kit, he explained, "I have until now avoided mention of him, ma'am, as he is recently deceased—but I feel that it would be cathartic to speak of him to such sympathetic company.

"We were just a year apart, so we felt for each other much what twins do, though in temperament he was much different from me. He died of the influenza a month ago, surviving his wife by only a day, and orphaning their only child, Pamela, not quite five months old."

Fumbling in her reticule, Miss Roche extracted a serviceable handkerchief, with which she dabbed her eyes and murmured emotionally, "Oh, the poor little darling!"

Concerned, Paige said sympathetically, "What a tragedy! Who cares for her presently?"

Sighing, David responded, "I am her sole guardian, but as I must return to the Continent, she resides with my mother. It is not entirely a satisfactory arrangement...."

"Oh, yes," Paige recalled. "You mentioned that your mother is not in good health."

"Yes, she herself is still recovering from the influenza, and is much weakened," he confirmed regretfully.

"Oh, dear. Oh, dear!" Kit cried. "How can you leave them?!"

"It is not easy, ma'am, for my cousin and heir, Sylvester, is not to be relied upon. His habits run to dissolution and his only concern for his family lies in extracting money to cover his debts. If only I knew of someone in London who could affectionately fulfill my role as guardian, I would bring my mother and the babe to town. I am uneasy about their being alone in that great house with just the servants to look after them."

Noticing that the discussion of these melancholy events had become too distressing for Miss Roche, who was now practically sobbing into her handkerchief, Captain Owens shifted the focus to what he hoped was a more salubrious topic. "What takes you ladies to London?"

Recognizing the motive behind his polite question, Paige

energetically launched into a succinct explanation: their recently widowed childhood friend, Lady Bragdon, was in need of company and had invited them for an extended stay.

"Is this your first visit to London?" he inquired predictably.

Simultaneously, Kit said, "Yes!" and Paige said, "No!" Paige allowed Kit to clarify this puzzling response. "This is *my* first visit; however, Miss Undershaw has had several Seasons there." Proudly, Kit added, "And had no fewer than three *very* eligible offers in her first Season."

"What? Only three?" Captain Owens grinned, glancing at Miss Undershaw with amusement.

Missing the light irony, Kit objected, "But she has had at *least* one in every year since!"

"And how many years is that?"

"Cad!" Paige gurgled.

Misinterpreting the exchange between the captain and her friend, Kit jumped to Paige's defense by pointing out that Miss Undershaw had just recently received a most flattering declaration from the local squire.

"The local squire!" David repeated enthusiastically, eyes agleam. "Surely you cannot have turned him down, Miss Undershaw!"

"You sound like my sister-in-law, for whom increasing one's status and worldly goods is the only reason to marry," disclosed Paige incautiously.

"Would this be Richard's wife of whom you speak?" the captain wondered incredulously.

"It can be no other, for he is my only sibling." Sighing in exasperation and pushing an escaping lock of hair from her eyes, she continued, "You have been frank with us about your situation, so I shall be frank about my own. Richard's wife is not the one I would have chosen for him, nor do I think Richard would have selected her for himself had there been an alternative. But Dorcas pursued him relentlessly, finally entrapping him in a scene which compromised her virtue, knowing full well that Richard would do the honorable thing. I realize, sir, that my brother is not blameless, but for all his thirty-two years he is quite naïve and never would suspect anyone of dishonorable intentions, especially a woman." Turning her head at an angle, she reflected, "But, then, he was raised with well-bred young women. Dorcas, sir, did not fit into this category. Though a distant, but respectable cousin presented her to society, no one was quite certain of her antecedents," she concluded ominously.

"How came he, then, to marry her?" the captain asked curiously.

"My understanding is that she enticed him into a secluded room by swooning in his arms as they were passing the door. She had artfully arranged for a friend to enter that room just as he was gently placing her onto the settee. Realizing that no explanation would serve, he immediately offered to put a notice of their betrothal into *The Gazette*. Of course Dorcas readily agreed," Paige recounted bitterly.

Appalled, the captain ejaculated, "But did he not see through her scheme?"

"No, and I fear that he still does not, and *I* do not wish to be the one to enlighten him. It has become impossible for me to be around her, knowing her true character. Moreover, *she* knows that I cannot like her, and as mistress of Waverly she has it in her power to make my life there intolerable."

"So you are running away?" the captain guessed perceptively.

"You could put it that way; however, I have always wanted to live independently, and this is my opportunity to do so. Miss Roche and I plan not to return to Waverly after our visit with Cornelia, though Richard and Dorcas know naught of this."

"Then," he wondered, "where will you reside?"

She quickly explained their plans to hire a suitable residence in London, then remove to Bath at the end of the Season.

The captain was thoughtful for a moment, then offered, "Why not lease my townhouse? It is on Berkeley Square, and will otherwise sit empty the entire Season."

Surprised into a social gaffe, Kit exclaimed disdainfully, "Do you mean to say that you, Captain, *own* a townhouse on Berkeley Square? Your prize money must have been substantial!"

Horrified at her companion's unguarded tongue, Paige interposed, "Kit, I am sure you did not mean to imply that the captain is not of the *haut ton*. After all, his father was the sixth Earl of Penllyn!" Turning to the captain for confirmation, she asked, "Is that not so, sir?"

Deducing that the time had come to clarify his station, Captain Owens admitted, "Yes, and I must confess that I am the eighth earl—my brother having held the title before me." Concerned that they would think he had been deliberately deceiving them, he added apologetically, "The title has been such an unwanted and recent acquisition that I scarcely remember *myself* that I am such an exalted individual."

Torn between embarrassment at her previous gaucherie and delight that Paige had become acquainted with such a highly eligible gentleman, Kit was initially speechless, then turned to Paige and said, "I am sure that someone of His Lordship's consequence must know that I intended no offense."

With twitching lips, "His Lordship" intervened solemnly, "I did not take it as such, ma'am." Then, catching Paige's amused eyes, he almost lost his composure and resorted to coughing fiercely into his handkerchief.

Kit, taking the coughing fit at face value, expressed hope that the earl had not contracted the influenza. Never one to ignore a matchmaking opportunity, she promptly began to tout Paige's skills as a nurse and recounted in oppressive detail the four or five occasions when she had witnessed the miraculous return of Paige's patients from death's very door.

Hoping to forestall an additional sickroom anecdote, the earl said gravely, "I assure you, ma'am, that it is not I who need nursing. It is my mother and niece who could benefit from her angelic ministrations."

Sensing an opportunity to prolong the contact between Paige and the earl, Kit impulsively suggested that if he could get his family to London, she was sure Miss Undershaw would see to their care.

Filling the astonished silence that followed Kit's impassioned avowal, David lightly riposted, "I am certain that Miss Undershaw would fulfill those responsibilities creditably; but it is a duty I could not ask of anyone outside the family."

This was the very thing Miss Roche wanted to hear! The plots of the romantic novels she was addicted to now swam before her eyes—and before she knew what she was about she found herself suggesting that the earl *make* Paige a member of his family.

The earl wondered dryly, "And how do you suggest I accomplish that? Pass her off as a recently discovered third cousin?"

Swept away by her fantasy, Kit continued, "Why, *marry* her, sir! . . . Of course, this would be a marriage in name only, but it would solve *your* need for a suitable surrogate guardian 'til you return from the Continent, and Miss *Undershaw's* problem of finding a home without upsetting her dear brother!" (Kit felt no compulsion to mention that it would also solve her *own* problem of seeing Paige comfortably established, for it was certain that the captain and Paige would eventually discover the mutual *tendre* they had already developed.)

Accustomed to Kit's occasional flights of imagination, Paige clapped her hands in glee and responded, "But of course! How stupid of us not to have thought of it! It answers every concern." Thinking to share this joke with the captain, she turned to him in amusement and encountered a distracted, meditative expression.

The captain's mind was in a whirl. At first the suggestion had seemed preposterous, but second thoughts now led him to quite a different conclusion; marriage to Miss Undershaw could certainly relieve him of his most pressing concern. She was of a highly respectable family, and though he had been acquainted with her for a shockingly brief time, he found her to be a most resourceful yet compassionate individual. He had few reservations about leaving his mother and niece in her care—certainly fewer than he had about any of the other persons he had considered. Moreover, this plan would also be to Miss Undershaw's benefit: as his wife, she would have a temporary refuge from which to establish herself independently in society ... "temporary," because of course the marriage would be annulled when (if!) he returned from the war. Though time was short, he felt certain he could arrange matters with his man of business in the two days he had remaining in England. His hardest task would likely be persuading the lady herself of the wisdom of the plan, for despite her individualism she was not without a sense of propriety. *Well,* he thought, unconsciously squaring his broad shoulders, *I must make a start on that now.*

Reaching over and gently taking Paige's hand in his own, he asked quite simply, "Well, ma'am, would you do me the honor of becoming my wife?"

Shaken by the patent seriousness of his manner, Paige quickly removed her slightly trembling hand from his grasp and stammered, "S-surely you jest, sir?!"

"I do not, ma'am. I am in earnest, for after a swift assessment of Miss Roche's proposition, I find myself agreeing with her that it would answer both our needs. Let me reassure you that I also agree with her that it would be a 'marriage in name only'; when I return, we should be able to procure an annulment with ease, for we would not have lived together as man and wife. Come, Miss Undershaw," he added persuasively, "where is your spirit of adventure? Can you not see the advantages this union would have?''

Paige was in turmoil. Her emotions fluctuated between relief at the easy solution to her immediate problem, shock and fear at the impropriety of the suggestion, and glee at the thought of Dorcas's jealous reaction to the news that Paige had become a countess. She could not instantly reconcile these conflicting sentiments.

Reading into the earl's ready acceptance of her suggestion an affection for Paige that she had not anticipated, the ever-romantic Kit threw caution to the wind and pressed Paige to accept by reminding her that as a married woman she would be permitted the freedom she so desired.

This was just the right appeal to make to Miss Undershaw, who began to seriously consider the plan. However, she could—and did—foresee several obstacles and began to voice them. ''Whatever will our families say when they find us so suddenly wed to strangers?''

Anticipating this objection, the earl had his answer ready. ''May I remind you, ma'am, that I am no stranger to your brother? Based on my brief encounter with him a twelvemonth ago, I believe he would not look unfavorably upon our union, though he might be surprised at its suddenness. During our conversation he had several times mentioned his ''most delightful younger sister,'' whom he hoped I would soon have the opportunity to meet. As for my own parent, my mother will welcome you to her bosom as soon as she realizes that you and she are cut from the same cloth. You must believe that she has been plaguing me for years to marry and settle down. I am certain also that she will support the story we must circulate to silence society's tabbies: that we have long been acquainted and have been secretly betrothed this last year.''

With a touch of desperation, Paige continued, ''Well, then there is the matter of the marriage settlement.''

''Yes, I have considered that, also. As soon as possible

after our arrival in London, you and I will meet jointly with my man of business, who will, I am certain, work out a mutually satisfactory arrangement. I assure you, Miss Undershaw, that I am a wealthy man, so you need not worry about being provided for.''

Huffily, Paige retorted, ''I do not need to be provided for, sir, as I am a wealthy woman in my own right! What *I* am concerned about is the effect this marriage may have on your heirs.''

''I can assure you, ma'am, that none of my *deserving* family will suffer financially because of our marriage.''

Somewhat mollified, she went on, ''But surely, sir, all of this cannot be arranged in the time available before you set sail. When will that be?''

''Two days hence; but my solicitor, Mr. Oakes, is exceedingly capable, and my uncle is a bishop (I never thought I'd rejoice in *that!*), so we need have no difficulty in obtaining a special license.''

Left with no further significant objections, Paige reluctantly acquiesced, much to the relief of Kit and the earl, who had both been holding their breath. Then, cognizant of the honor he had done her by asking her to become his wife, she gazed directly into his anxious gray eyes and said softly, ''My lord, I would be honored to become your . . . temporary wife.''

''You've made me a happy man, Miss Undershaw,'' the captain assured her sincerely, raising her hand to his lips.

Witnessing this scene with a profound sense of self-satisfaction, Kit gushed, ''Oh, my dear Paige, I am so happy for you! You'll make a beautiful bride!''

''Doing it too brown, Kit,'' the prospective bride said, laughing. ''This is more of a business arrangement than the culmination of a storybook romance.''

''As to that,'' the earl noted, ''we will be approaching London within the hour, and had best occupy ourselves with working out the details of our promising agreement.''

With a merriment that relieved the tension that had filled

the carriage, the three coconspirators mapped out the next two days—and they were to be full indeed, with business arrangements to be made, families and friends to be notified, the opening of the earl's townhouse, and the wedding itself.

Chapter IV

CRANING their necks as the carriage turned onto Park Place, the excited female occupants competed like children to be the first to catch sight of the Bragdon townhouse. Kit suddenly bounced on her seat, pointed madly out her window, and cried, "There is number twenty!" However, it was Jack Coachman who had actually seen it first, for the coach was already slowing so that it could be maneuvered into a favorable position for unloading.

As the vehicle came to a halt, the earl descended first; but before he could give his hand to one of the ladies the door of number twenty was flung open by one of the most beautiful women he'd ever beheld: ravishing black locks framed an exquisite heart-shaped face, which was animated with undisguised delight. His immediate thought was that this must be the ladies' recently widowed friend, Cornelia, for her divine figure was outfitted in a mourning dress of black twilled French silk. As he continued to gaze at her in admiration, she bubbled, *"Soyez les bienvenues, mes chères amies! Mais, qui est ce beau cavalier?"*

Stepping from the coach, Paige laughingly admonished her betrothed for being so awestruck by Cornelia's beauty that she failed to hand her down. Then she rushed into Cornelia's fragrant embrace. "Ah, your French improves! I am convinced that you mean to serve our country as a spy in Paris!'' Paige joked affectionately.

''Compliments will not deter me from my object, *ma chérie,* which right now is to learn the identity of this handsome soldier with whom you seem so familiar!'' her hostess retorted.

To her chagrin, Paige found herself blushing fetchingly to the shade of her rose-colored velvet pelisse. To cover her discomfort (for Paige was not ready to reveal the extent of her relationship with the earl), she changed the subject and gushed, ''I will first have you meet the love of my life,'' and rushed to the coach to extract Snow's basket, which slipped from her grasp as she hastily turned to show Cornelia its contents.

Confusion ensued as the lid sprang open to give Snow his first taste of freedom since he was lured from under the chair in the Cock 'N' Hen's parlor. In a flash he was streaking down the street, pursued by the quick-footed earl, who finally managed to snatch his quarry from an untimely demise under the wheels of a tradesman's wagon.

Though partially distracted by an effusive greeting from Kit, Cornelia did not fail to note the relief that flooded Paige's face as the soldier and kitten emerged uninjured from under the cart. As the two disheveled males returned to the ladies, Cornelia glanced penetratingly at Paige and inquired without the trace of a French accent, ''I wonder whom you were more concerned about—the soldier or the cat?''

Puzzled at Cornelia's intent, Paige replied promptly, ''Whatever do you mean? I am naturally concerned with both of them.''

Trusting her intuition, Cornelia was sure that there was something more to the relationship with the soldier than Paige was willing to admit; but she decided to wait until they were alone to press for an explanation. Instead, she said *''Mais oui!''* Then, gracefully gesturing toward the approaching earl and his frightened charge, she added, "Do make me known at once to these two brave gentlemen!"

As Penllyn neared, Paige reached out her hands to receive the cat, who at first refused to disengage his claws from the coat of his savior. Gently coaxing Snow into retracting his needle-sharp nails without damaging the superfine wool of his jacket, the earl placed him in Miss Undershaw's outstretched arms. As she accepted the now purring kitten, Paige smiled up at the earl and teased, "I am again in your debt, sir—and will now repay you by introducing you to the woman you have been unable to take your eyes off since our arrival."

Turning to Cornelia, she queried rhetorically, "Lady Bragdon, may I present Captain Owens, Earl of Penllyn?"

Brushing Cornelia's hand with his lips, he murmured graciously, *"Enchanté, madame."* Then, more solemnly, he continued, "Allow me to express my condolences on your recent bereavement."

At these last words, Paige and Kit exchanged stricken glances as they realized that in their joy at seeing Cornelia again they had forgotten her situation.

"Thank you," Cornelia replied with composure. "Already my grief has been lightened by the arrival of my two dearest friends." She then smiled encouragingly at both these ladies, who heaved grateful sighs of relief.

Shivering slightly, Cornelia turned back to the earl and asked, "Will you come in? I have Welsh cakes for tea, and suspect those might be favorites of yours, my lord."

Mentally noting that Lady Bragdon was intelligent as well as beautiful, David replied, "The Welsh cakes sound tempting, ma'am; however, while there is still light I must find lodgings." Bowing to the other two ladies, he took Miss Undershaw aside briefly and said, "I shall call on you in the morning, for we must see my man of business as soon as possible. Can you be ready at ten?"

As she nodded affirmatively, he squeezed her slender

fingers and hopped into the carriage, shouting directions to Jack Coachman.

Entering the house, the ladies were admitted by Grimsley, the Bragdons' very correct butler, into a room that reflected the tastes of its mistress—elegantly simple. The best French period pieces mingled charmingly with solid English hardwoods. No trace of Prinny's latest preference for Oriental exotica intruded on the ambiance.

Cornelia asked the butler to postpone serving the tea for half an hour, while Kit and Paige were shown to their rooms to refresh themselves. Paige was delighted with her accommodations: Cornelia had remembered her fondness for bright colors and had put her in the yellow bedchamber. As the maid unpacked her trunks, Paige sat at the dressing table, planning how much of her extraordinary arrangement with the earl she would reveal to her hostess. As she pinned back several errant locks of hair, Paige was struck by the absurdity of trying to keep any secret from Cornelia that Kit was already privy to; for though Kit possessed many fine qualities, keeping her tongue about anything that hinted of romance was not one of them.

Together again in the drawing room, Cornelia graciously accepted her friends' belated solicitude regarding her husband's death but refused to dwell upon it, emphasizing that Tracy himself—always optimistic and high-spirited— would have wanted his lively wife to enjoy her future rather than mope about, mourning his passing.

So, with a gleam in her eye, she inquired of Paige, "What role does the dashing Earl of Penllyn play in *your* future?"

Kit, relieved at the opportunity to shift to the topic most occupying her own thoughts, launched into a detailed description of Paige's arrangement with the earl. Paige toyed with the idea of boxing Kit's ears when she heard her predictably embellished account but knew she would be able to correct misrepresentations when Kit ran out of superlatives.

To Kit's satisfaction, Cornelia was appropriately amazed at Paige's acquiescence to this daring marriage proposal and even choked on her tea when Kit described the earl on his knee in the carriage, clasping Paige's hand in uncontrolled passion and begging her to marry him. Paige also choked and almost began to wish that the narrator of this fairy tale had succumbed to her "chill" at the Cock 'N' Hen.

Finally, unable to keep silent another minute, Paige interrupted, protesting, "Cornelia, truly this is just a 'business venture.' Do not let Kit cloud your mind with her romantic notions. Surely you can see that the earl and I are both past the age of sentimental nonsense."

Unable, as true friends often are, to resist prolonging their dear ones' agitation, Cornelia objected to Paige, "Oh, pray do not say so, for I am as old as you are and have every intention of one day finding romance again."

These words recalled Paige to the practicality of the arrangement she had made. "I wish you well, Cornelia, but I guess I have not a romantic nature. This situation suits me admirably, for when the earl returns from the Continent I will have established myself in society and have the freedom to come and go as I desire. Of course, the annulment will give the tabbies something to talk of, but it will be merely a nine-day wonder. By then I will have fulfilled my responsibilities to the earl and his family and will feel good about it."

Kit and Cornelia, separately and to different degrees, felt that the annulment need never occur but wisely kept their hunches to themselves.

Always interested in fashion, Cornelia turned the topic to the wedding dress and, to her friends' surprise, withdrew a well-worn sketchbook and swiftly designed a dress suited to the occasion. Paige was astounded by her friend's ability to capture precisely what she herself would have desired. It was a high-waisted, ankle-length creation of ivory silk, trimmed with nile-green ribbon threaded through delicate lace. Though the neckline was somewhat lower than Paige was accustomed to wearing, she declared with admiration, "It is perfect! But it cannot possibly be done up in one day's time."

'Au contraire!' Cornelia objected. "I know the perfect dressmaker, who will, I am sure, oblige me. We can stop by there tomorrow morning."

"Oh, dear, I fear I cannot, as I have an appointment with Penllyn's solicitor. Will it be too late if we do it after nuncheon?"

With a secret smile, Cornelia confidently assured Paige that her dress would be ready in time even if the fitting took place in the evening. Amazed at such certainty on Cornelia's part, Kit inquired if this were Cornelia's very own modiste. Disregarding the nod that confirmed this, Paige protested, "But even if she is your own dressmaker, we cannot keep her up all night sewing!"

Cornelia replied with a knowing look, "Oh, but she will have some help."

The arrangement for a fitting having been completed, the topic shifted to a discussion of the ladies' families and mutual friends. Cornelia coerced Paige into revealing the unpleasantness of Richard's situation. Knowing how close Cornelia and Richard had been as children, Paige was not surprised by the intensity of her friend's distress upon hearing that Richard was unhappy.

If only Richard had married someone with Cornelia's fine sensibilities, Paige mused, with fleeting wishes for Dorcas's early demise. Ashamed at her own lack of charity, Paige searched for something positive to say about her sister-in-law and finally owned that Dorcas *had* done wonders with the garden at Waverly.

The rest of the night, which included a sumptuous dinner, was spent in that comfortable coze that Paige and Kit had so been looking forward to when stranded at the Cock 'N' Hen.

Promptly at ten the following morning, the earl arrived in a hired chaise. Paige looked fetching in a walking dress of dove-gray bombazine trimmed with claret-colored braid. Her three-quarter-length redingote reversed the colors—being wine-colored with gray velvet bands and tassels. A matching beret-styled velvet hat featuring an ostrich plume was perched at a jaunty angle on her dusky-brown locks.

As he touched her arm to guide her down the steps, the earl commented on her dashing appearance: "I can see now that I need not worry about my friends questioning my sudden decision to wed, for when they clap eyes on my choice of bride, all questions will be silenced."

Exhilarated by the bright morning and the compliment, Paige laughed and said, "Oh, just the right note to take, my lord! I am in high spirits and feel a light flirtation is just what we need before our serious business discussion."

"What?!" he exclaimed in shocked accents. "This, from the woman who gave me a severe set-down on this very subject in the parlor of the Cock 'N' Hen?"

Paige drew back from him in mock horror. "Oh, no. I fear I must reconsider this marriage, for I cannot abide men with long memories who are constantly reminding me of previous statements I have made which contradict present ones," she retorted gaily.

"Vixen!" He laughed, inwardly delighted with the variety of her moods.

Her air of levity was contagious, and the ride to the solicitor's was spent in cheerful banter.

Their arrival at their destination, however, caused a constraint to develop between them, as each became aware of the reality of their momentous decision; and they ascended the stairs to Mr. Oakes's offices in silence.

That personage himself came forward to greet them, and Paige was immediately put at her ease. He was a jolly, plump man with intelligent pale blue eyes behind thick spectacles and a shiny bald pate. He seemed not the slightest bit disturbed at the nature of their business and assured Paige that since he had been the Owens family solicitor for some twenty years, he would have their, and her, best interests at heart. Paige instinctively felt she could believe him, for he was not in the least condescending. Rather, he welcomed her questions and suggestions and incorporated them into the final marriage settlement.

The major provisions of this contract were that Paige's inheritance would remain separate from Penllyn's monies and therefore remain under her control. Though she would draw upon his funds for expenses for the household and his niece, Pamela, Miss Undershaw was adamant that her personal needs be provided for by her own substantial income. During the earl's absence, the management of Penllyn and the other family landholdings were to be the concern of Mr. Oakes and the bailiffs of those properties.

As they concluded the discussion of this unconventional contract, Mr. Oakes nervously cleared his throat and ventured, "Now, my lord, what are your wishes concerning your will?"

The earl was obviously more comfortable with this subject than was his solicitor, for he promptly began to outline the changes he wanted made. His cousin Sylvester was to receive nothing but the entailed estates and their income. The remainder of David's property and monies (less five thousand pounds per annum) would be held in trust until the infant Lady Pamela came of age. To fulfill the role of guardian for his niece, he had already obtained the consent of his close friend Jerry, Lord Hadley, and was now hoping that Paige would agree to jointly serve with that gentleman.

At the thought of the earl's possible demise and the heavy responsibility she would be left with, Paige momentarily panicked and had to control an absurd impulse to turn to her betrothed and tell him that she would under no circumstances marry him unless he promised to remain alive until the annulment. Then, imagining the look on his face were she to speak these thoughts aloud, she began to giggle, much to her horror.

"You find the thought of acting as coguardian to my

niece amusing?" the earl questioned, raising his dark eyebrows.

"Of course not," Paige objected, still laughing. "It was only that I had not previously thought of your death."

"Oh, so it's my death that occasions such mirth?" he postulated, raising his eyebrows even higher.

"No, no! Oh, dear, I only seem to be making things worse. Richard is right—I do have the most inappropriate sense of humor. It is best now that we get back to the business at hand before I start laughing again," she barely articulated as laughter once again overcame her. There being nothing quite so contagious as an uncontrollable fit of giggling, the earl and Mr. Oakes finally succumbed, and soon all three were wiping their streaming eyes.

Regaining his composure first, the earl declared, "Well, I see that I cannot count on you two as mourners. But can I count on you, Miss Undershaw, to be Pamela's guardian?"

Recalling the seriousness of the request, Paige instantly sobered and replied, "Yes, sir, of course. I hope I am worthy of the trust you bestow upon me."

David was relieved to hear this, for although Jerry was the finest of fellows, he did possess a streak of irresponsibility which would be offset by Paige's sense of duty and sound reasoning. Since Jerry had agreed to act as the earl's witness to the marriage ceremony, David would have the opportunity to see, before his departure for Belgium, how these two guardians got on together.

At this point, Mr. Oakes intervened to ask the earl who was to receive the five thousand pounds per year he had mentioned before. Looking vaguely uncomfortable, David mumbled in a low voice, "My widow," then quickly asked when Mr. Oakes could send the completed documents around to be signed.

As it took a full minute for Paige to realize that she was the "widow" to whom this bequest was made, she raised no immediate objection. But as the meaning of his words fully penetrated her brain, she startled the gentlemen by banging her fist on the desk and declaring, "But that is absurd! As your wife in name only, I have no claims on your estate and I will not see your rightful family denied their full due."

Mr. Oakes, pretending an intense preoccupation with some papers on his desk, waited curiously to see how the earl would handle this determined young woman.

Knowing better than to try to convince Paige that it was for her sake he was leaving her the money, David argued instead that his own feelings required it. "If I die at the hand of the Frenchies, ma'am, you will be the only wife I ever had, and it would please me to know that I have left you with something other than the burden of the responsibility of my family."

These words were spoken with such sincerity and intensity of feeling that Paige would have been lost to all sensibility if she had continued to reject his wishes. So she conceded defeat on the matter, saying softly, "If it means that much to you, sir—my lord, I mean."

Having borne witness to the easy and affectionate camaraderie between these clients, Mr. Oakes became the third person of their acquaintance who cherished hopes that this "temporary marriage" would become a lasting one. Assuring them that they would have the papers early in the morning, he escorted the couple to their waiting chaise.

When Paige arrived back in Park Place, she found that she had an unscheduled hour which she could put to good use by writing to inform Richard of her plans.

A good half hour was spent pondering how truthful she should be in her disclosure. It pained her to lie to Richard; however, she felt that if Richard and Dorcas knew the true nature of her arrangement with Penllyn, the result would be a series of arguments. Richard would be forced to defend his sister against Dorcas's charges that Paige was an impetuous hoyden who would ruin the Undershaw name.

Having decided that the full truth would not serve, Paige

used her natural ability with words to weave a tale of a rapidly intensifying affection between herself and Captain Owens, culminating in the decision to wed before he returned to war. The rest of the letter was factual enough to relieve her conscience—it described David's recent elevation to the Penllyn earldom and her new responsibilities in caring for his mother and orphaned niece. Satisfied with her efforts, Paige was just sealing the missive when luncheon was announced.

In the early afternoon the three ladies set forth to the Bond Street modiste who was to fashion the wedding dress. Paige's apprehension at having her person inspected and assessed by an unfamiliar dressmaker dissolved as she was introduced to the owner of the establishment, a tiny elderly woman with an air of calm competence.

Kit kept wiping her red-rimmed eyes as ivory silk was draped about Paige's figure and tucked to reveal the outlines of the enchanting garment in Cornelia's sketchbook. Cornelia herself was unable to remain just an observer to these ministrations and was soon assisting Mme. Claudette. If Paige and Kit had not been preoccupied with their own thoughts, they might have found something remarkable in Cornelia's behavior or in the dressmaker's easy acceptance of it. With two sets of deft fingers arranging and pinning, the fitting was soon concluded, and the ladies were able to go on their way with the promise that the dress would be delivered in time for the eleven o'clock wedding service on the morrow.

The rest of the afternoon was spent purchasing shoes, flowers for Paige's hair, and other incidentals for the ladies.

David also had a busy afternoon. He had decided to tackle the most difficult of his tasks first—obtaining the special license. His uncle, the bishop, had the uncanny knack of making David feel as though he were in short pants again. Mumbling his way through a short defense of his hasty decision to wed, David left with the license and his uncle's reluctant agreement to officiate at the nuptial ceremony.

His next stop was at his house on Berkeley Square. He had already sent word to the Cappers, longtime retainers of the Penllyn family, that the house was to be opened, so they were not surprised to find their new master on the step.

Capper, having known David since his infancy, greeted him with an enthusiastic clap on the shoulder, followed immediately by a self-conscious bow. "Straighten up, man," David commanded his butler with a grin. "Please do not start fawning over me now that I am the earl! Where is that saucy wife of yours? I want to tell you, together, some extraordinary news."

The two men went to the library, where they found Mrs. Capper removing the last of the Holland covers. He bade them be comfortable, then told them of his marriage plans and requested their help in assisting their new mistress with anything she might require.

Mrs. Capper could barely suppress her curiosity about the new countess, a fact David was quick to note. "You will like her," he offered with a twinkle in his eye. "She is much like my mother, who I know is a favorite of yours"—as though that explained everything. And it did, in their eyes.

At this point Mrs. Capper ventured to inquire after the health of the dowager Lady Penllyn. Concern darkened David's face as he replied that her health could be better, but he counted on Mrs. Capper's fine cooking to set things right again.

Both Cappers' faces lit up at the obvious implication that Lady Susan would soon be with them. Responding to their animation, David confirmed, "Yes, she is to join you, and is bringing Evan and Louisa's daughter, Pamela."

"Ah, the poor thing!" exclaimed the butler sympathetically. "We will see to her comfort." Then, perking up, he added, "It has been a long time since we've had a babe to spoil." Winking at the earl, he said, "You were the last, sir."

As he rose to take his leave, David promised to bring his bride around to Berkeley Square after the ceremony to meet them and to make arrangements for hiring the full staff.

Feeling the need to walk off his accumulated energy, David dismissed the hired chaise and set out on foot to his lodgings.

Tomorrow at this time he would be a married man! Sentiments that he had not had time to reflect upon now rushed to his consciousness. He had always supposed he would marry for love, though he never would have admitted it to his friends, who disparaged such romantic notions. Though he liked and admired Miss Undershaw, he certainly was not in love with her—for this was not how he'd imagined love to be. While he enjoyed her company, he did not think of her when out of her presence. Neither did he have a longing to slip his arms around her tiny waist and steal a kiss. It saddened him to think that he would be reciting the sacred vows of marriage with an absence of proper feeling; and that he should be asking her to do the same.

Coming to an abrupt halt in the middle of the street and narrowly avoiding being run down by a buck on horseback, the earl was struck by the realization that it was not too late to undo their plans. His mother *had* assured him that she could manage quite well at Penllyn; and perhaps he had misjudged Sylvester—surely if David died, his cousin would not take advantage of his mother's and Pamela's vulnerable situation.

David conjured up an image of Sylvester's ruddy countenance, framed with flaming red hair and with close-set eyes so dark as to be almost black. Reflecting on this picture, the earl remembered that although his cousin could be charmingly attractive when it suited him, his overall air was one of furtiveness—and he had aged prematurely from too much gaming and drinking. Pausing again, the earl shook his head to erase this image and decided he simply could not trust Sylvester.

Then whom could he rely on? Lord Hadley? No; Jerry would likely soon marry and David could not burden his friend (and the unknown Lady Hadley) with a child not their own. Moreover, the possibility existed that Pamela would be ignored when the Hadley offspring began to arrive. But if his reading of Miss Undershaw was correct— and he felt sure that it was—David sensed that even if she were to marry again, she would see to it that Pamela received responsible and loving care.

With a sigh he recommitted himself to his original course of action. This decision coincided with his arrival at his hotel, and before he could change his mind again, he sealed his fate by hastily writing a long letter to his mother, conveying the plans he had decided upon and instructing her to set out for London as soon as possible.

Paige's own second thoughts came later in the evening, as she prepared to retire for the last time as a single woman. For her, not marrying for love was not the concern, for she was not at all sure she was capable of that emotion (having never experienced it). Besides, as a realist she was aware that most marriages among people of her class were not love matches—Cornelia's for one, and Richard's for another. What disturbed her was the fear that instead of gaining the independence she sought, she would lose what little she already possessed.

Upon reflection, it was rather likely that the earl would not survive the hostilities, for Napoleon was a desperate man and would certainly wage an all-out effort to regain his empire. And if Paige's reading of the earl were correct, he would insist on being in the thick of battle, thus increasing his chances of being killed. Then she would be left with the guardianship of his niece and the care of his elderly mother, tasks that would certainly restrict her activities more than she would like.

Releasing her hair from its uncomfortable confines, she began to brush it in agitation. *What have I gotten myself into now? Perhaps there is still time to extract myself, though Kit would never forgive me. Well, then she can marry him! She'd make a wonderful mother, and is certainly an excellent nurse. Moreover, it would answer all her financial needs.*

Donning her red dressing gown, she was reminded of her first encounter with the captain and smiled to herself to think of how Kit might have reacted under the same circumstances. Poor Captain Owens! To be confronted with an hysterical female, shrieking incoherently, in his tired and disconsolate state. No, Kit would never suit him, for they would not find the same things humorous.

Then there is Cornelia, Paige mused. Though she could not doubt that the earl would find marriage to Lady Bragdon attractive, this was also an unsuitable alternative, as Cornelia was still in deep mourning.

As Paige snuffed out her candle, she realized that she could not let the earl down. She had given him her word, and she would not go back on it. (In addition, she *had* sent that letter to Richard!) There was nothing for it but to become Countess Penllyn on the morrow.

Everyone was up early for a hearty breakfast, as there were many things still to be done in preparation for the wedding. The household staff bustled about cheerily, glad to have some relief from the oppressive atmosphere of mourning. Snow seemed to sense that something special was about to occur, for he was permitted to weave about the legs of the ladies, rubbing affectionately against their skirts.

Kit was already sniffling at the thought of being parted from her friend, though Paige would not remove to Berkeley Square until the arrival of Lady Susan and Pamela, which would not be for at least a fortnight. Cornelia, denied the long visit from both her friends that she had anticipated, had begged Kit to remain indefinitely with her. Loath to leave Paige, but realizing she might be in the way at the Penllyn residence, Kit had reluctantly accepted the invitation.

They had scarcely left the table when the gown arrived, earlier than they had hoped. It was even more lovely than they had expected, and they rushed upstairs to inspect it. Kit and Cornelia dismissed the disappointed abigail so they could fuss about Paige themselves. While Kit dressed Paige's hair, Cornelia adjusted the gown.

As they were attending to the last details of Paige's toilette, the banished abigail reappeared smugly, bearing an elegant leather case and an accompanying card for Paige. "This was just delivered by His Lordship. He asked that you open it immediately."

Puzzled, Paige slowly opened the case while her two friends clustered about her, bursting with curiosity. Inside lay the most exquisite emerald pendant any of the three had ever seen. "Read the card!" insisted Kit. Paige, momentarily dazzled, allowed Kit to open it for her. But as the silence grew, Cornelia realized that Kit had become too choked up to reveal its contents to the others; so she snatched it from her friend's grasp and read aloud, "To match my wife's beautiful eyes. Penllyn."

Anticipating that Paige was about to protest such an expensive gift, Cornelia lifted the pendant from its nest of satin and fastened it around Paige's slender neck, where it lay sparkling against her alabaster skin.

Touching her gift wistfully, Paige declared, "But he should not have done this. It is not a real marriage, and, besides, I have no gift for *him*. I shall return it after the ceremony," she said decisively.

Kit and Cornelia knew better than to disagree or argue with her. Their mutual hunch was that David could handle any protests that Paige might make, and that the emerald would find its way permanently into Paige's jewel box.

David arrived at the church before the ladies, coming directly from delivering the necklace. To his amazement, Jerry was already there, having misunderstood the hour of the ceremony.

"So you're going to go through with it!" Jerry greeted him. "I never thought you would beat me to the altar, for you've shown no inclination in the past to get leg-shackled. This bride of yours must be a prime article for you not to wait to wed her until you return."

David retorted playfully, "Ah, but if I were to leave her unwed in Town with you about, I fear I might lose her to your charm."

Toying with his artfully arranged cravat, Jerry responded, "No, seriously, David, why are you marrying in such haste? She is not increasing, is she?"

Considering Paige and David's actual relationship, this suggestion was so ludicrous as to cause the earl to guffaw heartily. He was wishing Paige were there to share the joke.

David hated lying to his friend but felt it would be awkward for Paige if too many people were in possession of the facts, so he merely responded, "No, that is not the story. What we are putting about is that Miss Undershaw and I have been acquainted for many years, and were secretly betrothed this last year. I will fill in the true details to you when I am back, and must ask you not to press me further now."

Respecting his friend's wishes, Jerry ceased his questioning—for the moment, anyway. However, being a lover of intrigue, he vowed to become better acquainted with the new Countess Penllyn and was sure (if he did) that he could piece together the details of the story before David's return.

His first opportunity came immediately, as the ladies arrived that moment. "Good God!" Jerry expostulated, beholding the enchanting trio before him. "If any one of these beauties is to be your wife, I see no need to further question your motives.''

David scarcely heard him, for he was caught up in his own admiration. Although indeed all three ladies looked lovely, his eyes were immediately drawn to Paige. He had expected her to turn herself out elegantly but had not anticipated that she would resemble the exotic bride of his dreams. Her brilliant green eyes put the emerald to shame, and the flowers in her hair exuded a heady perfume.

Dazed, he failed to hear her initial greeting. Jerry's elbow in his ribs recalled him to his senses, and he stepped forward to draw her aside. ''You look bewitching,'' he exclaimed, still awed. Then, more confidingly, he suggested that they address each other by their Christian names—quickly adding, ''For the sake of appearances.''

Before responding, Paige surveyed her future husband with an appreciative eye. Mimicking him, she complimented, ''And you, my lord, are bang up to the nines! Just tell me your Christian name, and I will oblige.''

Bowing, he said, ''David Owens at your command, my lady,'' gray eyes twinkling down at her from under curling black lashes.

''My dear David, your flirtation is wasted. After all, we are about to be wed.'' His reply was interrupted by Lord Hadley's demand to be made known to the future countess.

Placing his arm gingerly around his betrothed's waist, the earl made the introductions.

Just then the distinguished white-haired bishop appeared, and the introductions were repeated. Ushering the party into the chapel, David's uncle suggested that they get on with the service, as he was a busy man.

Paige found herself focusing on Kit's loud sobs as the service progressed. She wondered what in the bishop's monotone delivery could have inspired such a reaction, as she herself felt removed from the proceedings. Suddenly Paige felt everyone looking at her and realized a response was called for.

"I will," she intoned, hoping they had reached this point in the service. As the bishop droned on, she surmised that she had said the correct thing and determined to pay more attention to the remainder of the ceremony. As the next requirement of the rites was for David to take her hand in his, this was easy to do. The pressure of his fingers against hers called forth an agitation she had not expected to experience.

Looking directly into her eyes, David spoke his vows with such conviction that it heightened her discomfiture. Paige's own vows were repeated in a less steady voice than she had planned. Fortunately, no one noticed her quavering speech, as a voice began howling in protest at the back of the chapel. All heads turned to espy an outraged Snow prancing down the aisle, waving his tail like a flag.

His destination appeared to be the earl, whom he had not seen in over a day. Lord Hadley stepped hastily forward to shoo away the animal, dropping the wedding ring in the process. While Jerry retrieved the ring, David scooped up the hissing cat and told his uncle to proceed.

As the point had arrived to place the ring on Paige's finger, David handed the startled bishop the cat while he carried out this action. Paige was barely concealing her mirth, and to Kit and Cornelia's horror, she burst out laughing at the sight of Snow clawing the clerical vestments. David, having a firmer control over his emotions, whispered in her ear that she should relieve his uncle of his burden— and throughout the rest of the ceremony, Snow looked on, purring contentedly, from the comfortable position in the crook of his mistress's arm.

As the final words were said, David brushed his lips against his wife's cheek; then, catching sight of Jerry's speculative look, he kissed her again—this time, full on the lips. The sensation was so pleasurable that the length of the kiss exceeded what was called for. Paige stepped back, breathless, looking at him in confusion, and encountered a gaze that was no more steady than her own. This trancelike state was soon disturbed by fresh sobs from Kit, felicitations from Cornelia, and meowing from Snow, who had been somewhat crushed in their embrace.

Laughing self-consciously, Penllyn suggested that they be on their way to Berkeley Square, as he only had an hour before setting off for the coast.

Once there, Paige and the Cappers took to each other within minutes: she enjoyed their cheerful demeanor, and they were impressed with her informality. Promising to return the next day for a complete tour, Paige was handed into the carriage by David and they set off for Park Place.

The first few minutes of the trip passed in awkward silence, which Paige broke by turning in vexation to her husband and saying, "I am sure, David, that I am not going to like marriage to you at all, if it is going to mean that we no longer have anything to say to each other. I have often observed that marriage alters a relationship, but I had not known that the effect was so immediate. I already miss our easy companionship."

Smiling ruefully, David confessed, "I have been silent because there is something I want to say to you, but I cannot find the words for it." Adjusting his collar as though to relieve its tightness, he made an attempt at speech. "I . . . um, want to . . . um, apologize, Paige, for . . . well—the kiss."

Trying to lighten the moment, Paige queried, "What is there to apologize for? You *are* my husband, and, anyway, I rather enjoyed it."

"Well, dash it all, I did, too, but my apology is for extending it beyond what was necessary to provide the correct impression."

"Then why *did* you prolong it? I will own having wondered at the time."

"I am really not certain," he offered. "I had thought that I was proving to Jerry that our relationship was one of long standing and deep affection."

"And now you do not think that was the reason?" Paige interjected.

"No. If I am honest with myself, I think that rationale does not completely answer." Staring sheepishly at her, he admitted, "I was surprised at how pleasurable it was."

"Oh? You did not expect that kissing me would be pleasurable?"

"To tell the truth, I had never really thought about it until I did it."

Theatrically pressing her hand to her heart, Paige sighed facetiously. "And here I harbored hopes that you had found me irresistible, and that all last evening you lay awake anticipating the moment of our embrace."

"Baggage!" teased the earl, grateful to his wife for preventing him from making a more complete gudgeon of himself.

Therefore it was in high spirits that they arrived at the Bragdon townhouse. The earl did not enter, as he was already behind in his schedule, so the newlyweds bade each other farewell on the stoop.

Surprised to find tears pricking her eyes, Paige admonished Penllyn to be courageous but not foolhardy, for she would greatly miss his friendship. The earl soberly assured her he would heed her advice; then, eyes agleam, he suggested a parting kiss, since they had both enjoyed it so in the chapel.

Paige, curious to discover how it would feel a second time, nodded her assent and stood on her tiptoes as Penllyn bent toward her. This time the kiss was sweet and poignant, and Paige found a tear escaping her control. Brushing it away with a gentle touch, David said, "Do not fear for me. My men say I am like a cat, for I seem to have many lives. I will soon be back to relieve you of your responsibilities before they become a burden." With that, he bounded into the carriage and was off.

Chapter V

PAIGE'S first several days as a countess were spent making domestic arrangements. Kit had accompanied her to Berkeley Square for the thorough tour and agreed with Paige that the Cappers seemed so capable and competent that she could leave the hiring of the servants entirely in their hands.

At the end of the week a letter arrived from Waverly, and Paige took it to her bedchamber—where she opened it with some trepidation.

Dearest Sister [it began],

You continue to shock us! I had never imagined that my madcap little sister would be the one to land one of the most eligible members of the *ton!* I must say, Babs, you will certainly have to change your hoydenish ways now that you are a countess. But I do not think Penllyn will keep you reined in too closely, as he did not seem like a high stickler to me. As I thought at the time of meeting him, but never mentioned to *you* (as my praise of him would have turned you away from him), he has just the sense of humour to appeal to you. I wish you very happy!

Dorcas is more skeptical than I because of the suddenness of the union and has insisted we make haste to

London to ensure all is well. (This is the very excuse she wanted to remove to Town; however, she does not know that *I* know this is a ruse to rejoin the life she likes best.) I am afraid I am sometimes dull company for her.

Paige snarled at this expression of self-deprecation and turned back to read the closing paragraph.

So we will leave for Grosvenor Square in two days' time and will call upon you once we are settled in. By the by, you may be amused that Dorcas has voiced the suspicion that you are increasing. I want to prepare you for her thorough scrutiny of your person when next we meet.

> Your loving brother,
> Richard

Paige was delighted that Richard would soon be in Town and relieved that he had accepted the story her last letter had conveyed. Still, she frowned at the thought of Dorcas's prying into her own circumstances. Much as Paige disliked her, she respected Dorcas's shrewdness and was afraid that her sister-in-law would ferret out the true nature of the marriage.

Her musings were interrupted just then by a maid announcing that Lord Hadley was below, asking for her.

Paige entered the drawing room to find her two friends and their caller engaged in a lively discussion of the latest *on-dits*. Kit had never seemed so animated. Her hazel eyes sparkled as Lord Hadley imitated the Prince Regent's attempts to lower himself onto a settee with his corset creaking in protest.

Cornelia, holding her sides, spluttered, "Oh, that is so like him! I haven't been so diverted since before poor Tracy's accident. I knew there would be joy again in this house once my friends arrived—they always attract such delightful people."

As the merry trio detected Paige's presence, Cornelia begged her to do her imitation of their former neighbor, Jane Singleton, the squire's bran-faced sister. Paige demurred, protesting that her performance could in no way compete with Lord Hadley's.

"But you must!" Kit pleaded, which puzzled Paige—since Kit customarily frowned on satirical portrayals of their acquaintances. Curious to discover the reason for her friend's uncharacteristic request, Paige obliged.

Grinning and bobbing her head toward her audience, Paige walked toward the harp and announced in a high-pitched, squeaky voice that she would play and sing an original composition in the Italian tongue. The sounds emanating from both the instrument and her mouth were so cacophonous that all three listeners had to clap their hands over their ears. Lord Hadley howled in delight and began to applaud vigorously. At this outburst Paige stopped, gave him a severe but slightly cross-eyed look, and said in Jane's grating voice, "Please, sir! I have not finished!" and resumed her noisemaking. This was too much for Cornelia, who was having trouble catching her breath as she rocked back and forth on the edge of her chair. Kit had started to hiccup and needed to be patted on the back by Lord Hadley.

Snow seemed to be the only one of the room's occupants not enjoying the proceedings. Every hair on his body stuck straight out and he began spitting in the direction of the harp. Catching sight of this phenomenon, Paige ceased her torment and began laughing herself. At that moment tea was delivered, which seemed to recall to everyone that this was a house of mourning. As the grim-faced butler turned to leave, he eyed the harp suspiciously and inquired of his mistress if she wanted him to summon the tuner. Kit, who had the least control on her emotions, began to twitter at this speech, and soon the other three found themselves once again in the throes of merriment. The butler threw back his shoulders and exited with dignity, shaking his head at the peculiar ways of the Quality.

As Cornelia poured out the tea, Paige asked Lord Hadley if there was a specific reason for his visit.

"Yes, Countess Penllyn. I wanted you to know that as David's closest friend, I am at your service should you need a male's assistance."

"I am very obliged, and pray do not be surprised if I take you up on your offer."

Not wanting to overstay his welcome, Jerry quickly finished his tea and took his leave, promising to pay a morning call later in the week.

As soon as he was out of hearing distance, Paige declared, "I like him!" Turning to Kit, she added, "And perhaps I can ask him to introduce you to his eligible friends."

Cornelia seconded Paige's suggestion while Kit blushed a rosy hue and stammered, "S-surely someone as handsome as Lord Hadley would not want to be bothered with a dab of a nobody like me."

In unison, her devoted friends scolded her and began pointing out her considerable virtues—thick, silky red hair; large, gold-flecked hazel eyes; a generous mouth; and a curvaceously full figure.

Close to tears, Kit flashed, "Don't be silly! I'm a dowd with cast-off clothing and no portion."

Cornelia intervened, "As to your portion, the man who loves you will not care a whit for that—and as soon as my shop is opened I shall see you turned out in the first style of elegance."

Paige, thinking she cannot have heard correctly, repeated, "As soon as you open your *shop?!*"

Clapping her hand to the side of her head in vexation, Cornelia replied, "Oh, dear, I had not wanted to tell you about that just yet!"

Kit, now picking up the thread of the conversation, exclaimed in horror, "Cornelia, you *cannot* be thinking of going into *trade!* It is so improper." Then, suspecting the worst, she blurted out, "Can Lord Bragdon have left you poorly provided for?"

Laughing, Cornelia responded, "Do not fret, dear Kit; I have a substantial income. However, I find myself bored with the prospect of reentering the social world I have never particularly cared for. What I need is to have a purpose in my life beyond my family."

Eyes glowing, she described her business idea. "I shall have the finest dress shop in London! There are so many women who just copy fashion, who do not buy things that suit their personalities and figures. I intend to be my sex's Beau Brummell—creating gems out of common stones." Smiling reminiscently, she continued, "I can't tell you how many times at a ball I have mentally disrobed the female guests, and have redressed them in far more suitable and attractive raiment. I've often suspected that if some of the debutantes had been exposed to my advice, they would have not needed a second Season."

Paige put her arm around Cornelia's shoulders and said soothingly, "I sympathize with your desire to make use of your talents, which are considerable. But how are you to do this without creating a scandal—for it is unseemly for *men* of our class to enter trade, let alone *women*."

"Exactly so!" confirmed Kit with a vigorous nod.

"And that is what has me in a quandary," Cornelia confessed. "For I have found the shop that I wish to purchase, and shall lose it if I do not come up with a solution that will avoid scandal. You see, Madame Claudette is retiring, and she would like me to take over the premises and her staff. I must find an additional thousand pounds and a way to conceal my own identity."

Paige, thrilled with the prospect of having a problem to solve, suggested first that Cornelia could hire a Frenchwoman to oversee the shop for her. Then, evaluating her own postulation, Paige reconsidered, "No, that will never do, for you will soon be pulling caps with her over the management of the establishment.''

"*Exactement*," Cornelia agreed. "*Tu a raison*."

Paige, struck by the perfection of Cornelia's accent, ejaculated, ''That's it!''

Two pairs of puzzled eyes widened in disbelief as Paige pirouetted about the room. ''You can disguise yourself as a French modiste! A blond wig to hide your raven hair, and no one will recognize you.'' As an afterthought she added, ''And I will provide your thousand pounds, of course, so *that* is no obstacle.''

''But that is ingenious!'' crowed Cornelia. ''I shall make myself up to resemble an older woman—five and thirty at *least*—and my name shall be . . . Madame Lisette, and I shall have recently arrived from France in a rum-runner's boat. Oh, you are too good!'' she declared, hugging Paige.

Kit found it hard to enter into the spirit of the celebration, for she could only imagine the blotch on Cornelia's character were her subterfuge to be found out. Their mood was not to be dampened, though, and the rest of the evening was spent in an elaboration of their scheme.

Over breakfast Paige produced a list she had prepared in her bedchamber the previous night of the tasks that were required to set up Cornelia in business. In grave tones she read it aloud.

''One: Inform Madame Claudette of intent and means to purchase shop. Two: Visit Mr. Oakes to draw up agreement of sale. Three: Open business account for C. and transfer one thousand pounds into it from my own account. Four: Wig.''

Cornelia's reaction to Paige's effort was one of profound admiration. ''Methinks it ought to be *you* starting this business, for you are shockingly organized.''

''Nothing more than any good financier would do to protect her investment,'' Paige chortled.

"I know your list makes sense, but it all sounds so stuffy—except for purchasing the wig. So we will do that first!" Cornelia declared purposefully, flinging her napkin onto the table. "Besides, I would like to approach Madame Claudette as 'Lisette' and see if she can penetrate my disguise."

This plan agreed to, the ladies set off for Bond Street, where a suitable peruke was purchased; Madame Claudette was gratifyingly taken in by the transformation wrought in Cornelia; and Mr. Oakes nimbly negotiated the terms of the sale. By nuncheon, Cornelia's enterprise was thoroughly launched.

Animated by the ease of their success, the three friends returned to Park Place. It was fortunate that Cornelia had removed her wig prior to the homecoming, for as they entered the foyer, Grimsley announced in ominous tones that they had a visitor. Upon inquiring who that might be, Cornelia was informed that the dowager Lady Bragdon had been waiting this half hour.

Pleading the headache, the quick-thinking Miss Roche headed for her bedchamber, while the quick-footed Cornelia blocked her way, pleading, "Please don't desert us—you are the only one of us she will like!"

Raising her eyebrows in mock offense, Paige wanted to know what rendered her own person so unlikeable.

"You don't cower," was the instant explanation. Then, casting a look at *Kit's* insulted countenance, Cornelia amended, "That is, Paige, you are too outspoken for my mother-in-law. She believes that women our age should have no ideas of their own, and must defer at all times to the 'wisdom' of elder women—or to men of *any* age."

Paige groaned as she and Kit were uncompromisingly thrust into the drawing room, where they confronted a dour-faced female of immense proportions—who scowled menacingly at the trio and demanded, "Where *were* you? It is most unseemly for a recent widow to go gadding about!"

Terrorized, Kit took a step backward and attempted to maneuver herself behind the taller Cornelia, only to be startled back into her original position by the dowager's demand that she be made known—"instantly!"—to Cornelia's guests.

Cornelia decided that it was easier to introduce her friends than to explain where she had been. As expected, her mother-in-law took an instant liking to Kit, comparing her to her own youngest daughter, who had done her prescribed duty by marrying well and raising a brood of red-haired progeny.

Upon hearing that the other guest was a countess, the dowager ceased extolling her own daughter's virtues and smiled stiffly, congratulating Paige on her "conquest."

Paige considered giving her a set-down for her officiousness, but as she did not wish to cause an upset for Cornelia, she accepted the congratulations with seeming complaisance.

A very awkward silence ensued, which was broken by Grimsley's announcement that nuncheon was served. Unfortunately the dowager had no previous commitments, so she joined them. During the meal, Kit (a circumstance for which Cornelia was greatly obliged) entertained Cornelia's mother-in-law with the latest gossip from Surrey. Pleased to discover that her daughter-in-law had such a biddable person as a friend, that formidable woman prepared to leave in restored spirits, even complimenting Cornelia on her tasteful attire.

As the dowager rose from her chair, Paige noted with mingled horror and amusement that the skirt of their departing visitor's black gown was covered with Snow's white hairs. No one dared to tell her, so the parting took place on terms of amiability.

When the door was safely closed behind the caller, the beleaguered trio collapsed with sighs into their chairs. "Phew!" Cornelia shuddered. "We are done with her for a while, as she only calls on me once a month to make sure I am not doing anything to disgrace her family's name." This remark, of course, sent the ladies into whoops of laughter as they individually considered the dowager's probable reaction to learning of the morning's activities.

Exhausted after having been on their best behavior for over an hour, all felt the need for quiet repose, and as they separated to retire to their respective chambers, Grimsley handed Paige a letter that had just arrived.

It was a day for mothers-in-law, for the writer was Penllyn's mother, Lady Susan. After what she had just experienced downstairs, Paige felt fortunate in her husband's relations, for the tone of the letter was warm and welcoming.

She would be arriving in a week's time and was looking forward to meeting "the courageous and caring woman who would put the needs of others above her own—and who can beat my son at chess."

Instantly, Paige decided that she would like David's mother, not only from what she said, but from the way she penned her letter—for she wrote large and left much white space (which in Paige's experience indicated that she was generous and outgoing. In fact, it was the very opposite of *Dorcas's* crablike penmanship).

Placing the letter in her reticule, Paige decided to go 'round to Berkeley Square on the morrow, to ensure that the place would be in readiness for Lady Susan's arrival.

Not feeling sufficiently fatigued to take a nap, Paige picked up a copy of *Ladies' Monthly Museum* and scanned it restlessly. Throwing it aside impatiently, she realized that what she needed was an audience for her observations about the day's events. Admittedly feeling a little foolish, she called Snow to her and began prattling to him. His reaction was not gratifying, as he dozed off promptly and could not be revived even by a vivid description of the dowager Lady Bragdon.

"Traitor," she whispered to the ball of fur in her lap. "Your master would not be bored by this narrative—he would find it excessively diverting. . . . That's it! I will pen a letter to him, for it will relieve his tedium of waiting for action.''

Collecting her writing materials without disturbing Snow's repose (on her lap) occupied the next ten minutes but did not reduce the energy that she poured into her colorful account of the day's happenings. She chuckled to herself as she reread her graphic description of Kit's attempts to make herself invisible to Cornelia's tartar of a mother-in-law. She concluded by relieving David of his anxiety about his mother, pointing out that Lady Susan's polite letter was written in a firm, clear script indicative of robust health.

As this was her first letter to her husband, she found herself in a dilemma about how to conclude it. "Love" would not do, for the word had never been spoken between them (except as required during the marriage ceremony); just "Paige" seemed too curt; "Yours truly" too impersonal. Chewing on the end of her quill, she eventually made her selection and wrote, "Your friend, Paige."

Content that she had accomplished all she could for the while, she decided to imitate her feline friend and curled up on her bed.

Chapter VI

THE next morning Paige woke to a day that betokened the arrival of spring. The birds were in full voice, and, attracted by their gay chattering, she flung open the window and deeply breathed the sweetly scented fresh air.

Suddenly a wave of nostalgia swept over her as she thought how beautiful Surrey must be right now. If she were home, she would have run down to the stables to take her lively chestnut mare, Wildflower, for a spirited gallop through the dew-soaked fields. Paige could almost feel the wind on her face and her hair blowing free.

Sighing as she realized that no such ride could be had in London, Paige decided to take a brisk walk to Berkeley Square, then perhaps continue on to Bond Street to purchase a new spring bonnet. Breakfasting early, she was gone before Cornelia and Kit had arisen.

The ''brisk walk'' she had anticipated became, in fact, a leisurely stroll, as she stopped periodically to exclaim over a patch of crocuses or a single snowdrop. Therefore, it was just after ten when Capper opened the door to admit her.

Beaming, he ushered her inside while simultaneously calling for his wife. Like two proud parents showing off a firstborn, they steered her through the immaculately gleaming downstairs rooms, which smelled of beeswax and lemons.

Paige was suitably impressed with their efforts and was anxious to see the quarters being readied for her mother-in-law and Pamela.

Mrs. Capper escorted her upstairs, where the newly engaged chambermaids were dusting and putting out fresh linens. Pausing before they ascended to the second-floor nursery, Paige requested Mrs. Capper's advice on which of the maids might serve as her personal abigail until a permanent one could be engaged.

"I hate to put her forward (because she is my own niece), but I do think Sally would suit you, my lady," Mrs. Capper replied readily, as though she had already anticipated this request. "She is particularly skilled in the dressing of hair, and has an unerring eye for colors. She has even had experience as a lady's abigail," she added, then stopped speaking, lowering her eyes and twisting her apron in her work-worn hands.

"How is it that she is now but a chambermaid, then?" Paige inquired, puzzled.

Mrs. Capper blurted out defensively, "Ah, she's a good girl! She never stole anything." Then, more hesitantly, she continued, "It's just that she can't hold her tongue when her mistresses *would* dress too young for their years, or would insist on carrying a turquoise reticule with a fuchsia dress."

Paige, controlling an impulse to gag at this last description, declared that she was quite in agreement with Sally's point of view and asked to be introduced to her before leaving.

The nursery had been done up charmingly in soft colors and fabrics, and Paige commented with surprised delight, "Oh, this is just right! Too often a nursery is a glum place that doesn't offer the bright visual stimulation young children thrive on. I can see you love and understand babies."

At these words the housekeeper beamed with pride and mentally saluted her new mistress for recognizing the feeling with which she had prepared the room for the poor little orphan. Her response, however, was a polite thank-you and a curtsy.

Returning to the first floor, Mrs. Capper remembered that Sally was likely to be found in the dowager's bedroom and suggested to Paige that they look for her there.

Stepping into that room, Paige had no difficulty discerning which of the maids might be Sally. In the middle of the chamber stood a tall, slender blonde who was giving orders for the mattress to be turned. Her hair was honey gold and fell about her face in a profusion of ringlets. Paige suspected that if this vision were indeed Sally, jealousy of her beauty might have been another reason for her mistresses' dismissal of her.

When Mrs. Capper called out, "Sally!" and this angelic creature turned around, Paige's prognostications were confirmed. Following the introductions, Sally declared, admiring her new mistress's stylish ensemble with rapt eyes, "Oh, I will enjoy waiting on you, my lady. You know how to deck yourself out right proper!"

Unconsciously beginning to preen, Paige was struck dumb by her new abigail's next comment, which was, "And in no time at all I can fashion a hairstyle that really becomes you, so you'll do justice to your outfits."

Recovering from her first reaction (the word *insolent* had crossed her mind), Paige laughed and said, "You may have encountered your first failure, for my hair resists all efforts to tame it."

Sensing that Sally was about to elaborate on the deficiencies of Paige's present hairdresser, Mrs. Capper whisked Paige into the hallway and expressed her hope that her mistress would stay for a nuncheon. Finding the hour a little early for that repast, Paige requested instead that she share a cup of tea with the Cappers in the parlor. As they entered it, with Mrs. Capper in the process of simpering at the honor being done to herself and her husband by their mistress, a loud pounding at the front door captured everyone's attention.

The Cappers exchanged puzzled glances as the pounding

continued. "Whoever can that be?" wondered Mrs. Capper. "We have not yet restored the knocker."

"Whoever he is, he is certainly rudely insistent," observed Paige as the knocking became louder.

Their curiosity was soon gratified, for Capper had reached the door, pulling it open to reveal a well-dressed gentleman of medium height, whose not unattractive face was flushed from his assault upon the door.

"Master Sylvester!" exclaimed Capper (in less than enthusiastic tones, Paige noted), while simultaneously a sigh of vexation escaped Mrs. Capper.

"So that's David's infamous cousin," Paige whispered to the housekeeper as she swept forward to greet the first of her in-laws.

Before Paige had reached the door of the parlor, Capper announced in chillingly formal tones, "Sir Sylvester Owens."

"Sylvester!" Paige said welcomingly, extending her hand. "I am David's wife, Paige."

Taking her hand in his cold, clammy one, he bowed over it in silence. Releasing it, he raked his hard, opaque eyes over her entire being, concluding his inspection with a curt, "Servant, ma'am."

Paige suddenly felt chilled to the bone, as though Lucifer himself had just taken her measure and was making plans for her. . . . Shaking off this sensation, she cordially invited her new cousin to join her for tea and turned to Mrs. Capper, saying, "I will take tea with Sylvester in the drawing room—and we can finish our conversation later."

The housekeeper focused a malicious stare on this unwelcome caller and reflected that Sir Sylvester always meant mischief. Deprived of the treat of taking tea and conversation with her new mistress, she flounced off to the kitchen, where she noisily prepared the tea impedimenta.

In the drawing room, Paige was frantically searching her mind for an opening remark other than "I understand that you lead a life of shocking dissipation." Disappointed with herself for falling back on convention, she resorted to, "How very kind of you to pay me a bride call."

"I would have come earlier, but I was visiting friends in Yorkshire and only returned yesterday," Sylvester intoned in a drawl approaching boredom.

Again silence reigned, but Paige sensed that he wanted to say more, so she did not attempt to fill it. While waiting, she studied him objectively. He could have been anywhere between thirty and forty, though the lines on his face and the fleshiness of it led her to believe he was closer to the latter. His most outstanding feature was his blazing red hair, a color Paige had always associated with charmingly volatile personalities—that is, in combination with green or blue eyes. However, Sylvester's cold black orbs gave his face a diabolical cast.

As her eyes moved down his face toward his thin-lipped mouth, he shifted in his chair and murmured, "Forgive me if I seem impertinent, cousin, but I was rather taken aback to learn that David had got leg-shackled, especially to an unknown such as yourself. How came this about?"

Fortunately, Sally appeared just then with their refreshments, and Sylvester's preoccupation with the maid's physiognomy provided Paige with the opportunity to prepare her fictitious account of her courtship. Her strategy was to keep her tale succinct, having observed that she was usually able, herself, to detect others' prevarications by the excessive quantity of words they employed. Adopting the tone of a dreamy romantic, she sketched out the progress of their relationship, which supposedly had developed in the limited time David's leaves had allowed.

Sylvester listened attentively, but with an air of disbelief, commenting sarcastically, "My esteemed cousin is even more remarkable than I had thought, for he seems to have contrived a technique for being in two places simultaneously."

Paige had not been so foolish as to hope that there would be no inconsistencies in her story but felt equal to the challenge implicit in Sylvester's remark. Sighing wistfully, she replied, "Yes, is he not remarkable?! Why, I do believe there is nothing he cannot do." (Paige mentally noted that she needed to thank Kit for serving as her model of a disarmingly innocent ingenue.) Reminding herself that the less she said, the less trouble she would embroil herself in, Paige turned the conversation back to him, smiling winningly.

Sylvester narrowed his eyes, suspecting that this young woman was not the naive country chit he had expected her to be—and that she was pretending to be. *Damn her,* he thought. *All I want to ascertain is how close I am to being removed from first in line of succession to the earldom. She doesn't appear already to be breeding, for she has not that glow about her—which means that something might yet happen to prevent her from ever bearing David's heir.* He had a head for mischief, and although no solution currently presented itself, a close association with the bride might reveal an opportunity. He inwardly reviewed his repertoire of social behaviors and chose "charm." Affecting a boyish grin, he said sympathetically, "Oh, you must sorely miss this paragon. I know I am but a poor substitute, but I am at your disposal should there be anything you require, dear cousin. David and I are very close, and he would want you to rely on me in his absence."

Paige was not disarmed by his patina of charm, for she noted that his smile did not reach his eyes—and wondered what deep game he was playing. "Why, thank you, Sylvester. It is so nice to know that I shall have an additional protector." As his eyebrows rose questioningly, she continued, "My brother is, at this very moment, on his way to Town—and then of course there is Lord Hadley."

"Lord Hadley?" he exclaimed speculatively, as a spark flashed briefly in his obsidian eyes. "What an attractive fellow," he observed gratuitously.

As Paige refilled their cups, Sylvester queried, "I collect by the absence of the knocker that neither you nor my Aunt Susan is actually in residence here?"

"I intend to move here when Lady Susan and her granddaughter arrive at the end of next week, but for the present I reside at Park Place with Lady Bragdon."

"Oh, the unexceptional Cornelia!" Sylvester drawled. "I once laid my heart at her feet—and had it stomped on."

Paige could not wonder at this but decided not to say so. Instead she remarked, "I suppose you will be glad to see your Aunt Susan. When was the last time you saw her?"

"Several years," he admitted. "I understand that she has not been well. How did you find her when last *you* saw her?"

Momentarily nonplussed, she almost admitted that she had never met her, but since that did not fit in with the tale she had woven of a long courtship, Paige deftly sidestepped his question by saying, "Her most recent letter, which I received just yesterday, was most encouraging."

Expressing his gratification with this news, he rose from his chair, pleading another engagement.

No sooner had he quit the room than Mrs. Capper knocked and asked if it would be convenient to hold their chat now.

It was, so Paige invited her to be seated. Paige suspected that they both had the same topic (Sylvester) on their minds, and that one of them was as eager to impart information about him as the other was to hear it. "Is there anything else you would like to discuss besides the preparations for Lady Susan's arrival?" Paige ventured curiously.

"Indeed there is, ma'am, and although it could be thought forward of me, as a servant, to talk with *you* of your relations, I feel it my duty to make some things known to you in the absence of your husband."

"By all means. You are a devoted retainer of my husband's family and I trust your judgment and discretion."

Recognizing this statement as permission to proceed, Mrs. Capper said carefully, "Sir Sylvester is not a credit to the family. He has run through his own funds and would do the same with the earl's if he were permitted. And

money is not his only problem,'' she intimated darkly.
''He has a shocking reputation with the ladies. I would
advise you not to be too much alone in his company.''

''I appreciate the risk you took to be frank with me.
What you say confirms my reading of him, and I will be
guarded with him. But unfortunately, since he is an in-law,
I must be civil to him.'' Sighing, Paige continued, ''I have
some experience with disagreeable relations, and have
devised several strategies for handling them: boring them
with pointless anecdotes; pleading the headache and escaping to my room; playing badly—and loudly—on the
pianoforte; serving stale buns with weak tea. So,'' she
twinkled, ''as in the latter case, you may be called upon to
serve as my accomplice.''

Satisfied that Paige would be able to deal with this
scoundrel, Mrs. Capper felt comfortable moving on to
matters of the household and asked her mistress when she
planned to move in.

''As we expect Lady Susan on next Friday, I should
install myself on the day before so I can welcome her
properly.'' This was approved of, and the rest of their
business was dispatched with ease.

As she set out for Bond Street, Paige was happy to
realize that she was becoming easy in her new role as
countess.

During the next week Paige was busier than she could
ever remember being at Waverly. As the opening of
Cornelia's shop was imminent, the three friends spent long
hours contriving strategies for attracting as customers members of the *ton*. All three were not of the same mind on
how to achieve this, so their discussions were lively and
punctuated with such tactless remarks as ''That crow?!''
''How gauche!'' and ''Your taste is all in your mouth.''
It's a wonder the friendship survived, and even more
extraordinary that eventually a firm plan was agreed to by
all.

Miss Roche and the Countess Penllyn were the first

customers on opening day, both to lend their support and their names, and to get themselves outfitted for the coming Season.

Richard and Dorcas's arrival at Grosvenor Square made another demand on Paige's time. Though thrilled to see Richard, she was horrified to discover that Dorcas had abandoned her coldly indifferent attitude toward her in favor of a high-handed sisterly concern. This change in behavior was apparent at their first meeting in London, when Richard and Dorcas paid a morning call in Park Place.

"My dear countess," Dorcas gushed, rushing to embrace her startled sister-in-law. "Let me look at you!" she said brightly, stepping back and focusing her eyes directly at Paige's midsection. Paige could scarcely refrain from thrusting out that portion of her anatomy. Instead, she glanced at her brother, who could not resist winking conspiratorially at her.

"You look well, yourself, Dorcas; the trip from Waverly does not appear to have tired you," she said reservedly. Then, with significantly more warmth, she threw her arms around her brother's neck. As was his custom, he picked her up and twirled her off her feet. As she was set back on the floor, Paige caught a disapproving look pass from Dorcas to Richard.

Nothing's changed, thought Paige. *She still resents my closeness with Richard. But she'll conceal her dislike of me now that I am a countess—at least to my face.*

This was exactly Dorcas's plan. Like so many women of inferior birth, she both resented, and aspired to be of, the *Beau Monde*. Despite the major liability of her birth, her assets were a well-favored countenance and figure, marriage to a baronet, and a singular drive to improve her station.

She was just twenty years of age, but there was not a shred of innocence in her large brown eyes. Her mouth, though full and sensual, turned down at the corners, giving her a mulish, pouty look. She called attention to her full-breasted figure by wearing snug and daringly low-cut gowns. (Occasionally at social gatherings, as the men clustered around Dorcas, Paige contented herself with the thought that Dorcas's figure was exactly the type to run to fat at an early age.)

As Dorcas mulled over ways to ingratiate herself with Paige, Richard beamed at his sister and exclaimed, "Marriage seems to agree with you, m'dear. You look all the crack."

This was the opening Dorcas was wanting, and she stepped toward Paige, spilling over with effusive compliments.

The countess was wearing a high-necked apricot lingerie gown trimmed with peach-colored eyelet embroidery that exactly matched the ribbons in her hair and the slippers peeking out from her fashionably ankle-length hemline. Dorcas found much to admire in this ensemble and begged for the name of Paige's dressmaker.

Paige, snickering inwardly, conceived a plan to spread the word about Cornelia's dress shop. Knowing that Dorcas enjoyed violating confidences, Paige would insist that she keep secret the name of the brilliant Mme. Lisette, to ensure that everyone was not as well dressed as they. Adopting an air of reluctance, she gave her the name and direction of the shop, then added, "Dorcas, I know I can trust you not to say anything, or the place will become unbearably crowded."

Mentally compiling a list of acquaintances who would be indebted to her for this valuable hint, Dorcas assured Paige, "Your secret will go no further. Of course I will have to tell my dresser, but will threaten to cast her off without a reference if she breathes a word of it."

The vehemence with which this promise was made convinced Paige that her investment was secure, and that Cornelia's business would pick up as soon as Dorcas had paid a few morning calls.

At that moment Kit tripped into the room to say her hellos. It was no surprise to Paige that Kit was immediately drawn aside by Dorcas, who undoubtedly hoped to pump her for information. For once, Paige was not concerned, since Kit had promised not to divulge the true account of David and Paige's relationship; and Paige knew that a promise from her loyal friend was as good as if chiseled in marble.

Paige was, in fact, grateful for the chance to talk to Richard privately, for she wanted to know how much of her letter he had divulged to Dorcas. But before she had the opportunity to pose her question, Richard hustled her into a distant corner, saying, "See here, Babs! I must tell you what I have said to Dorcas about your situation. You know how she disapproves of you, so I could not tell her the truth—that you and the earl had become acquainted only four days before your wedding. So I, er, that is, um, well, I concocted a different version of your relationship."

"Get to the point, Richard!" Paige begged with an air of desperation.

"You may not like this, but I've told her that you've actually known Penllyn for several years and that the seed of a deep caring was already present when you accidentally encountered each other on the journey—where, thrown together for two whole days, it blossomed into love."

Richard was halted in his narrative by the skeptical look on his sister's face. "How did she react to this story?" Paige wondered apprehensively.

Hemming and hawing once again, Richard said, "Well, you know Dorcas. She accused you of weaving a Banbury tale in order to cover up a planned elopement. . . ."

"Whyever did she think I would run *off* to be married—to such a respectable catch, too?" Paige interrupted. After a moment's reflection, she answered her own question. "Oh, no! Do not tell me that she has resurrected that theme of my being ashamed of her because her father was a cit—and that the hasty wedding was held purely to exclude her from attending."

Hanging his head, Richard confessed, "Just so." As

Paige's bosom began to heave in indignation, he quickly reminded her that Dorcas would likely overhear them if she did not keep down her voice.

Recovering her countenance, Paige bit back the disparaging remark she had been about to utter and commended her brother on his wisdom in concocting this tale. "Although I appear vexed, I am most grateful to you, for the version David and I have put about is similar—and so, as a member of the family, Dorcas will be able to corroborate what she hears in society."

On the other side of the room, Dorcas was becoming bored with Kit's prattling, for it contained no tantalizing tidbits about the earl and his marriage. It seemed necessary, therefore, to reclaim her husband so they could move on to their next morning call, with her cousin, Lottie Morrow. That nosy lady could be counted on to share details of goings-on unknown even to the subjects themselves.

Rising majestically from the needlepointed Queen Anne chair that had served as her perch for the last quarter hour, Dorcas cut Kit off in midsentence and shrilly announced their departure. Paige hugged Richard consolingly, then walked with them to the door, promising to call on them within the week.

Before Paige knew it, the day had arrived for her to remove to Berkeley Square. Her first night there she experienced difficulty sleeping, although every comfort had been provided. Deciding she could make better use of her time than to thrash about, waiting for sleep to come, Paige lit a candle, propped up her pillows, and reached for the leather-bound diary Cornelia had bestowed on her as a "belated betrothal gift." Perhaps if she wrote out her thoughts she could exorcise the cause of her sleeplessness.

In a bold hand she found herself describing her feelings about her new situation. Wife, aunt, and daughter-in-law: all these were roles with which she'd had no experience. *How well will I carry out these responsibilities?* she queried of herself. She guessed she would muddle through on her own but, surprisingly, found herself missing David's comforting presence. . . . He would tease her out of her anxieties. With a start, Paige realized that she was lonely—a feeling that had been foreign to her at Waverly, where she'd had Kit and Richard at hand.

In a sense, she'd had a prolonged childhood, with all her favorite playthings and people about her. But those days were gone forever. She was beginning a new chapter, entitled "adulthood," which she could write either fearfully or with confidence—it was up to her. Much comforted by knowing what her choice would be, she felt herself relaxing and blew out the candle.

It was midday when Sally bustled into her mistress's chamber to announce that the coach from Penllyn had arrived. Paige jumped up from her writing table and rushed to the looking glass to ensure that her appearance could give her mother-in-law no offense. As she had feared, her reflection revealed an untidy lock falling about her face. In exasperation she turned to Sally and moaned, "Do something!" Sally's nimble fingers quickly pinned the wayward strands into place. Clucking softly, she reminded her mistress that time must be set aside to fashion a style more suited to her poker-straight hair. Paige wished she had thought to do so the previous evening and determined to make amends that afternoon—as soon as her husband's family was settled.

The sound of an infant's cry drifted up the steps as Paige hurried down them. Arriving at the bottom, she encountered effusive and tender greetings being exchanged between the Cappers and the arriving party. Her mother-in-law was easy to recognize, as she stood a head above the others.

Paige stepped forward as a lull settled upon the group. "Lady Penllyn, I am Paige. I've been so looking forward to meeting you. I trust your journey was not too exhausting."

As the two ladies clasped hands, Lady Susan exclaimed with approval, "My dear! How glad I am that you've joined our family." Stepping back and raising her lorgnette, she studied her new daughter with interest.

"Oh, no!" Paige gasped laughingly. "Not another inspection! Do I pass muster, ma'am?"

"Yes! You're as lovely as David described, though I do believe your eyes have *more* facets than the Owens emeralds. Now, I should quite like you if you would stop calling me 'ma'am' and 'Lady Penllyn.' Can you not call me 'Mother'? I understand your own has passed away, so she cannot take offense."

Paige hesitated before replying, "How kind of you. I would like to please you, but I cannot feel fully comfortable with your suggestion—"

"Of course," interrupted Lady Susan smoothly. "In my instant liking of you, I had momentarily forgotten your actual arrangement with David. How would 'Lady Susan' suit you?"

"Admirably," Paige responded promptly.

Another wail emanated from a tiny blanketed bundle, and all eyes turned toward the sound.

"And this, of course, is Pamela," stated the proud grandmother. Nurse stepped forward to present her charge, who ceased crying as soon as she was the center of attention. As Paige bent to get a closer view, gurgles of satisfaction filled the hallway.

Enthralled with the exquisite beauty of the violet-eyed infant, Paige held out her arms to cuddle her, saying, "Oh, how enchanting she is! So unlike other infants I've seen. Usually they resemble little old men with their bald, fuzzy heads and pinched features."

As Paige cooed to the responsive Pamela, she was aghast to hear the sound of ripping fabric, followed by the sensation of sharp pinpricks in her leg. Looking down at her ravaged skirt, she wailed, "Oh, no—Snow!" That animal was attempting to scale the heights of her billowing skirts to take his rightful place in her arms.

Capper, stifling a guffaw, came to the rescue, disengaging the jealous feline while Paige restored Pamela to her nurse.

Stroking the cat's head, Lady Susan observed, "Looks like someone's nose is out of joint."

Paige hoisted the cat from Capper's arms and presented him to the gathering. "This is Snow—a cherished member of the family, who ought to be in the kitchen, as *we* ought to be in the drawing room. Mrs. Capper, if you would show Nurse to the second floor, we will retire for refreshments."

As Paige and Lady Susan entered the drawing room, the latter said, "I do hope the refreshments include tea. I've been longing for a strong cup for some hours."

Noting the strain on her face, Paige felt uneasy about having kept her standing so long in the chilly hall. This compounded an already developing sense of guilt which had originated when Paige had realized that perhaps she ought to emulate Lady Susan's mourning dress instead of outfitting herself in the cheery jonquil confection Cornelia had prepared for this event.

"Tea it is," Paige replied, and as if to confirm this, Capper entered with the elegant service.

After the first soothing sips had been taken, Paige raised the question of mourning dress that had been weighing so heavily on her mind. Lady Susan was appreciative of Paige's sense of familial duty but quickly put Paige's mind at ease. "Stuff and nonsense!" the dowager declared firmly. "You never even met my son Evan, so why should you mourn him? Besides, I am cheered out of remembering my grief by bright colors—and that dress is one of the most exquisite I've ever seen. I used to be quite the belle myself, you know. . . ."

As Lady Susan went on in this vein, Paige surveyed her thoughtfully. Her black traveling dress contrasted sharply with her snow-white halo of hair. Huge violet eyes dominated her abnormally gaunt face, and her skin looked chalky.

Because of Lady Susan's vigorous personality, Paige had almost forgotten that she was still recuperating from a serious illness, heartbreaking grief, and a long journey. As the dowager's reminiscences wound down, Paige inquired if she were ready to retire to her room for a refreshing nap.

Lady Susan accepted this suggestion with gratitude and let Paige take her arm to escort her to her chamber.

Chapter VII

THE weeks following Lady Susan's arrival were full ones. Friends and acquaintances began drifting into Town as the Season got into full swing. It was apparent that Lady Susan was highly regarded by the *Beau Monde,* for the Berkeley Square drawing room was never empty of callers.

Chief among them was Sir Walter Townsend, an older tulip of fashion and longtime acquaintance of Lady Susan. The dowager brightened in his presence, for his striking raiment and sparkling conversation reminded her of the carefree days when, as newlyweds, she and her husband, along with Sir Walter and her dear friend, Lavinia, were recognized as leaders of the young married set.

One early May morning, while Sir Walter, ensconced in his favorite chair overlooking the blossoming dogwoods in the park, was reassuring Paige and her mother-in-law that no news about Wellington's troops in Belgium was better than bad news, Capper announced the arrival of Miss Catherine Roche.

Paige jumped up eagerly at the entrance of her friend. "Oh, Kit!" she exclaimed. "You must have known I needed you." Three pairs of eyes regarded Paige with anticipation and, sensing their scrutiny, she laughingly apologized for being so dramatic—for all she needed was some assistance in picking up a dropped stitch in the blanket she was knitting for Pamela.

The two friends were soon bent over the soft pink wool. Shifting his gaze from the spring scenery to the more attractive picture before him, Sir Walter reflected how rejuvenated he felt in the presence of Paige and her friends. His adored Lavinia's passing, two years previously, had taken the edge off life, and he'd found himself losing his pleasure in such important areas as the color of his waistcoat, the folds of his cravats, and the cut of his coats. However, since meeting the new Countess Penllyn and her charming friends he had found himself ordering a new cherry-striped waistcoat from his tailor and berating his valet for the lack of stiffness in his shirtpoints.

His reverie was interrupted as Capper appeared once again to announce a visitor. This time it was Lord Hadley. Kit started so violently at these words that she lost the stitch she had just managed to retrieve. Paige suppressed a pejorative exclamation, then glanced at her friend speculatively. What she observed was a flushed countenance and trembling hands flying up to pat her hair. *So that's the way the wind blows!* Paige reflected. *And to think I had no idea. In coping with the new demands on my time I fear I have been neglecting my friends. Perhaps I can do something to make amends. . . .*

Motioning toward the vacant cushion on the settee next to Kit, Paige began to atone for her sins. "Lord Hadley," she called out silkily, "pray do be seated."

Accepting the seat offered, Jerry settled himself a few inches from an exceedingly flustered Miss Roche. Fortunately for Kit her agitation was not detected, for Jerry's eyes never left the lovely face of the countess.

As usually occurred when this trio got together, merriment abounded. Lord Hadley was particularly entertaining today, for the previous evening he had attended a ball in honor of Phillippa Coates, a new debutante. Both ladies were eager for a description of this ingenue. Lord Hadley prefaced his reply by saying, "Neither one of you two pretties need worry about being cast into the shade by Miss Coates." (Kit blushed to the roots of her hair at this encomium.) "Her most striking feature is the sheer quantity of her. I found myself imagining millions of silkworms working their little hearts out attempting to produce sufficient yardage to cover her ample proportions." Gratified by Paige's howl of amusement, he continued in this vein, next describing her dancing ability.

"During the first set, in which she was partnered by her broomstick of a brother, Phillippa lost her balance and trod on his toes, causing him to scream with pain and expostulate, 'You clumsy ox!' Whereupon Miss Coates burst into tears and ran from the room, causing the chandelier to quake ominously."

As her giggles subsided, Kit felt it necessary to offer some sympathy to the unlucky debutante. "It appears that *she* was not the only clumsy one at the ball; her brother's verbal bungling far exceeded her own gracelessness."

"Well said, Kit! Your tenderheartedness does you great credit," Paige approved warmly. "Do you not agree, Lord Hadley?"

"I *quite* agree. In fact, Miss Roche, I am not as harsh as my tongue would make me appear. It was I who led Miss Coates out for the next dance, after she returned to the ballroom."

"Well done!" Both ladies applauded in unison. Jerry beamed with pride at this paean, reflecting that what had seemed a sacrificial duty the evening before now greatly added to his consequence. The grin on his face and the sparkle in Paige's eyes were recorded by Sylvester, who had just entered the room behind Capper.

Though she was as unhappy to see her nephew as was the rest of the company, Lady Susan greeted him politely. Nodding to everyone, he settled into a chair near his aunt and attempted to extract from her useful information about

David's wife. He had found that lady herself cool and nonconfiding.

Determined that this visit would not be an unprofitable one, he selected his words carefully. "What is the latest news from David? As a besmitten bridegroom, I am sure he writes to his wife every day."

"Neither of us has received a word from him, and we are quite worried," Lady Susan admitted forlornly. "I hope nothing has happened, for he is usually a regular correspondent. But then, I'm somewhat reassured by my friends, who tell me that no letters have yet come through from Wellington's troops. What have *you* heard?"

Annoyed at this ambiguous piece of information, Sylvester snapped, "Nothing, for you know I despise anything to do with the military."

"No stomach for a forthright fight, eh?" interjected Sir Walter, rousing from his doze in the sunlight.

Lady Susan, ever the diplomat, intervened, saying smoothly, "I'm sure it's not the action Sylvester abhors, but the incessant talking about it. I find it quite boring myself."

Pulling his six-foot-four-inch frame from his chair, Sir Walter rose to take his leave. As he bent over Lady Susan's hand he muttered, "Can't abide that fellow. I'm off to Watier's." As he said his good-byes to the others, he invited Paige to ride with him early on the morrow. Paige agreed, saying she looked forward to some exercise.

With that as an opening, Lord Hadley recalled the object of his visit and requested Paige's company in St. James's Park that afternoon. Mindful of her duty to Kit, Paige resorted to a bald-faced lie, saying that though she would enjoy the outing, she had promised to drive out with Kit—but if Lord Hadley would not mind providing a mount for Miss Roche, they would both accompany him. Lord Hadley was all amiability and inquired of Miss Roche her preference for her horse's temperament. Paige jumped in to answer for her friend, declaring, "Kit is much too modest to admit to being a very fine horsewoman, and she should have a horse with spirit.''

As Kit's mouth opened and closed in mute shock, Lord Hadley extolled: "Excellent. Fireball it is, then, for Miss Roche.'' He said his farewells, promising to call for the ladies at four-thirty.

Paige anticipated Kit's protestations over this arrangement and quickly forestalled her by whispering, "Lady Susan is looking fagged. I must do something to rescue her from that bounder—you can rake me over the coals later.''

Approaching Lady Susan and Sylvester with an air of keen interest, Paige snapped her fingers in front of Sylvester's face and said, "I know who you remind me of! I have been trying to think of it this half hour, and it has just come into my head: Mr. Nailor! Richard's and my tutor.'' She settled herself companionably on the love seat across from her quarry and pulled Kit down beside her.

With enthusiasm she launched into a detailed description of that pedagogue and his unsuccessful attempts to control the Undershaw brats. At each observation she made of Mr. Nailor's ineffectiveness, Paige prodded Kit in the ribs and invited her confirmation with, "Isn't that so, Kit?'' Each time called upon, Kit dutifully nodded, but she was puzzled by her friend's uncharacteristically laborious and long-winded narrative. Surely Lady Susan would think her new daughter a veritable gabblemonger.

Glancing uneasily at the dowager, Kit was surprised at the smile playing around the corners of that lady's mouth and was astonished when she opened it to say, "But my dear, this is fascinating! Do tell us more about your use of the globes!''

At this interruption, Sylvester leapt to his feet, suddenly remembering an appointment with his tailor, and was soon gone from the drawing room. Lady Susan stood up and embraced her daughter-in-law. "Well done, my love. I don't think I could have endured another minute with him.

I'm going upstairs now to nap, and no doubt will dream of childish pranks at Waverly.''

As the door closed behind Lady Susan, Kit turned to Paige and said in anguish, *"Fireball?* What few horses I have ridden have had names such as Pacific, Lullaby, and Good Girl! You *know* I am not an accomplished rider, and I shall make a fool of myself—if I make it into the saddle at all.''

"Nonsense! My dear, you have a respectable seat—and a dashing new riding habit. Lord Hadley will be unable to take his eyes off you.''

Close to tears, Kit said violently, "Do not be absurd! Lord Hadley only has eyes for *you*—not that it signifies in the *least* to *me!''*

Paige did not believe a word of this impassioned speech but seized upon it as a means of convincing Kit to accompany them. "I'm glad you mentioned that,'' Paige replied. "I have been uncomfortable lately with his attentions and do not want to be alone with him—so your company this afternoon would be much appreciated.''

Aghast, Kit stammered, "Has he . . . has he . . . said . . . anything . . . improper?''

"No. But I do not want to give him the opportunity to do so. You can be of great service to me in chaperoning us.''

Being of service to Paige was important to Kit, but her overriding concern was still to avoid becoming an object of ridicule. Her agitation was almost palpable, and since Paige could not bear to see her friend in such misery, she offered to let Kit ride her own mount, Wildflower, if they discovered that Fireball's behavior lived up to his name. Kit's memory of Wildflower was that this mare was not exactly docile, but she felt it would be mean-spirited to reject Paige's well-intentioned offer. So, feeling slightly more comfortable about her mount, and suddenly desirous of experiencing the headiness of actually riding by Lord Hadley's side,

Kit gave her consent and departed to prepare for this adventure.

By the time she confronted the horses that afternoon, Miss Roche had recovered her confidence. She knew she looked smart in the new habit Cornelia had designed for her. Her short, perfectly cut moss-green jacket and matching skirt hid her opulent femininity and made her feel almost svelte. She was delighted with the rust velvet collar and trim which exactly matched her hair. Upon those shining locks perched an original millinery creation featuring several curled ostrich plumes, which gave her the appearance of added inches.

"Fireball it is," she proclaimed, having decided he looked no more fierce than Wildflower. Next came the moment Kit had been thinking about all afternoon. Lord Hadley lifted her into the saddle, commenting as he did on her trim ankle. Kit felt almost smug as she watched the groom assist Paige to mount, though she had to admit that Paige looked most becoming in her ruby-red costume. The black frogging and epaulets gave it a military look which enhanced her slimness. If her brightly colored habit did not cause a stir in the park, her ruby-veiled, high-crowned beaver hat would certainly excite interest.

As this colorful group set off for the park at a decorous pace, Kit stole glances at "Jerry," as she tended to call him in her thoughts. His curly chestnut hair glistened in the afternoon sun, and he looked tall in the saddle, though he was in fact slightly below average in height. As they entered the park he pulled up beside her. His nearness and the genuine interest in his sea-green eyes nearly caused Kit to unseat herself, but she surprised herself by bringing Fireball quickly under control. Jerry's "I see the countess did not exaggerate your equestrian skill" would ring in her ears for the next several weeks, and she unconsciously imitated Paige as she replied spiritedly but mendaciously, "It is a pity we cannot spring them here, for Fireball and I would both welcome a gallop."

As Kit well knew, this would be impossible. At this fashionable hour, their pace was dilatory and constantly interrupted by hails from acquaintances. Lord Hadley stopped to exchange words with the Duke of Dorset on his magnificent white horse; and, shortly after, Paige espied Richard and Dorcas in their smart phaeton.

At the sight of his sister, Richard enthusiastically shouted, "Babs!" and reined in.

In her "Mme. Lisette"–designed outfit, up until now Dorcas had felt herself to be the most strikingly attired female in the park. As she registered the dramatic perfection of Paige's and Kit's attire, she scowled malevolently. "Really, Richard, your sister continues to make a spectacle of herself, when everyone knows that muted colors are in style!"

Innocently he countered, "Why, I think she looks quite dashing—and, by George, so does Miss Roche."

"Who is their escort?" Dorcas asked, anxious to change the subject. The answer was forthcoming, as introductions were made. Annoyed that Lord Hadley seemed more interested in Paige than in herself, Dorcas took an instant dislike to him. As she was contemplating how to give him a set-down, a most intriguing gentleman reined in his horse as if to join the party.

"Cousin!" he directed at Paige, as his eyes wandered to Dorcas's ample bosom. Paige's acknowledgment of the greeting was chilly, but she soon made Sir Sylvester Owens known to her family. Receiving a warm greeting from Sir Richard—and an even warmer one from his wife—Sylvester decided to cultivate this acquaintance.

Wasting no time, he called in Grosvenor Square early the next morning. He was not overly distraught to learn that Sir Richard was not at home, for he thought Lady Undershaw would be freer with her disclosures without her husband's inhibiting presence. There was no concealing that Dorcas was a bigger handful than Sir Richard could manage: she was a lady who thrived on excitement, while her husband seemed rather naive and staid.

It was Sylvester's good fortune that Dorcas's cousin Lottie was there, as that intrepid gossipmonger was at the moment of his entrance passing along a tale originating with the servants at the Penllyn townhouse. Lottie's dresser's niece was an underparlormaid there and said wagers were being made belowstairs as to who would bed the countess first—Sir Walter Townsend or Lord Jerold Hadley.

Drawing a breath to continue this defamation of Paige's character, Lottie was interrupted by a sharp warning from Dorcas. "Hold your tongue, woman! Sir Sylvester is the earl's cousin."

"And as such," Sylvester intervened smoothly, "I naturally have his best interests at heart. I, too, have heard rumors about Lady Penllyn and her admirers," he lied, hoping to encourage further confidences.

This succeeded, as Mrs. Morrow added, "You must know, then, that Lady Penllyn is in the habit of entertaining that notorious rake, Hadley, unchaperoned. Why, just last week Meg's niece accidentally intruded on them in the library. He was leaning familiarly over her shoulder, as if about to kiss her neck. And they didn't even have the grace to blush when they were discovered. Brazen, I call it!"

Dorcas had initially been enjoying this recital, for she'd never really liked her uppity sister-in-law. However, it suddenly occurred to her that if scandal besmirched Paige's name, she herself would be adversely affected. Rallying herself, she said chidingly, "Lottie, are you going to believe everything the servants tell you? You know they lead such dull lives that they'll make even the most commonplace occurrence a *cause célèbre*. My sister-in-law may not be the most refined lady, but she would not play her husband false within a month of her wedding."

"I see you are a sensible woman and a loyal family supporter," flattered Sylvester, seeking to further ingratiate himself with Dorcas. "I'm sure you are right, and there is some logical explanation about Hadley. Now that I am privy to this information I will discover the truth and put the rumors to rest. I would appreciate your informing me of any other incidents, and assure you that you can trust my discretion."

Sylvester spent ten more minutes alternating between flattering them both and name dropping; then, not wanting to outstay his welcome, he bowed over their hands and promised to call again soon.

Unaware of the mischief being done to her reputation, Paige had enjoyed an invigorating gallop with Sir Walter and returned home tousled and sparkling. As she passed Lady Susan's room on the way to her own, her mother-in-law merrily called for her to enter.

"Good news! David is well, and there are two letters for you from him! I've just read the one for me."

Though Paige was sincerely glad to hear this, she felt a momentary twinge of guilt that she hadn't thought of her husband during the past two days. "Oh, that is happy news indeed! Where might I find these missives?"

"I put them on your dressing table, as I knew you'd be coming right up to change your costume."

"Then I'll be off to read them. I trust you will excuse me for such an important errand."

Entering her chamber, Paige was amused to find Snow curled in slumber atop the letters, as though wanting to make sure he did not miss whatever news there was of his master. Not wishing to wake him, she attempted to ease the envelopes from under him and was rewarded with a hiss.

"Sorry, boy, but I need those letters." Seeming to understand, he began to make amends by licking her hand with affection.

"Come, Snow, and sit on my lap, and I'll make us both current on our lord's activities."

It was not hard to decide which envelope to open first,

for one of them excited her immediate interest. It was crumpled, dirty, and seemed to beg for her attention. Its contents, however, bore no relationship to its container; David wrote lightly and entertainingly:

Dear Most Esteemed Wife,

I have now been in Brussels for two days, and you were right to fear for my safety. My life has been several times in jeopardy since my arrival. My first night I was accosted by two camp followers who wished to have the silver lace from my dress uniform for their own. Yesterday I was almost forced to suicide to extricate myself from a boring tea given by Lady Vidal. Then last night I was struck on the left shoulder by a flying wineglass thrown in a cavalier manner by a drunken lifeguardsman. As long as Wellington remains in Vienna (and Boney in Paris), I fear I will continue to be subjected to such harrowing experiences.

Actually, my dear, life is fairly routine here in Brussels. Allied troops are trickling into town, but there is as yet no sign of a major battle. I am growing restless at this inactivity and the excessive time available for lugubrious memories. I'm reminiscing about the last time I was melancholy. A green-eyed chit was able to distract me, and I have several times found myself longing for her company.

How are you bearing up under your new responsibilities? Do you have regrets? I know my mother and Pamela's arrival is imminent. Do not be put off by my mother's crotchetiness, for she has not been herself since her illness and Evan's death. Ply her with tea—she loves it!

Should you need reinforcements, I hope you will call upon Jerry. I asked him to render you any assistance in his power, and he is an obliging fellow.

I am constantly reminded of Snow. His distinctive hairs tenaciously adorn several of my jackets. Give him a hug for me (but wear a white dress!).

Although there are a lot of my countrymen (and women) in Brussels, I am feeling a bit homesick and would welcome hearing from you. I plan to write to you at least once a week.

This letter is longer than my usual ones, for I don't know how to close it. I've thought of "Your obedient husband" (but I'm not very obedient); "Yours forever" (but actually "Yours temporarily" is more to the point); so I've settled on something my heart can truly acknowledge—

Your friend,
David

For a reason she couldn't fathom, tears pricked Paige's eyes, and she turned quickly to the second letter.

Dear Paige,

Your recent letter cheered me. I wish I'd been there to see the dowager Lady Bragdon. Thank you for the encouraging words about my mother's health. I hope your instincts are correct. Do pen me a complete description of your first meeting with her!

I am writing this in haste, as I have just been summoned to Old Hookey's headquarters—it seems our renowned leader has a special assignment for me to perform. Do not fear, for I doubt it is dangerous. Boney remains with his forces in Paris.

Your friend,
David (Glad we agree about that.)

Paige put down this letter with a sigh and looked pensively at Snow. "There, you see, you had nothing to worry about: your master is hale and hearty. Still, I feel somewhat uneasy; 'special assignment' has an ominous ring to me. But then I am unfamiliar with military terminology. *You* are a male. What think you of all this?"

Sensing that a response was called for, Snow yawned and stretched his sinewy body languidly.

"So, you think I have no reason to worry, eh?" Paige concluded reasonably. "I will report to Lady Susan that all is well."

Chapter VIII

THE receipt of the letters seemed to lift the little nagging worry that had periodically plagued Paige since David had left. He was in no danger; he'd soon be home, and she would be free to pursue her own life, which would henceforth be enriched by her friendship with the Owens family.

The next morning found her in a celebratory mood. She plumped up her pillows and rang for Sally, requesting that a hearty breakfast be sent up to her. While awaiting the tray, she decided to make current her journal. She'd been coming home so late from the round of parties and balls that she'd lacked the energy to reflect on them—and there were some interesting observations to be recorded. Just last night she had witnessed Lord Hastings challenge a young buck to a duel for having insinuated that Miss Hastings's virtue was no certainty. As Paige struggled for words to capture the rage in Hastings's eyes, Sally entered with an aromatic assortment of dishes which it appeared would serve three persons.

As Paige eyed the array hungrily, Sally chortled, "I told Cook to heap it on, as you had that ravenous glint in your eyes when you ordered."

"You are a wonder, Sally! You take care of all parts of me: my hair has never looked so neat; your mending is undetectable; and you encourage, rather than discourage, my hearty appetite. I am so glad you have agreed to serve me permanently.''

Grinning in acknowledgment of the compliment, Sally retorted, ''Well, you certainly do look better since I've been taking care of you,'' then scurried quickly out of the room to avoid the pillow flung at her from the bed.

As Paige was scraping the last morsel of food from her plate, there was a knock at her door and Richard's voice yelled, ''Babs! Are you decent? May I come in?''

Scrambling for her dressing gown, she called for him to enter. Paige, who hadn't seen her brother in two days, was struck by his worried, distracted air. Not being one to mince words, she inquired, ''What ails you, brother? You look as if you've aged five years in two days.'' Hoping that it had nothing to do with Dorcas, she added, ''Bad news from Waverly?''

''I almost wish it were,'' her brother blurted out. ''It is a delicate matter. I am at a loss what to do.''

Motioning him to a chair by the sunny window, Paige summoned Sally and requested that coffee be sent up. ''Now, tell me what this is all about, and how I can help,'' she offered encouragingly.

''Well, you know how I am about clothes. All I know is whether they look nice—not how new they are or how much they cost. And then Jasper comes waving a sheaf of bills at me and declaring I will be broke within the year unless this spending stops. . . .''

From this disjointed speech, Paige deduced that Dorcas had been running up bills in amounts that Richard's man of business felt uneasy about paying routinely. To confirm her suspicions, she interrupted to ask, ''Has Dorcas been running up large dressmaker bills?''

''Well, yes, that is what Madame Lisette says, but, um, er, Dorcas says she never bought half the items listed. I cannot believe Dorcas would be dishonest with me, but

Mme. Lisette was so convincing as she went over the account with me."

Paige gasped, "You *saw* Madame Lisette?!"

"This is too sensitive a matter to entrust further to Jasper. I had to attend to it myself."

Again, needing to be sure she understood the situation, Paige summarized, "Madame Lisette described each garment, but Dorcas still insists she didn't purchase them?"

Richard nodded. "She will own the four muslin dresses, but she insists she did *not* purchase the sable pelisse, the pink sarcenet ball gown, and a turquoise riding habit—but they add up to a shocking sum. Moreover, I can't remember if I've ever seen them."

"*I* have," Paige intoned bitterly. "She wore the sable over the pink sarcenet at Carlton House several weeks ago. And I saw the habit only yesterday." As Richard's face paled and he dropped his head into his hands, she added, "I am sorry, Richard. I would just as lief spare you this pain."

Straightening up with an air of resolution, Richard said, "Thank you, Babs, for confirming what I feared was the truth. But I blame myself for not providing proper guidance. After all, she is only three years out of the schoolroom. I will speak to her about a clothing allowance; I'm sure she will see the wisdom of it."

"A clothing allowance may be just the thing," Paige commented, not really believing her own words.

As he got up to leave, curiosity overwhelmed Paige, and she heard herself asking, "What thought you of Madame Lisette?"

Richard's eyes lit up. "A most charming and understanding woman. I felt as though she comprehended the delicacy of the case and took pains to be diplomatic. . . . Strikingly beautiful, too, in a foreign sort of way."

After Richard departed, Paige decided to pay a call in Bond Street. . . .

She was in luck. Cornelia had retired to her private

sitting room at the back of the shop to partake of a light repast. The shop itself was a veritable squeeze, Paige noticed with an investor's delight, as she threaded her way through to join Cornelia.

"So I hear you've passed your greatest test," Paige chided the successful entrepreneur.

Cornelia knew instinctively that Paige was not referring to the crowds out front. "Yes, I managed to spend a full half hour with your brother and he did not recognize me. . . . But, more important, what sort of viper can he be wed to, who repudiates her honest debts?" she pondered, her blue eyes shadowed with trouble. Not waiting for an answer to this rhetorical question, Cornelia continued, "One so kind-hearted and gentle as he deserves someone more sincere and refined."

Since Paige had already spent more than a year feeling similarly, and was anxious to get to the details of the transaction between Cornelia and Richard, she quickly agreed, "Just so! . . . But are you sure he did not recognize you? He described you as 'strikingly beautiful, in a foreign sort of way.' "

"Richard said *that?* I never thought he much noticed ladies."

Paige replied, "He doesn't. And that is what worried me, because you, Cornelia, are the only woman whose beauty he has ever publicly acknowledged."

Cornelia could not let this pass. "Richard said I, I mean I, Cornelia, was beautiful? When?"

"I think it was the Season you became betrothed to Lord Bragdon."

"Before or after?"

"Why is that so important?" Paige remarked, thoroughly puzzled.

Recognizing that she had betrayed an inappropriate amount of interest in Richard's opinion of her, Cornelia tried to circumnavigate these dangerous shoals. "I always suspected that I was in my best looks during my engagement. Your news would confirm it. . . ." she trailed off weakly.

This was not a satisfactory answer, but Paige was too preoccupied to pursue it. "So you don't think he recognized you, and we have no fear of a scandal erupting over the ownership of this shop," she attempted to confirm.

Cornelia nodded and turned the subject to the financial side of the business, summarizing the new customers and the total amount of their purchases.

"Lady Cowper!" Paige repeated excitedly. "But that is famous! To have a patroness of Almack's frequent the shop so soon! In no time you will be the female equivalent of Weston's."

Since Cornelia only smiled wryly at this, Paige observed, "But it is no fun to see them dressed only in the shop. Let us go to Almack's this very Wednesday and observe your finery in motion!"

Cornelia protested, "But I have not been anywhere these five months. Moreover, I am still in mourning."

"But I am persuaded that it is perfectly acceptable for you to attend if you do not dance."

Cornelia could not but agree. "You're right. I have not had any fun in my life recently. A few more months of this and I shall become as dour-faced as the dowager Lady Bragdon herself." With resolution she rallied, "Kit and I will call for you at nine-thirty."

Though many of the Notables were in Brussels, the assembly rooms were crowded, and Kit, whose first visit it was to Almack's, was not disappointed. A waltz was being played, and she was transfixed by the sight of so many beautiful ladies whirling about in the arms of their handsome partners. Looking down in appreciative wonder at her own dress of filmy gauze over a pomona-green underskirt, Kit likened herself to Cinderella at the ball.

The comparison seemed even more appropriate as she spied Lord Hadley approaching the party. He was definitely the man of her dreams in his black frock coat, satin knee breeches, white waistcoat, and silk stockings—all of which he filled out to perfection. So lost was she in this fantasy that she imagined he would greet her first and formed her face into a glowing visage of welcome. This pose drooped instantly, as Lord Hadley brushed past her to clasp Paige's hand in greeting.

Paige was quick to perceive Kit's wilting posture and resolved to intervene. "Ah! Lord Hadley. So glad you are here! May I impose on you to take care of my friends while I have a word with my brother and his wife, whom I see across the room?"

Agreeing to do it with alacrity, he protested, "To have Miss Roche and Lady Bragdon on my arms is a privilege, not an imposition."

Amused, Cornelia tapped him on the shoulder with her fan and twinkled, "Flirting with recently widowed ladies is not at all the thing, Lord Hadley. So I'll assume that your compliments are intended for Miss Roche."

Fervently hoping this were so, Kit gently laid her hand on his proffered arm and gazed surreptitiously at his strong profile.

Across the room, Dorcas's eyes narrowed into slits as she observed Paige's approach. "Why, I see your sister has again made a spectacle of herself—flaunting your mother's diamonds," she hissed.

Richard could see nothing amiss in Paige's turquoise silk gown and diamond earrings and necklace, and he said so before he kissed his sister's cheek in greeting.

"Babs, I did not expect to see you here tonight."

"I did not expect to be here, actually, but I felt that Cornelia needed to get out among friends before the bloom faded from her cheeks."

"Oh, is Cornelia here? Where might I find her?"

Receiving directions, he hastened off, leaving Dorcas and Paige to deal together. Left alone with her nemesis, Dorcas wasted no time taking her sister-in-law to task for interfering in her affairs.

"How dare you turn my husband against me!" she accused passionately. "You never could stand the fact that I had replaced you in his affections—so you make mischief wherever you can."

Paige was calm, having expected this tirade, and responded, "What is it I have done now to displease you?"

"You have taken that shop owner's word over mine!"

"Nonsense, Dorcas. I do not discuss your affairs with shopkeepers. Whatever can you be talking about?" she queried innocently. "Can you mean the discussion I had with Richard about Madame Lisette?"

"That's it exactly. You've leant credence to her charges that I owe her a ridiculously extortionate sum."

"Don't you?" Paige responded coolly.

"Whether I do or not is no concern of yours. And I would welcome your not intervening in something which is strictly between my husband and me."

"If you make no cause for intervention, you need never fear it," Paige moralized, and held out her hand to Sir Walter Townsend, who had approached unnoticed.

Dorcas, who found Sir Walter too foppish for her taste, made her excuses and went off to find more desirable company.

"Are you two meeting on Putney Heath in the morning? I'll serve as your second, for she looks to be a tamperer of pistols."

"I know I should affect ignorance of your meaning, but I am beginning to exceed my tolerance for her, and feel just guilty enough about it to need confirmation of my view from others," Paige confided.

"Perhaps a dance will put your spirits aright," he suggested, leading her to the floor, where a set was just forming for a country dance.

Seemingly oblivious to the lure of the music, Cornelia and Kit sat chatting with Cornelia's acquaintances. Kit had refused several offers to dance out of misplaced sympathy for her friend. Sir Walter, observing this from the dance floor, winked at Paige and said, "Methinks Miss Roche will miss the chance of a lifetime if she does not soon unchain herself from Lady Bragdon's side. I've been watching Lord Hadley glance in that direction several times, and suspect he would beseech one of the patronesses to present him as a waltzing partner if only the lady looked more willing."

"How perceptive of you, Sir Walter. Will you be my accomplice in a plan to remedy it?"

"With pleasure, my lady. Tell me my role."

Seconds later the two conspirators approached their target. Kit's attempt to refuse Sir Walter's invitation to make up the next set was brushed aside by Paige, who uttered one word: "Nonsense!" She quickly added, "Now that I am here to bear Cornelia company you can have no possible objection—unless you wish to offend Sir Walter."

Horrified to think Sir Walter might take her refusal personally, Miss Roche rose at once. As the dancing commenced, Paige and Cornelia watched their friend's natural grace cast all the other ladies into the shade.

Kit had barely recovered her breath from her first dance when her hand was claimed for the next by a fashionable young gentleman. "Why, I do believe our Kit is a success!" crowed Cornelia.

"Yes, thanks to Sir Walter, who has much finer sensibilities than I had realized. I can now better understand Lady Susan's strong affection for him. He is very good for her, you know; she is always much more cheerful after his visits."

"Oh, look!" Cornelia exclaimed as a waltz struck up. "Lady Cowper—in *my* gown, by the by—is presenting Lord Hadley to Kit as a partner."

Paige glanced across the room to where Sir Walter stood and encountered a collegial smile of satisfaction.

Kit was in raptures. The pressure of Lord Hadley's hand against her waist sent her pulse racing and left her bereft of all powers of speech. Fortunately, Lord Hadley was so delighted to have such a graceful and tiny partner after the elephant-footed females he had been dragging around the room that he initially forgot to make conversation.

Suddenly he remembered his reason for asking Miss Roche to dance. Ever since Penllyn had implied a mystery about his marriage, Jerry's natural curiosity had been piqued. Since the countess was not increasing, the only other explanation he could come up with for the hastiness of their union was that it was some sort of marriage of convenience. This idea greatly appealed to Jerry, for he found himself attracted to David's lovely wife and, rake though he might be, could not in good conscience pursue the countess if David's affections were engaged. He had called frequently at Berkeley Square, hoping that clues supporting this theory would present themselves, but the countess's demeanor was all that could be expected of a devoted wife. Consequently, Jerry had decided to focus his quest for the truth on the ingenuous Miss Roche, who might unknowingly reveal the actual state of affairs. And this could be a pleasant task, since she was not an unappetizing morsel of femininity.

As a man in the petticoat line, he prided himself on his understanding of women and had taken pains to analyze Kit's character. She was a loyal person who would be staunchly protective of her friend's secrets. But being the gentle and uncomplicated soul she was, she would likely presume that, if Paige had confided in *her*, David had likewise entrusted *his* closest friend with the facts of his marriage. Therefore Jerry's strategy was to pretend that this was so and get her to confirm his suspicion.

"I was glad to see our countess dancing," Jerry opined meaningfully to Kit. "No sense pining away for her husband, given the nature of their marriage. . . ."

Deflated that her trance should be broken by talk of another woman (albeit her closest friend), Kit reacted to only a portion of his statement, mumbling, "Yes, she has too much spirit to pine away."

Before Lord Hadley could restate his observation, the music ended, and he escorted her back to her companions.

As the next dance commenced, Paige observed with distaste Sylvester's soliciting of Dorcas's hand. Involuntarily she was struck by how well they suited, both physically and by temperament—he with the fire in his hair and the blackness in his soul, and she with the darkness in her hair and the flame in her eyes.

"This is too dull a gathering for you, I warrant," Sylvester remarked to his partner as they drew close enough in the dance for conversation.

"And for you, no doubt," came the reply. "I suspect you'd rather be gaming and whoring."

Somewhat nonplussed by this unladylike response, Sylvester smirked and challenged, "What does the wife of the estimable Sir Richard know of gaming and whoring?"

"I was not always his wife," she said tantalizingly, before their steps parted them.

Unused to this type of unbridled interchange at Almack's, Sylvester forgot his purpose in furthering his relationship with Lady Undershaw and found himself speculating about her womanly charms, which he owned were considerable. Perhaps there might be unexpected benefits to his course of action.

In any case, he now had an additional motivation to be more in her company. Wasting no time, he invited her to drive out with him in the morning and was gratified by her ready acceptance.

On the drive home, Paige noticed that Kit was unusually quiet and pressed her for the reason behind her silence.

"Oh, it is just the heat and the stuffiness of the rooms," Kit intoned listlessly. As she noticed Cornelia and Paige exchange doubting glances, she quickly added, "Which have given me the headache."

Cornelia was instantly all solicitation, for Kit never

suffered from megrims. "My dear! You must be on the verge of some serious illness, for were it not so, you could only be exhilarated by the success of your first appearance at Almack's."

"I do not count it a success to have my dance partner speak solely of another!" Kit snapped, then burst into tears.

"Am I to understand that *one* (of your many) dance partners has ruined your evening by his insensitivity?"

"Yes—I mean, no; he's *not* insensitive."

"Of course he's not," Cornelia crooned soothingly, totally at sea. "Of whom are we speaking?"

"Nobody," sobbed Kit into Cornelia's shoulder, casting Paige a beseeching look.

"There is no need to discuss it now, Kit," Paige said reassuringly. "Why do you not join me for tea tomorrow." To Cornelia, she announced with a wink, "I need a domino for the Prince Regent's upcoming masquerade. Is it suitable for me to come by your shop in the morning?"

Both plans were agreed to as the carriage drew to a halt at Berkeley Square.

Despite the late hour at which she'd retired, Paige set out early for Mme. Lisette's, wanting to have some quiet time to talk to Cornelia about Kit and Lord Hadley. As she approached Mme. Lisette's private sitting room, her progress was momentarily forestalled by voices from within, one of which was both masculine and familiar. Identifying its owner, she barged in on Cornelia (as Mme. Lisette) and Richard, who were sipping coffee and eating croissants.

The flaky, buttery pastry smelled delicious, and Paige was about to help herself when her brother intervened, saying in shocked accents, "Babs! Whatever are you doing, barging into the private chambers of Madame Lisette?!"

Unperturbed, Paige riposted, "Well, at least I am an investor in this enterprise. What can be *your* excuse?"

Richard's fair skin took on a pink hue as he undertook

his explanation. "I have come to order something special for Dorcas's natal day, and was kindly invited to take coffee with Madame." Then, wanting to distract attention from himself, he queried, "But what can you mean by being an 'investor'?"

"It is quite simple, my dear brother. An excellent modiste needed some money to set up her shop, and I came to her aid. And since every time I wear one of her creations you have praised my attire, I daresay you can have no mistrust of my business acumen."

"No, as usual your taste is infallible," he complimented his sister, while taking in Mme Lisette's enticing beauty. His frank admiration of Cornelia did not escape his sharp-eyed sibling, who found herself developing a sense of unease.

Rising to take his leave, Richard said, "Well, now that my business has been completed, I will let you get on with yours. Babs, will I see you tonight at Lady Grenville's?"

"Yes, I've accepted that invitation. Do save a waltz for me—you know you're my favorite dancing partner."

"Of course, my dear. *Au revoir*, ladies."

Seeing Richard settled so amiably with Mme. Lisette caused Paige's original mission to become of secondary importance. Taking possession of his abandoned chair and biting into a chocolate croissant, she fixed Cornelia with an interrogatory stare and quizzed, "How long has this been going on?"

Somewhat stiffly, Cornelia huffed, "If you mean Richard's visits to my shop, the answer is—a week. Why do you look at me with such a suspicious gleam in your eye? I cannot help it if he wishes to order clothes for his wife."

Being perfectly frank with her longtime friend, Paige admitted to wondering if there were more to the relationship than a series of business transactions, for Richard normally detested a personal involvement in the world of fashion. "He obviously admires 'Madame Lisette.' What think *you* of his attentions?"

"Rest your mind. I think that Richard is merely lonely in the City (as I'll own *I* am) and finds himself unknowingly drawn to a sensibility which understands his. After all, we were used to confide in each other as children."

Regretting that her suspicions had made her sound accusatory, Paige decided to agree with Cornelia's analysis but cautioned her, "Methinks now that you are going into society more, where you and Richard will encounter each other frequently, the less you have to do with him as Madame Lisette the better. If he sees you in the morning as Madame Lisette and in the evening as Cornelia, it will be no time till he penetrates your disguise."

"Your point is well taken," Cornelia admitted. "I will try to avoid close contact with him in my present role. But I must own I will miss his open admiration of me. . . . Speaking of admiration, whose is it that *Kit* would desire? I was much puzzled last night."

"Can you not guess?" Paige teased. "You were always the one to sniff out potential matches. As a matter of fact, I am surprised that you need to ask *me* about this one."

"Oh, you are right. I *am* losing my sense of smell. It must be my advanced years. So do not keep an old woman in suspense—tell me who it is!" Cornelia pleaded.

"Indeed, you are so enfeebled with age that half the men at Almack's last night needed to be constantly by your side in case you required their assistance to rise from your chair or retrieve a dropped handkerchief. So I am not letting you off so easily—you must make a guess as to who has captured our Kit's heart."

Cornelia, reviewing the possibilities (and knowing Paige well enough to realize that she would not reveal her "secret" unless Cornelia made an intelligent stab at a hunch of her own), decided on Lord Hadley, whose name seemed to come up more often than that of other gentlemen in Kit's conversation. "Do not tell me it is Lord Hadley, for he is obviously enamored of *you*."

Her friend let escape an exasperated sigh. "Well, I see

you have not totally lost your perception, for you are half-right.''

"Oh, so it *is* Lord Hadley. Then I am *totally* right."

"No, you are still half-wrong. He has no interest in *me*, other than as the wife of his best friend . . . though I *did* pretend to Kit that he had made advances to me, in order to get her to accompany Jerry and me for a ride."

"Oh, you rustics are so naive. Some of the most notorious affairs started when men became 'interested' in the wives of their best friends." Cornelia, while saying this, admitted to herself that she was enjoying the turn-about in the conversation—Paige's thinly veiled accusations about Mme. Lisette and Richard had, in a different guise, been thrown back at the accuser.

"I would rather not argue about that, for it does not signify," Paige insisted, sniffing in annoyance. "What we need to do is put our energies into forming a scheme to help Kit ensnare his heart—without her knowledge, of course."

Cornelia protested, "But it *does* signify. If you have already captured his heart, he will not want to give it to another."

"Well, I will own that he seeks me out frequently, and though you and I differ as to his intentions in doing so, perhaps we can put his visits to good use."

"By that glint in your eye, I can tell that you have not lost your knack for contriving solutions to seemingly insoluble problems. What is your plan?"

Eagerly (for, of course, there *was* one), Paige disclosed it. "I will invite Kit to come stay with me, saying that Lady Susan wishes to see more of her, as she is always cheered up by her presence. Kit will not refuse an act of mercy, and Lady Susan will fall in with my plan—for she is fond of Kit and has a highly romantic sensibility. With Kit in residence at Berkeley Square, she and Lord Hadley will be more in each other's company—and he will soon discover the many fine qualities she has that would make her a good wife. If, indeed, Lord Hadley does have an interest in me, I will discourage him by talking much of my love for David and how greatly I miss him," Paige concluded.

"Yes, that should serve. It also answers another concern *I* have had lately—leaving Kit alone all day while I am here."

"Then this seems to be a strategy that will universally please. I will ask her at tea this afternoon, after discussing it with Lady Susan. Now that that's out of the way, I was in earnest about needing that domino. Would you create something out of the ordinary? I have one of my premonitions that Prinny's masquerade will be a significant evening."

"You do, do you? That feeling of yours is rarely wrong. . . . Perhaps I should make plans to attend after all. I am so weary of my unexciting and proper existence. What better way to add some spice to it than to attend a masquerade, where my identity can remain hidden!"

"That is just the thing for you! I could see you were longing to dance last night, as your foot was constantly keeping time to the music. With your identity concealed, you need not sit out the dancing."

Just then the bell on the shop door tinkled, signaling the arrival of an early customer, so Paige took her leave, satisfied with her morning's work. With some time to spare, and a reluctance to head directly to Berkeley Square, she decided to walk to Richard's with the hope of mending fences with Dorcas.

But she was too late, for Dorcas and Sylvester had left for Hyde Park moments before Paige arrived.

Sylvester thought Dorcas was looking exceptionally striking in a low-cut lavender dress. Small wonder that many eyes turned to look at them as he tooled his daring high-perch phaeton down the park's main thoroughfare. Dorcas was exhilarated by the speed of the vehicle and the attention of its driver. *I have been too long without an adventure*, she mused to herself. Casting a sidelong glance at Sylvester, she reviewed his attractions. Though he was not so handsome or wealthy as Richard, he was more daring and stimulating. His eyes showed his appreciation of her physical attributes and her spirited nature. *He* would probably take her to Vauxhall Gardens and even more interesting and dangerous places. Furthermore, in time he could become an earl; Richard had no such prospects.

Never one for subtlety, Sylvester stared meaningfully at her bodice and declared, "That style quite becomes you, Lady Undershaw. I am delighted to see you shun the custom of wearing a fichu—it would be a shame to hide such bountiful endowments."

"You seem to have the eye of a connoisseur, Sir Sylvester," Dorcas said provocatively.

"I will own that I settle only for the best."

"And do you usually get it?" Dorcas teased.

"Usually."

"Oh, then there have been times when you've failed?"

"Rarely with the ladies. Occasionally at cards, when I've been dealt a bad hand."

"Oh, I am very lucky at cards, but, alas, I have not found a sufficiently challenging game since I returned to London," Dorcas noted wistfully.

"Then you have not yet been to Lady Bouchet's gaming house, I collect," Sylvester remarked in disbelief. "I would have expected that someone with your vivacity would have sought out such entertainment."

Dorcas was thrilled to have her character so accurately read and appreciated. Richard's devotion to her was gratifying, but he did not understand her restless nature and need for variety; instead, he tried to squelch it.

"I would be happy to introduce you to the pleasures of Lady Bouchet's," Sylvester offered. "Whenever you wish."

Though this was an almost irresistible offer, Dorcas hesitated accepting it, fearing Richard's displeasure and uncertain of the propriety of such conduct. Stating her reservations, Dorcas invited Sylvester's rebuttal. To her surprise, he agreed that these obstacles were formidable but came up at once with a plan to overcome them. He knew of a certain house that provided private rooms for high-stakes games. Participants were obligated to forget the identities of their fellow players, and this code had never been violated.

Dorcas was intrigued by this alternative but fought the desire to accept, fearing she might lose the respectability she had worked so hard to attain.

Sensing her discomfiture, Sylvester added, "Though I cannot violate the code and give you names, I assure you that some of the most respected members of the *ton* have tried their luck there."

"But where can I tell Richard I am going?" Dorcas wondered aloud.

"Why not select an evening when he already has an engagement?"

"I know of no such engagement right now, but I believe he must go to Waverly within a se'nnight, so perhaps I can get away then. . . ."

"Excellent! I shall escort you whenever you give the word. I daresay there is no fear of encountering your sister-in-law at these affairs," he interjected smoothly. "She strikes me as being too prim and proper to disport herself."

"On the contrary, I have always found her too hoydenish for my taste, but she seems to have tempered that trait since she married your cousin," Dorcas reflected.

Keeping his original reason for cultivating Dorcas in mind, Sylvester inquired whether there were any new rumors circulating about the countess.

"No. She seems to exhibit no preference between Lord Hadley and Sir Walter."

"But they are still very much on the scene?" he asked with relish.

"That is what Lottie says," Dorcas reported uninterestedly as they returned to Grosvenor Square.

Ignorant of Dorcas and Sylvester's deepening relationship, Paige greeted Kit at teatime searchingly. Her friend seemed in remarkably good spirits considering her despondency the night before. Lady Susan had been apprised of Paige's plan for Kit and had agreed enthusiastically to support it.

As Paige poured out the tea, Kit remarked on Lady Susan's absence.

Paige replied, "She is resting. I fear she has not fully recovered from her own touch of the influenza, but I believe you can be of great service in restoring her to full health. What would you say to removing to Berkeley Square for the express purpose of nursing Lady Susan? I've noticed that your visits leave her in restored spirits."

The prospect of being once again useful appealed strongly to Kit. She had spent a sleepless night assessing her lot in life and had arrived at the conclusion that, having no wealth and only an acceptable countenance, she must seek employment as an elderly female's companion. Therefore, the offer to nurse Lady Susan was a godsend, for it would give her the means to obtain both a highly respected reference and introductions to possible employers.

Not wanting to disclose to Paige her life plan, which could only meet with vociferous objection, she simply responded, "If Lady Susan needs me, I am at her disposal." She then added, "I doubt if Cornelia will miss me, as she is at the shop so often. But I would like to confirm this impression before giving my final answer."

Realizing that Kit would take umbrage if Paige revealed she had already discussed it with Cornelia, Paige agreed that by all means Cornelia must be consulted.

During the next hour of conversation, Paige was thwarted in her numerous attempts to lead Kit to unburden herself of her feelings for Lord Hadley. Kit seemed so unagitated with Paige's references to Jerry that Paige began to think she had mistaken her friend's heart.

Had she but known it, Kit's feelings for Hadley were even stronger than Paige imagined. However, in the wee hours of the morning Kit had resigned herself to the hopelessness of her passion. Lord Hadley was quite evidently above her touch, and she had been foolish to develop a *tendre* in the first place. Since she could not have him, she would have no other. This resolution to accept her unrequited love with equanimity lifted a great weight from her shoulders. Now she felt she could face him without stammering and blushing. She could just be herself. On the walk back to Park Place after tea, Kit felt even more certain of her course, for she had just endured several references to her beloved with nary a fluttering in her breast.

After Kit's departure, Paige retired to her room to compose a letter to keep David *au courant* with the latest happenings in London.

She began by assuring him that his mother's health improved daily (despite what she had told Kit) and that Pamela prospered. A soft meow from the counterpane reminded Paige to also report on the antics of their feline charge. His latest devilment accounted for his presence in her chamber, for he had been banished from the kitchen after garnishing a tureen of soup with the remains of a mouse.

On a more somber note she related Dorcas's most recent folly. Waxing eloquent on her sister-in-law's less than admirable traits, Paige realized that the adjectives she was employing could as easily serve to describe Sylvester, and she pointed out this observation to her husband.

Wanting to end in a festive vein, she regaled him with anecdotes about the season's activities. Feeling that her stories lacked sparkle, she lamented to David her inability to emulate the brilliant satirical sketches of Jerry. She then went on to sing this friend's praises and finished just as Sally came to dress her for dinner.

Chapter IX

PARTIES continued throughout the following month, each one gayer than the last. Paige's journal reflected an increasing satisfaction with her lot. Her impulsive decision to wed a virtual stranger had resulted in all the benefits she had hoped for and none of the problems she had feared.

As the Earl of Penllyn's wife, she received invitations to the Season's most exclusive events. In addition, she was in a position to accept any of those that struck her fancy, because even if Lady Susan chose not to accompany her, her married status allowed her to attend alone with no eyebrows being raised (except in admiration of her countenance).

Her responsibilities to her new family were greatly alleviated by Kit's presence in Berkeley Square. Kit took seriously her role as Lady Susan's companion. She danced attendance on her at all hours of the day or night, refusing to leave her side even when Paige desired a private coze with her mother-in-law. When not with Lady Susan, Kit could be found in the nursery, cosseting Pamela to such an extent that Nurse had begun to complain to Paige that Miss Roche was spoiling the baby and interfering with the rigid schedule that Nurse knew to be proper for infants. But since Nurse was genuinely fond of her, she would conclude these outbursts with a request that nothing be said to ''dear Miss Roche.'' The presence of another felicitous female in the isolation of the nursery far outweighed any potential harm to the child.

At first Paige felt that she had inadvertently put too much of a burden on her friend, but when she saw how much Kit thrived on her duties, Paige decided not to feel guilty. As a matter of fact, Paige had never seen Kit look so well: she was in high bloom, with a perpetual smile of satisfaction, and her overall aspect bespoke a newly discovered self-confidence. In short, she seemed to have found her niche in life.

Kit and Lord Hadley, who was still a frequent caller, appeared to have forged a new relationship. Whereas previously Kit had been scarcely able to utter a syllable in his presence, she was now all garrulity. The tone of their conversation was one of fond brother and sister, and a favorite topic was Jerry's love of irresponsible masculine pursuits. Paige often had to conceal a smile as Jerry meekly accepted Kit's reproofs for endangering his health by staying out till all hours and consuming large quantities of alcoholic beverages.

The thought of a dab of a woman like Kit scolding a nonpareil like Hadley was so diverting that Paige feared he might provide entertainment in other drawing rooms by mimicking Kit's sermons. But these fears seemed unfounded, for he took no action to avoid Kit's company (as he did Miss Coates's) and often sent her, as well as Paige, posies for special occasions. All this led Paige to conclude that the *tendre* she had suspected Kit of developing for Lord Hadley had been a figment of Paige's imagination.

Lord Hadley found his visits to Berkeley Square continually refreshing. One never knew next what novel crime he would find himself accused of by the delightfully upright Miss Roche, who seemed to disapprove of all his favorite activities—boxing, shooting, gaming, and womanizing.

Of these four vices, the largest share of his time was spent on gaming. Though he continued to play at White's and Watier's, he increasingly frequented the gaming halls in the Pall Mall district. He found he was addicted to faro, and, unlike most of his friends, his luck was holding—so he felt confident enough to accept invitations to private parties where the play was deeper still. This had unexpected benefits, for ladies felt more secure attending these select affairs, and thus Jerry was able to combine his second most favorite activity with his first.

When not playing, he would often attach himself to the comeliest lady present, hoping she might succumb to his irresistible charm. Here, too, he was having a run of luck—his latest conquest was the ravishing Druscilla Robertson, whose elderly husband was at present rusticating.

One night, as she lay in his arms, Jerry was surprised out of his mood of drowsy satiation by Druscilla's request for the name of a moneylender who was discreet and offered low rates. Shocked into full wakefulness by this unorthodox question, Jerry expostulated, aghast, "Good God, Druscilla! I hadn't realized you were so badly dipped."

"I am not," she replied indignantly. "*I* know when to quit. Unfortunately, one of my friends is not so disciplined."

"Of course, m'dear, quite so. You caught me when my wits were not fully engaged. How much does this friend owe?"

"Five thousand," confessed the lady sheepishly.

"Five thousand!! How could he?"

"*She*," Druscilla corrected.

"A lady?! That is even more shocking."

"Although she is entitled to call herself a lady, there's some question about her behavior warranting that title."

"I should say so, if she is unable to cover her debts," Jerry affirmed contemptuously. "Who is this irresponsible female?"

"I am not sure you would remember her. She was at Lady Blackstone's last Wednesday . . . though, come to think of it, you might, for she has a figure which stops men dead in their tracks."

With a sinking feeling in his stomach, Jerry realized that the only woman he'd seen last week who fit that description was Countess Penllyn's sister-in-law.

"You can't mean Lady Undershaw!" he groaned.

"Oh, you have guessed—and I promised myself I wouldn't reveal her name," she said in mock despair. "Give me your word of honor that you won't carry this tale to the Countess Penllyn. Dorcas says she's an interfering schemer who'd relish the news as a way of alienating Dorcas from Richard's affections."

"You have my word," said a very worried Lord Hadley. "But I cannot recommend a moneylender in this situation. You must persuade her to confess her dismal state of affairs to her husband. Having a peal rung down on one by one's husband must be unpleasant, but not as bad by half as becoming entangled in the coils of a moneylender. Every one of them is unscrupulous."

"Yes, I've told her that myself, but she insists that her punishment will be a return to Surrey, and that to her is a worse fate than anything she can imagine."

"So if I don't give you the name of a moneylender, she's going to find one somehow? Well, I still will not be a party to it," he said firmly, jutting out his chin.

No longer in the mood for amorous activities, Jerry began to dress, feeling that a walk to his rooms would clear his brain and help him decide how to deal with this disturbing news.

As he walked the dimly lit streets, he examined his feelings toward his best friend's wife. He was excessively fond of her, for she was wont to say the most unexpected things, and he always enjoyed himself in her company—plus she was a looker, with an abundance of untameable silky hair (of course it was not the colorful shade of Miss Roche's, but that did not signify). She was, in fact, the sole woman with whom he'd ever contemplated matrimony—should it turn out that her present marriage was not all that it seemed.

He hated to think of the scandal that would redound to her if Dorcas's indiscretions were to become public knowledge. By the time he mounted the steps to his very comfortable lodgings, he had vowed to intercede in some way, while keeping his word to Druscilla that he himself would not be the one to tell Paige.

The problem was still on his mind the next day as he took the countess and Miss Roche for a drive. He toyed with the idea of enlisting Miss Roche as a confidante in hopes of getting her opinion of the countess's probable reaction to the news. But he valued her naiveté and therefore was loath to sully her ears with matters that could only disillusion her.

Thus he was still undecided what to do when they returned to Berkeley Square to join Lady Susan and Sir Walter for refreshments.

"Oh, Paige, thank goodness you are back! We have a muddle that I believe Sir Walter has sorted out, but it wants your approval," Lady Susan exclaimed immediately she spied her daughter-in-law.

"Good heavens! What is it?" Paige begged, alarmed at her mother-in-law's worried state.

"It's Molly. She's breeding—and her parent has disowned her. And Thomas wants to marry her, but he has no means to support a wife and child. . . ."

Grasping the situation at once, but wanting to confirm her conclusions, Paige interrupted her mother-in-law. "I collect that our maid Molly has been dallying with Thomas, the footman, which has resulted in the premature beginnings of a family. And you would like to help them, so Sir Walter has come up with a plan which needs my approval?"

"Just what I said," Lady Susan agreed.

"Shall I explain my humble plan to the countess?" Sir Walter offered. Receiving no objection, he outlined his solution. "The earl has several large estates. Certainly one of them must have room for a new tenant. I understand Thomas is not long from the country, and has not been happy with Town life. We were thinking," he said, gazing at Paige, "that you might inquire of the earl's man of business if there is such a vacancy."

"I shall do so this very day! Trust *you* to be able to make a complicated problem seem simple. Lady Susan has told me of the many times you extracted David as a youth from one scrape or another. It looks like we're once more obliged to you, Sir Walter," Paige said warmly.

Paige's little speech of thanks was not lost on Jerry, who began to see that Sir Walter might be the very person to advise him what to do with Druscilla's news. So when Sir Walter left for Watier's, Lord Hadley asked if he could accompany him.

As they walked toward St. James Street, Sir Walter ventured, "Got something on your mind, eh, Hadley? I thought you were uncharacteristically quiet—you didn't even make one disparaging remark about Lady Carrington's rout last night; and I saw you dancing with a young miss who possessed too many teeth for her mouth."

"Yes, ghastly, wasn't she?" Jerry chuckled. "You'd think her mama would have told her not to smile so much, lest someone mistake her for a pianoforte."

"Well, whatever is bothering you can't be all that serious—you've regained your sense of humor."

Jerry immediately sobered. "I'm afraid it is serious, sir, and I'd like your advice. I respect the quality of your thinking; and, as a close friend of the Owens family, I know you'll be discreet." Exhibiting the quality of his thinking, Sir Walter remained silent. Jerry then recounted in detail the information he'd become privy to the previous evening, ending his narrative by asking Sir Walter if he agreed that Paige should be informed.

Sir Walter pondered the matter briefly and replied, "Ordinarily I don't hold with carrying tales to relatives about family indiscretions. However, in this case I agree with your assessment of Lady Undershaw. She does not have the strength of character to extract herself from the consequences of her folly without besmirching the Undershaw name. Unfortunately, she has not the good sense of her sister-in-law; and it's on this good sense that we must rely. So since you cannot break your word and inform the countess yourself, I offer my services. I will make inquiries to confirm the information first, then seek a private meeting with Countess Penllyn. Of course I shall not mention that you were the source.''

To have the problem taken out of his hands so swiftly and completely momentarily exhilarated Hadley—but this was almost immediately replaced with a sense of guilt for having transferred his burden to other shoulders.

Sensing his young friend's dilemma, Sir Walter crowed, "By Jove, I shall get pleasure from this intrigue. Glad you came to me, my boy. I'll keep you advised of the progress I've made.''

Sir Walter's inquiries confirmed Druscilla Robertson's story, and he wasted no time in laying the facts before Paige.

Paige was angry. To think that the same clever mind that had connived and schemed to marry her brother should be so foolish as to fall into the hands of a moneylender. Why could she not have been unlucky in love and lucky in cards, instead of the other way 'round?

Recognizing that sitting around damning her sister-in-law was getting her nowhere, Paige resolved to confront Dorcas with her information and insist that she reveal her debts to Richard. Given the sum of money involved, Paige saw that as the only honorable solution.

Having decided to undertake this unpleasant chore immediately, Paige made an afternoon call to Grosvenor Square, secure in the knowledge that Richard was still in Surrey.

Ushered into the drawing room, she was again taken with the changes Dorcas had wrought in the furnishings of this spacious room. Gone were the ornately carved gilt-edged French pieces brought by her mother from France.

In their places were some lovely new Sheraton pieces, which mingled well with the Chippendale her father had fancied. Both Paige and Richard, who had never been fond of their mother's taste in furniture (but were afraid relegating her choices to the attic would imply disrespect), had been secretly relieved when Dorcas took matters into her own hands.

Caught up in her appreciation for the genteel ambiance of the room, Paige almost failed to notice Dorcas, sunken in an apple-green-and-gold-striped wing chair. Dorcas gave a weak wave of her hand to acknowledge her sister-in-law's entrance but did not speak. Paige thought she had lost weight; her eyes were more pronounced and the bodice of her gown was less tight.

"My dear, have you been ill? You look quite fagged," Paige declared.

Repositioning herself on the edge of her chair, Dorcas denied this assessment, offering in explanation that the heat had quite worn her down. Paige did not believe this statement, for it had been quite cool of late, but she decided to pounce upon it as a means of introducing the purpose of her visit.

"From what I hear, you have every reason to be feeling the heat! Is that moneylender breathing down your neck?"

At these words, all of Dorcas's usual passion reasserted itself, and she castigated vehemently, "You meddling sneak! Richard doesn't need you anymore and you just can't accept it! Look at you, standing there gloating," she spat out vitriolically.

Paige, though inwardly shaken at this outburst, managed to reply calmly, "I guess I need not ask if the rumor I hear is true. Your behavior is answer enough. When are you going to inform your husband of your losses? It is the only way out, you know."

A year's worth of pent-up resentment poured from Dorcas's pouty, sensuous lips. "What do you know of finding ways out?! You've always had all you ever desired.

Ringing the bell to summon a servant is the hardest task you've ever had to perform. Get out! Get out! I don't need your help!'' she shouted, rising from her chair and advancing menacingly toward Paige.

Though much daunted by this emotional display, Paige recognized that Dorcas was on the verge of collapsing and rushed forward to break her fall as she crumpled to the floor and burst into tears.

Tenderly supporting her sister-in-law to the settee, Paige was suddenly overcome with feelings of sympathy. After all, Dorcas was not yet twenty-one and was caught up in a life-style to which she had not been raised. She had virtually no one close to her to turn to in a crisis, and the strain must be intolerable.

When Dorcas's sobs had subsided, Paige reiterated in a warmer and more conciliatory manner her pleas for Dorcas to unburden herself to Richard. "Though he will be upset, he loves you and will forgive you."

Recognizing the truth in Paige's words, Dorcas eventually promised to apprise Richard of the depths of her folly when he returned that evening.

When Paige left Grosvenor Square, her anger had turned to pity. She vowed in future to be more like a friend than an adversary to her sister-in-law. It also occurred to Paige that by not accepting Dorcas, she had done Richard more harm than good.

For the first time in her life, Dorcas appreciated her sister-in-law's calm common sense. What had seemed an impossible solution now seemed reasonable. She would tell Richard, accept the consequences, and turn over a new leaf. She was still in this frame of mind when Richard's carriage pulled up at the door several hours later.

Her husband scarcely had time to shrug off his jacket before Dorcas fervently drew him into the library and told him all. His reaction was as Paige had predicted.

Much relieved, Lady Undershaw, with her debts settled by her husband, regained her looks within a few days.

Sylvester commented on her renewed spirit when next they met. She artlessly filled him in on what had transpired, expecting commendation. Instead, he bristled and chided her for bending to the will of her sister-in-law.

"When you are in your dotage *she* will still be running your life. You could have won back that money in no time, but now you've scuttled your chances of escaping Sir Richard's vigilance."

Much taken with this argument, Dorcas's peace of mind was disturbed. It was true that Richard now watched her closely and she was chafing under this observation and the constraints it placed on her activities. No more masquerades at Vauxhall! In light of Sylvester's comments, Paige's advice and sisterly concern now took on an undertone of condescension. The embers of resentment flared anew in her breast.

Dorcas was not to be denied another masquerade, however, for the Undershaws received cards for the Prince Regent's masked ball—the culmination of the Season's social events.

With Paige's encouragement, Cornelia sent an acceptance but fully intended to leave the ball before the unmasking occurred. She had purchased a new wig in a style and color that resembled neither her natural hair nor the peruke of Mme. Lisette. Her domino was cleverly pleated so as to conceal as much of her elegant figure as possible. To ensure that her costume would adequately protect her identity, Paige and Cornelia had tried it out on an unknowing Kit, who could not for the life of her put a name to "the pretty lady in the unusual lilac domino." When Cornelia tore off her mask, laughing—"You goose, it's me!"—Kit was astonished.

"I was completely fooled. That getup makes you look like an entirely different person—taller and thinner." Since that was exactly the effect Cornelia had been aiming for, her remaining reservations about venturing out for a night of fun in disguise dissolved.

The night of the masquerade was a perfect June evening.

The coachmen scarcely needed the street lamps to light the way to Carlton House, for the moon was full and cast pools of soft light on the cobblestones. As Paige, escorted by Lord Hadley, rode toward the ball, the feeling she'd had a month earlier—that this was to be a special night— grew even stronger. The scent of roses was heavy on the air and inexplicably a desire for romance stole over her. Instinctively she glanced at Jerry. Catching her gaze upon him, he smiled warmly and threw her a kiss. *Trust Jerry to pick up my mood,* she thought.

Never one to censor her own thoughts, Paige began to wonder if she could fall in love with him. He was really a dear—considerate and always on hand when she needed him. In addition, he was strikingly handsome, witty, and gratifyingly adoring. She was sure if she wanted him, she could have him—and keep him. But there was none of the magic she'd hoped for; perhaps her expectations of love were unrealistic. In any case, it was premature to be contemplating falling in love, for she would most likely be a married lady for several more months; and her scruples would not allow her to pursue a romantic relationship while she was still Countess Penllyn.

The rooms were already crowded when Paige arrived, but she had no difficulty picking out Richard and Dorcas seated on a settee near one of the few open windows. Despite their masks, Paige could discern that neither had succumbed to the gaiety. Both were visibly relieved when Paige and Jerry joined them. Dorcas soon inveigled Hadley onto the dance floor, giving Paige a chance to find out how things fared. Inclining her head in the direction of the departing couple, she inquired gently, "How are you two getting on?"

"We rub along tolerably," came the restrained reply.

"Just tolerably?" echoed Paige.

"Well, she is young and headstrong and doesn't like having her activities curtailed by an 'old man,' as she sometimes refers to me."

Remembering Cornelia's conversation about her age, Paige chortled, "It's too bad you and Cornelia didn't get together, for the two of you could keep each other company sipping the waters at Bath."

"You talk in riddles, Babs. What has Cornelia to do with my domestic situation?"

"Nothing, of course," said his sister airily. "But Cornelia fancies herself aging rapidly enough to be losing her faculties."

"What?!" spluttered Richard. "She *must* be losing her faculties if she imagines herself aging. Why, I've never seen her in such good looks. It's a pity she's still in mourning, for she'd be the catch of the Season."

At that moment, spying Cornelia's domino across the room, a spark of mischief sprang to Paige's eyes. Excusing herself for a moment, she dexterously threaded her way to where Cornelia was enduring an onslaught of questions from admirers who were attempting to discover her identity. Apologizing to her friend's coterie, Paige whisked Cornelia across the room to Richard, whispering, "I have kept your secret, but Richard is lonely and needs diversion. I think you're just the one to provide it."

Arriving in front of her brother, breathless with her find, Paige declared succinctly, "New friend of mine—fresh from the country—divert her—I'll be back," and quickly vanished, not daring to look back.

Had she done so, she would have seen a look of bewilderment on Cornelia's masked face. Before she could ponder Paige's motives in thrusting her before the one person most likely to penetrate her disguise, Richard launched into his role of "big brother entertaining little sister's friend."

Cornelia volleyed a barrage of polite questions about her stay in London and her relationship with his sister. Weary from the effort of inventing answers, she hit upon a way to catch her breath when she heard a waltz struck up. In her newly adopted high-pitched voice, she exclaimed excitedly,

"Oh, Black Domino, it has been my desire since arriving in Town to dance the waltz. It is still not sanctioned at our assemblies in Northumberland. Would you consider me bold if I asked you to partner me?"

Thinking that she *was*, but wishing to avoid the dour Dorcas a few minutes longer, he replied, "I would be charmed."

This interlude proved more pleasurable than he'd anticipated. He found it difficult to believe his partner had never waltzed before—for she did not stiffen as his arm encircled her waist, nor did he once catch her counting her steps. In fact, they waltzed together so perfectly that he had a blissful feeling of *déjà vu*. It had been so long since he had enjoyed dancing this much that he refused to analyze these thoughts and gave himself up to floating with the music and the Lilac Lady (as he had come to think of her).

Recalled to reality as the music ended, Richard eyed the lady suspiciously and asked if she were hoaxing him. Fluttering her eyelashes and glancing guilelessly into his deep blue eyes, she feigned ignorance of his true meaning: "I suppose you've detected that I have waltzed before; but it's only been with my younger sister, who's had a London Season."

Plausible though this seemed as an explanation for her dancing expertise, it did not account for the impression that he had partnered her before. Trusting himself to unravel the mystery through further intercourse, he decided not to express his continued disbelief and led her to one of the rooms where refreshments were laid out.

Meanwhile, Sylvester, dressed in a blue-gray domino, had recognized Dorcas in her scarlet one and claimed her hand for the waltz. Holding her rather closer than convention allowed, he set in motion his plan to seduce her. Having decided that Dorcas wanted a liaison but was resisting the desire to succumb, Sylvester had determined to force the event—and the mysterious nature of a masquerade provided the perfect backdrop.

Circling her closer and closer to the door to the terrace, he whisked her through the opening and into the moonlit shadows beyond. Safe in the solitude of the night, he ceased dancing, tightened his hold on her tantalizingly voluptuous body, and gave her a kiss that she felt all the way to her toes. Satisfied with her yielding response, he allowed his hand to rove inside her domino and brush against the bodice of her gown. This movement caused a gratifying reaction, for she clasped her hands against the back of his neck, forcing his lips more firmly against hers. Reading this correctly as a signal to proceed with his explorations, he did. Suddenly noises from the far side of the terrace reminded them that they were not in private. Hastily, they whispered promises of future meetings and returned to the ballroom.

So engrossed was Richard in trying to determine the identity of the Lilac Lady that he scarcely noticed the absence of his wife. After much thought, he determined that the lady's conversation reminded him of Cornelia; and her beguiling femininity of Mme. Lisette. Soon the suspicion began to grow that she was one or the other. If he were right, it would explain her air of secrecy, for by rights neither one should be at the ball.

Reflecting on Cornelia's personality, he felt it most unlikely that she would consider so improper an action as to dance at a ball while mourning a much loved husband. Besides, if his memory served him correctly, Cornelia was several inches shorter than the Lilac Lady. Having ruled out Lady Bragdon, he focused his analysis on the French modiste. There were certain gestures the Lilac Lady used that reminded him of Mme. Lisette—the way she tilted her head when she looked up at him, and the hand gestures she used when she was excited. Just as he was congratulating himself on mentally unmasking her, his brows creased and he remembered that this charmer's speech had no hint of an accent. He was further discouraged by the impossibility of a shopkeeper, no matter how beautiful, procuring an invitation to Carlton House.

Then he recollected that it was Paige who had introduced them. If he knew his scamp of a sister, she'd revel in dampening the pretensions of the *ton* by passing off a shopkeeper as a member of the Quality. Furthermore, *Kit's* card had been available, as that devoted lady had insisted on staying at home to nurse the infant Pamela, who was cutting another tooth. But that still did not explain the lack of a French accent—could it be that Mme. Lisette only affected an accent to impress her disdainful clientele? Certainly he knew that Mme. Lisette was fluent in French, and he suspected it would be harder for her to disguise her voice in that language.

"*Ce champagne est très bien, n'est-ce pas?*" he observed blandly.

Her response was immediate and natural: "*C'est certainement bien meilleur que le moyena, mais au Maison Carlton on s'attend au meilleur.*"

Evaluating the success of his strategy, Richard was pleased to note that the Lilac Lady's accent and pitch were the same as Lisette's. There was no mistaking that sultry throatiness. Delighted that he had solved the puzzle of the Lilac Lady, he resolved to relax and enjoy the presence of the one woman who played havoc with his senses.

It had been a long time since he had engaged in a flirtation, so he decided to take advantage of the situation. Cornelia was in the same frame of mind. Richard had always been her true love, a fact she'd been unable to confess even to Paige. She'd accepted Lord Bragdon, of whom she had truly been fond, only after ascertaining that Richard would never be able to think of her other than as his sister's playmate.

She knew that Richard was no fool, so when he'd questioned her in French she had purposefully responded (with a sense of abandon) as Mme. Lisette would have done, wanting to see his next move. He now had the air of someone whose suspicions had been confirmed. In short, he thought she was Lisette—so Lisette she would be. She responded to his flirting coquettishly, and soon both of them forgot their actual situations and gave themselves over to enjoying each other's company.

From across the room Paige looked on, pleased with the change in Richard's general demeanor. He seemed younger and less burdened than she'd seen him recently.

She herself was in a lighthearted, festive mood. She had stood up for every set and was sure her slippers were quite worn through. However, as the hour for unmasking approached, she recalled Cornelia's situation and was relieved to see her friend hastening toward the ladies' withdrawing room. Scurrying after her, Paige saw her safely out the door and into her carriage.

She had scarcely returned to the ballroom when Lord Hadley sneaked up behind her and untied the strings of her mask. Amused at such daring, she laughingly accompanied him in to supper.

The merriment lasted into the wee hours, and Paige was enjoying a mild flirtation with the handsome heir to a dukedom when Hadley called her attention to the late hour and the thinness of the crowd. Making apologies to her latest conquest, she allowed herself to be escorted to the waiting carriage.

From his relaxed position against the squabs, Jerry surveyed Paige's still animated form silhouetted against the just breaking light of early morning. "Enjoyed yourself, eh? How many hearts were laid at your feet tonight?" he inquired languidly.

"Well, if I count yours, *five*," she flung out saucily.

As the seductiveness of the evening had left him in a dangerous mood, Jerry almost declared his feelings for her, but he knew her response required a light rejoinder. So he contented himself with saying enigmatically, "Five is an impressive number for one evening."

"Oh, you're as accomplished a flirt as David said—and how many hearts did *you* capture tonight?"

"Counting yours?" he said with an earnestness belying his attempt at raillery.

"Oh, silly, *I* do not count. I am your best friend's wife. Have you forgotten?"

"Try as I might, I've been unable to," he confessed with a sigh.

Feeling as though the conversation were taking a forbidden direction, Paige blithely declared, "So, we agree that we cannot number me among your conquests this evening. How many, then?"

"Then you have beat me, for I can only count four—or three, really, for I am loath to include Miss Coates."

Paige gurgled, "Despite her mask, I recognized her at once, and fear another million silkworms have expired on behalf of her domino."

"For shame, Countess Penllyn. Where is your Christian spirit? Or have you used it all up by employing it on behalf of your brother?" Jerry baited her.

Guardedly, Paige inquired as to his meaning.

"The mysterious lady in the lilac domino—did not I see you purposefully thrust her to your brother's attention?"

Relieved that Jerry was not referring to her intervention into the matter of Dorcas's debts, Paige burst into laughter. Seizing on this as an admission of a direct hit, Jerry pushed to uncover the lady's identity.

"My lips are sealed," Paige responded firmly, relieved to see that the carriage had drawn up at her house.

"Well, at least tell me if she was a Cyprian," he begged.

Indignant, Paige reached for the door handle and chastised, "A Cyprian! How would I have made the acquaintance of a Cyprian?"

Afraid that she was so insulted that she would not wait for him to hand her down, Jerry leaped to open the door and jumped down before his coachman had descended the box.

As he helped her out, he said, "Forgive me for my impertinence, but I know there's a mystery surrounding the lady in lilac—and I mean to know what it is." Grasping her arm lightly, he whirled her to face him and declared in a loud voice, much buoyed by champagne, "I refuse to part from you until you give in!"

So embroiled were they in this _contretemps_ that they failed to notice the arrival of a gentleman in a hackney until a weak cough caught their attention. A thin, bedraggled figure stumbled toward them. Paige stepped back in fear as Jerry prepared to protect her.

Suddenly the quiet dawn was broken by an unearthly howl, as Snow streaked down the pavement and hurled himself into the arms of the menacing stranger, from whence he proceeded to lick the dust on that drawn face.

"David!" gasped Paige.

Chapter X

MANAGING a wan smile, the earl said haltingly, "I'm afraid if one of you does not offer me your arm, it will be *I*, not Paige, who gives in."

The sound of that familiar voice roused Jerry from his state of frozen surprise, and he rushed to his friend's aid, getting there just as David's knees began to give way. Paige, waiting only long enough to see if Jerry were capable of holding her collapsing husband, ran to open the door and summon Capper.

As Hadley assisted Penllyn into the house, Dickson, who had finished paying off the hackney driver, shouted, "Take care not to bump his right side, or you'll start his wound bleeding again."

The candlelight in the hallway clearly illuminated David's countenance, and Paige was stunned by his haggard appearance: his face was the color of ashes; deep grooves lined his forehead; and his gray eyes were dimmed with pain. His stooped posture and the additional streaks of silver in his hair made him look much older than the man she'd kissed good-bye three months earlier.

Recovering from her shock, she immediately took charge. "Dickson! What has produced this state?" she demanded imperiously.

"My lord was shot, and the surgeons have been unable

147

to remove the ball that is lodged behind his ribs. There was nothing more they could do for him in Brussels, so they sent him home to get proper care from Harley Street.''

Turning on Capper, who still wore his nightcap, the countess ordered him to send a groom to fetch Dr. Russell. "Tell him not to return without him. It is a matter of life and death!''

Noticing that Jerry was still standing in the hallway with David slumped on his shoulder, she scolded, "Fool! Can't you see he has not the strength to stand? Lay him on the couch in the morning room.''

When this had been accomplished with Dickson's help, Paige loosened David's collar and offered him the glass of brandy Capper had had the foresight to provide. A distraught Mrs. Capper, hovering in the doorway, inquired if she should awaken Lady Susan. Paige's brow furrowed, considering the idea, before she concluded, "I think not just yet, for it would be senseless to upset her before we know the doctor's opinion. But you can bring me a bowl of cool lavender water and some cloths to bathe his head. He seems quite feverish.''

Jerry, left with no duty to perform, reflected on the scene before him. Here was a side of the countess he'd never seen—a tender, wifely concern. Disturbed as he was about his friend's plight, he could not help but feel resentful that this paragon's attentions had been so abruptly diverted from himself. Guilt for these thoughts immediately overtook him, and he tried to make amends for them by gently removing David's travel-stained boots. He was rewarded by a smile of appreciation from the countess. Under these ministrations from his loved ones, the half-conscious earl soon fell into a restless sleep.

As the anxious gathering waited for the physician to arrive, Dickson explained how the earl had come by his wound. Penllyn had been sent into France on a secret spy mission. Having succeeded in obtaining the vital information he was after, he was on his way back to Brussels when an advance party of Ney's forces came upon him near Quatre Bras. Though his steed was faster than theirs, he could not totally outrun their ammunition and took a ball through the right side. Though losing a considerable amount of blood, Penllyn had clung to his horse and heroically delivered his information to headquarters before collapsing. Two abortive attempts to remove the ball had only served to further weaken him, so Wellington himself had insisted his brave hussar be returned to England, where he would receive the finest medical attention.

Dickson had no sooner finished his story than Capper announced Dr. Russell. One look at his patient and the esteemed doctor immediately banished everyone but Dickson from the room. Ten minutes later Capper was summoned to help Dickson carry the earl to his bedchamber. There the medical man painstakingly, but successfully, removed the ball.

The sun was high when he rejoined the vigilant group in the morning room. Calling aside the countess, Dr. Russell informed her of the satisfactory outcome of the operation but warned her that her husband's condition was very serious: he was weak from loss of blood and a high fever, and would require continual nursing for at least a se'nnight.

"Doctor, please be honest with me. What do *you* think his chances are for survival?" Paige asked bravely.

"If I had seen him immediately, they would be excellent, for the ball did not damage any vital organs. However, the ministrations of my brothers in medicine have so sapped his strength that his fate is now in the hands of the Almighty," he replied gravely and, Paige felt, a bit pompously.

Resolving to do whatever she could to assist the Almighty, she thanked Dr. Russell for not mincing words and received his instructions for David's care. She then ordered breakfast to be laid out for the doctor and Jerry and trudged upstairs to alert Kit and solicit her support for informing Lady Susan.

As it happened, Kit's support was not needed. David's mother reacted far better than Paige had expected. Though clearly upset by the news that her sole surviving son lay below, close to death, she retained her composure and insisted on taking the first vigil at his bedside, thus allowing Paige to get some sleep. Reluctantly, a very weary Paige agreed, but on two conditions: first, that Kit share the vigil; and second, that Paige be awakened at once if his condition worsened.

Too tired to undress, Paige flopped at an angle across her bed and fell asleep at once. What seemed like two minutes later (but was actually two hours), she was shaken awake by a distraught Kit.

"Is he worse?" Paige questioned, instantly awake despite the brevity of her sleep.

Tears trickling down her pale cheeks, Kit nodded affirmatively. "We cannot keep him still. Dickson is worried lest he commence bleeding again."

Paige struggled to her feet and walked resolutely through the connecting door to her husband's bedchamber. The stricken looks on Lady Susan's and Dickson's faces confirmed that Kit had not exaggerated David's condition. Their patient looked frail and lost in the huge Tudor bed. His arms flailed weakly against the pillows and his legs were tangled in the bedclothes.

Quickly taking in this scene, Paige realized that he must have been thrashing about for some time. "Dickson, did not the doctor give him laudanum?"

"No, ma'am. We dosed him with so much brandy during the surgery that there seemed not the need."

Paige, unaware of the ludicrous picture she made in her rumpled ball gown, responded severely, "There is need *now*, for he must be kept quiet. Lady Susan, do you know if there is any laudanum in the house?"

Shaken though she was by her son's condition, the dowager Countess Penllyn was able to recall that Nurse had just procured several vials to ease Pamela's teething.

Kit was sent to fetch one, and a dose was soon forced down David's throat. This had the desired effect, for he soon ceased his tossing, and his breathing became easier. Once her husband had settled, Paige turned her attention to the other occupants of the room.

She realized with horror that Dickson looked almost as bad as his master. *Poor man,* she thought. *He's been caring for him without rest for days.*

Aloud she commented bracingly, "Well done, Dickson. You've seen your master safely home and we are grateful. Why do you not take this opportunity while he's resting to replenish your strength with food and sleep? No doubt we will need you later, when this dose wears off. And, as it was a strong one, that won't be for many hours yet. We'll be sure to call you at once," Paige promised.

As Dickson left, Capper entered, whispering that Sir Walter Townsend was below. Paige seized on this announcement as a way of giving Kit and Lady Susan a respite from the sickroom. Realizing they would not go easily, she argued that Sir Walter really ought to be informed of David's return and condition—and that she herself was perfectly capable of sitting with David while he slept. "Besides, I will have Snow to assist me if anything goes wrong," she added, smiling.

As if to acknowledge this comment, Snow rose from his position at the foot of the bed and rubbed himself against Paige's skirts.

Left alone with Penllyn and Snow, Paige did some soul-searching. To think that she had been out partying and flirting while her husband was risking his life in defense of his country! Her thoughts had been solely for her own pleasure, and she had scarcely remembered the existence of the man whose name she bore and in whose house she lived. Disappointed with herself, Paige suddenly felt shallow and contrite. She was no better than Dorcas!

Having diagnosed her own foibles as being self-centeredness and frivolousness, she began contemplating a cure. She would devote all her energies to nursing her husband back to health. She vowed that when he recovered, she'd immerse herself in good works. She could volunteer to help at an infirmary for the indigent and perhaps offer counsel at a Magdalen House. Having made these decisions, she immediately felt in harmony with herself and more optimistic about David's recovery.

This optimism was tested severely over the next week, as David's condition showed no improvement. His periods of consciousness were few and far between, and he seemed to recognize no one. Dr. Russell frowned over his delirious patient and could find no words to reassure his family.

The whole household was plunged into gloom. The only cheerful visage on the scene was Sylvester's. Try as he might to adopt a mask of grim concern, he could not conceal his presumption that the earldom would soon be his. He had already ordered a new carriage against his expectations and had to fiercely restrain himself from having the Penllyn crest affixed to it.

As the word was out that the earl was on his deathbed, Sylvester's credit soared. Suddenly all the ladies who'd previously spurned him welcomed his advances. As the competition increased, Dorcas, anxious to retain her hold on him, threw caution to the wind and allowed him to bed her. This proved to be a more pleasurable experience than either had expected and would turn out not to dim with repeated encounters.

For the first time in a year, Dorcas was not on Paige's mind at all. Paige spent every waking hour at Penllyn's bedside, growing increasingly pessimistic. By the end of the week, he had lost nearly two stone, and they were scarcely able to get water down his throat. Feeling as though drastic measures were needed, Paige decided in the wee hours one morning to strike a bargain with the Almighty. If He would spare David's life, she promised to devote the remainder of hers to needy causes. . . .

She had no sooner made this pledge than David's

ravings became more comprehensible. Rushing to his side, she could make out the words "Maria," "good girl," and "never fail me."

Hearing the name of another woman on his lips momentarily made Paige regret her recent pact with God. Shaking this uncharitable thought from her head, she stroked his forehead and murmured reassuringly, "Maria has not failed you. All is well." These words seemed to have a soothing effect; and Paige had begun to speculate as to Maria's importance in his life when Lady Susan entered the room to take Paige's place.

It was two nights later when David regained full consciousness. Awakening from a nightmare of his desperate ride to Brussels, his eyes focused on a vaguely familiar feminine profile. This lady was gently stroking and talking to what looked to be a fur muff in her lap. As the mist lifted from his brain he recognized Miss Undershaw (no! his *wife*) and the cat from the inn. He could see there were tears in her eyes, and he heard her croon, "Ah, no, do not purr when your master lies on the brink of death. How can you be so unfeeling, wretched animal? I know you only knew him for a short time, but he did save your life."

Licking his dry lips, Penllyn decided to make his presence known. Raspily he murmured, "I see you have had a change of heart, for you no longer seem to find the prospect of my death amusing."

Turning toward the bed in disbelief, Paige saw that her ears had not deceived her. David's eyes were open and twinkling at her. Snow was unceremoniously dumped from her lap as she ran to the bed and clasped his hand between both of hers, drawing it to her cheek. "Thank God," she uttered instinctively. Then, seeking to amuse him, she added, "I've been afraid I'd have to appear in widow's weeds, and I look quite dreadful in black—though Sylvester's had several mourning outfits delivered already." The fresh tears in her eyes betrayed the lightness of her words.

The earl was not yet out of the woods. Though his

periods of consciousness increased, another fortnight passed
before the doctor would declare him on the road to
recovery.

As his spirits rose, Paige's declined, for it dawned on
her that she must soon leave the Owens family. She had
originally agreed to obtain an annulment immediately upon
David's return, but naturally his condition had made that
course impossible. Now that he was close to regaining his
full health, her continuing residence with him could jeopar-
dize the annulment. After all, only a door separated their
bedchambers. Society could understand that marriage to an
absent or ailing husband was not likely to have been
consummated but would be more skeptical once word was
out that the earl was on his feet again. So it must be done
quickly.

Somehow the idea of setting up an independent household with Kit had lost its original appeal. Paige discovered
that she liked the warmth, caring, and even the obligations
of family life. It took her back to the days at Waverly
when her parents were alive. She would sorely miss Lady
Susan, Pamela, and the Cappers.

As David was not yet able to join the family for dinner,
Paige made it a point to sit with him every evening and
update him on the quotidian activities of the household.
She was at her most entertaining when she described
Sylvester's visits.

"I think you have misjudged him," Paige chided her
husband. "He is, above all others, concerned with your
health. His own is dependent upon yours, though inversely.
Poor man! The range of his emotions far exceeds anything
I would have expected. For when we describe the hearty
breakfast you've consumed, he is thrown into the pits of
despair. And we are forced to admit that your fever
persists, in order to revive his spirits.

"For our own amusement, your mother and I have
developed this technique into a new parlor game we play
with him, which we privately call 'Who Will Be Earl?'"

First Lady Susan feeds him a distressing piece of information about your health. Then I counter with a more optimistic vignette. He's so disturbed when he takes leave of us that he's twice forgotten his hat and once failed to recognize that the elegant coach at the doorstep belonged to him.''

In appreciation of these tales, David roared with laughter and, holding his bandaged side, accused his wife of being in cahoots with Sylvester. "You mean to see me in my grave yet, for you put me in danger of reopening my wound with your witty observations.''

"How clever of you to have guessed! If only I could think of a method to make you sneeze, I would be well on my way to earning the thousand pounds Sylvester has promised me if you die.''

Laughing even more heartily and clutching his rib cage, David wheezed, ''A few more remarks such as that, and a sneeze will not be necessary!''

"Nonsense! You've grown so strong that you could take another ball and still survive. The doctor says you'll be able to dress and join us downstairs by the end of the week—which means that you and I should discuss our 'arrangement.' ''

"Arrangement?'' he queried.

"The annulment.''

"Good God! Was I that bad a patient that you're anxious to be rid of me so soon?''

"Actually, you *were* a bad patient,'' she said frankly, "but that is not why I brought up the subject. Given the nature of our marriage, it would be unseemly for us to be living together once you are about.''

Innocently, he repeated the word—"Unseemly?''—and had the satisfaction of provoking one of her rare blushes.

"You know what I mean, David.''

"No, truly I do not. Are you afraid that I will sneak through the connecting door and claim my rights?'' He leered wolfishly.

"Oh, so you and Sylvester have, after all, something in common: ravishing unsuspecting women," she observed unperturbedly. "But do be serious, David. People will be more understanding if we announce an immediate annulment, for they will think that we married in haste because you were going off to war but then upon your return found we do not suit."

Do not suit?! he thought. *That is patently absurd. We share the same values, we laugh together, and are perfectly matched at chess.* . . . He supposed, like most women, she was more attracted to the smooth charm of an accomplished flirt, like Jerry. He hadn't been so numbed by pain that he'd missed the significance of their little exchange the night he returned home. *Well, I saw her first and I'm going to give him a run for his money. He's got a three-month start on me, but if I can keep her here as my wife for a while longer, I'll have the advantage.* Perhaps he could convince her it would create more of a scandal to get an immediate annulment. . . .

"More likely, people will say you don't want to be bothered tending an invalid husband," he finally responded somberly, lowering his gaze.

"Oh, no, David, you do not believe *that*, do you?!" she cried passionately.

"Of course *I* do not. I am merely suggesting how it might appear to others."

To herself, Paige acknowledged the truth in these words. She had already owned her own frivolousness, and perhaps society saw her the same way. She just couldn't bear others thinking of her as a feather-head who thought only of her own needs and wants. In horror, she realized that Kit's companionship with Lady Susan could be viewed as a ploy on Paige's part to free up more time for herself. Well! She would prove to herself and others that she was made of sterner stuff . . . she would not appear at another social event until David could accompany her.

Not recognizing the inconsistency between her musings

and her words, Paige declared resolutely, "I care not for others' opinions of me; however, I do feel it would be inconsiderate of me to leave your nursing solely on Lady Susan's shoulders." Then, not wishing to be seen as capitulating, she added absurdly, "You *are* very demanding."

Guessing Paige's motive for this last comment, David decided to ignore it. "So does this mean you are willing to postpone the annulment for a while?"

"Yes, until we make several public appearances together."

"Very wise." He nodded, as if in awe of her sound reasoning.

Later that day, Lady Susan found her son in a pensive mood. It did not take much probing to elicit its cause. David had always had an open relationship with his mother and welcomed her opinions. He told her of his scheme to get Paige to remain so they could become better acquainted.

"Better acquainted for the purpose of making your marriage a permanent one?" she guessed, delighted.

"Yes, but I fear that her affections may already be engaged."

"Hadley? Did she admit to this?"

"No, but he is an engaging fellow, and she seems to be on easy terms with him," he said, depressed that his mother was able to identify his rival so quickly.

Lady Susan considered the matter and offered, "At first I thought Paige was trying to make a match between Miss Roche and Hadley, but recently Kit has been absent from their excursions. As Kit is more in Paige's confidence, I will ask her opinion of how things stand," she declared, and went off to do so.

David thought this was a good scheme but decided to do some investigating of his own.

When next Jerry visited the sickroom, David made sure they were alone so he could surreptitiously quiz his friend about his feelings for Paige. "Old man, I haven't thanked you adequately for squiring my wife this Season. It must have seriously limited the number of flirtations you were able to carry on. So it's likely a relief to know, now that I am home, you'll be your own man once again.''

The stricken look on Jerry's face as the meaning of these words sunk in caused David's stomach to turn over. *Damn*, he thought, *it's worse than I suspected. Though I know if I ask him directly, he will give her up, I prefer to win her through competition rather than through default.*

Jerry took a moment to conceal his dismay before responding, ''While I am relieved to have you home, I don't relish giving up the company of the most charming woman in London. Being seen often with a woman of such substance has added greatly to my consequence among the mamas of the *ton*, you know.'' Then, seeking once and for all to learn the truth about the Penllyn marriage, he continued, ''You certainly found a gem of a wife; and I'm anxious to hear the details of your courtship, which you promised to confide to me as soon as you returned.''

David had not bargained for Jerry's pressing him on this point and was at a loss as to how to respond. Obviously, Paige had not taken Jerry into her confidence, and David found himself momentarily cheered by the implications of this. He also found in this a reason for not divulging the information Jerry sought. ''When I said those words to you before the wedding ceremony, I had forgotten that it was not my story alone to tell. I will feel more comfortable entrusting you with *our* story when I have Paige's permission.'' David liked the ring of this last statement, as it had a possessive quality to it which, from the look in Jerry's eyes, had not escaped his notice.

''Well, then, old man, I have no doubt I'll be hearing it soon, for once the countess knows she has *your* permission, she is bound to tell me. We've become famous friends in your absence.''

David winced at these words and swore to himself that Paige would not be the one to confide the truth to Jerry. However, he did not, of course, speak his mind. Instead, he brushed off his friend's presumption, saying, "That is, naturally, her decision."

A soft knock on the door heralded the arrival of Lady Susan, so Jerry made his excuses and took himself off.

Confounded by encountering the very person she intended to discuss with David, Lady Susan stammered an almost incoherent greeting to Hadley and tried not to look too relieved when he departed. Her hopes that her state of mind had gone unnoticed were dashed when David greeted her by saying, "Seeing as how Jerry's presence usually does not fluster you, I gather from your present behavior that you've come with a report of your talk with Kit."

"Oh, is it so obvious?" Lady Susan groaned.

"Only to me, dear, who knows you so well," he consoled affectionately. Obviously impatient to have her news, he patted a chair and said, "Sit here and tell me what I'm up against."

His mother's delay gave David the feeling that the news was not all he could want, and this was confirmed by her words. "Well, Miss Roche does think that Paige has developed a *tendre*—but it is of recent origin so it is not yet *well* developed. And Kit draws her conclusions from her own observations, not from Paige's confidence. So, do not look so down-hearted. There is still hope, and Kit feels that you are so much better suited for Paige than is Lord Hadley that she promises to throw her support on our side."

Sinking back onto his cushions, David bemoaned this intelligence and wondered if he could muster the strength needed to map out a winning strategy.

"Perhaps I ought to leave it up to fate."

"Nonsense!" his mother scolded in rallying tones. "We determine our own fate. If you want her, you're going to have to fight for her. And, although I may be prejudiced, your best weapon is to be yourself—after all, she was enough impressed with your qualities in two days' acquaintance that she agreed to marry you and take on your family. Imagine what wonders you can work by having her see you daily for, say, the next month. Didn't you say that she had agreed to stay on until you could be seen together in public?''

Receiving an affirmative nod, she continued, ''Then you need to delay your convalescence long enough to win her heart.''

David chortled, ''Only a mother could think her son shows to his best advantage in the sickroom.'' Snapping his fingers with sudden insight, he crowed, ''But where I *am* at my best is Penllyn! Hmmm. From the temperature in my room I gather it must be quite stifling in the streets— I'm sure the household could benefit from a few weeks in the country. And four days in a carriage ought to give me a chance to display my conversational abilities.''

Suddenly the spirit that had been rekindled by this seemingly perfect solution dimmed as he thought of the hardships the long journey might cause his mother and niece. ''But then there are probably several other solutions that will answer just as well, for I cannot ask you to undertake such an arduous trip when you have only just rid yourself of the last traces of the influenza.''

Laughing indulgently, Lady Susan pointed out that though *she* was fully recovered, David himself was not even allowed to venture downstairs until the morrow. Moreover, since David had never spent a summer in London, he was doubtless unaware that it was the unhealthiest of environments. ''We will all be better off at Penllyn,'' she concluded firmly, ''especially with Hadley either in Town or at his own estate.''

''Oh, but I intend to invite Jerry to join us, with the intent of besting him in country activities. You know how devilishly irritable he gets rusticating.''

"Sly as a fox, aren't you?" His mother smiled. "What date have you set for our departure, and what will you do if Paige refuses to go?"

"Can you not think of harder questions than those?" David teased affably, his spirits quite restored. "We'll leave the beginning of next week, when I have proved that I am stout enough; and Paige will be happy to accompany us because she's already told me that she's missing the summertime joys of the country. . . ."

As predicted, Paige was in transports over this treat, and preparations were soon under way for their removal to Penllyn. The only person disgruntled by the activity in Berkeley Square was Sylvester, who had overextended himself as a result of expectations that had proved to be illusory. Determined to find a way to drive a wedge between David and his wife so no heir would be produced, he wangled an invitation to his cousin's seat.

Chapter XI

UNLIKE the last time David had traveled the roads connecting Wales and London, this trip proved marvelously uneventful. Paige was enthralled with the mountainous Welsh terrain, so different from the rolling hills of Surrey. Their progress was periodically interrupted by orders to "Stop this instant!" so she could gather handfuls of the beautiful wildflowers found at this altitude. Hence it was close to dusk on the fourth day when they came upon one of the most romantic settings Paige had ever seen. The horses had just made a sharp turn in the road when she glimpsed patches of a dark blue body of water through the dense conifers. Again the command was given for the carriage to stop, which David countermanded by insisting that a better view was to be had just a few hundred feet farther.

As promised, the trees soon thinned to reveal an even more breathtaking scene than Paige had imagined. The waning sunlight sparkled on the lake's pristine surface like diamonds on a cloth of sapphire velvet. Gasping, she inquired of David if he knew the name of this charming tarn.

Looking somewhat amused, he furrowed his brow as if trying to remember it, finally drawling, "I believe the locals call it Mynyddlllyn."

Narrowing her eyes suspiciously, she queried, "Is that the lake's name, or did you just sneeze?"

"Since my life depends upon *not* sneezing, you can be sure it was the name of the lake," he replied with exaggerated seriousness.

Not rising to this conversational bait, she returned her gaze to the scene before her and discovered on the far mountainside an elegant residence. "Oh, how fortunate the owners of that home are, to be able to feast their eyes on this prospect whenever they so desire."

Lady Susan, who had been looking at the spectacle with an air of contemplative sadness, snapped out of her reverie at Paige's last comment and seemed on the point of responding to it when she caught David's eye and saw him shake his head warningly.

"I don't think you'll be disappointed in Penllyn's view," David predicted. "And if we don't soon get started, we'll be too late for dinner."

Though darkness had almost completely fallen by the time they reached their destination, Paige could see that the house was not the Tudor monstrosity she had expected, but a well-proportioned structure in the familiar E-shaped plan of the late Elizabethan period.

The entrance hall, which she guessed was quite large, seemed smaller by the presence of the entire serving staff, who had been summoned to meet their new mistress.

David was somewhat daunted by this assembled group, realizing that he would have to perform the introductions. As he had not spent much time at Penllyn over the past few years, he feared offending the newer members of the staff whose names and faces were not that familiar. To his relief, the butler, Williams, stepped out of line to accompany his master and new mistress as they ran the gauntlet. Williams had mastered the art of whispering without seeming to move his lips and was therefore able to provide David with the correct appellations. Upon approaching a diminutive and rather scared-looking young woman, Williams

surprised his master by stepping forward and very audibly
announcing that this was Mrs. Jones, the new cook. David
then remembered that Mrs. Morgan, who had filled this
lofty position previously, had been pensioned off just
before he had left to rejoin Wellington.

As the timid Mrs. Jones was presented to the countess,
Paige took pity on her and made a special effort to put her
at her ease. "Seeing as how I'm a new recruit here, also, I
think I can understand what you're feeling right now. I
imagine you're worried about making the right impression
at our first dinner, as I am. It must be concerning you to be
so long absent from the kitchen. If you'd like, you need
not wait till all the introductions are finished, but can get
on back there right now."

Gratefully, Mrs. Jones bobbed another curtsy and hurried off toward the back of the house. As the servants
looked at Paige with new respect, Lady Susan approved
the action, saying softly, "Not even in the house five
minutes and you've already won over the servants."

David's reaction to his wife's exchange with the cook
was one of self-congratulation, both in his choice of bride
and in his decision to remove to Penllyn—for she already
seemed to be unconsciously adopting the role of mistress.
Once she became immersed in this position, it would be
more difficult for her to give it up. He must remember to
talk to his mother about giving Paige free rein in running
the household, since out of habit the servants might defer
to the dowager countess.

When the rest of the servants had been dismissed, Mrs.
Rhys, the ramrod-thin housekeeper, offered in crisp tones
to show Paige her new quarters. David quickly intervened,
reserving that honor for himself, and escorted Paige to her
apartment, which was adjacent to his own. Spying a door
in her room near the wardrobe, Paige speculated out loud
as to whether that was the inevitable "connecting door"
between their chambers; and, at his nod, she twinkled,

"Are you going to give me the key now, or slide it under the door in the middle of the night?"

Lying convincingly, he announced that the key had been long since lost, and she would just have to take her chances. However, he understood that a chair placed under the doorknob would, while not preventing his entrance, at least announce it.

"Well, then, I guess it's a good thing I sleep with a pistol under my pillow," she countered devilishly.

"What?! And risk leaving Snow fatherless?" he queried playfully.

"Better to have no father at all than to have one who would take a woman against her will."

As, at that very moment, David espied through the window Snow on his way to the barn to make some conquests, David had no qualms declaring: "I don't believe he'd mind having a ravisher for a father."

"Speaking of 'ravishing,' I am frightfully hungry. Should we not be dressing for dinner?" Paige remarked, deftly turning the subject.

"Good God, you're right. It wants only a half hour until dinner," David exclaimed, glancing at his watch.

Paige was entranced by her first sight of the dining room. Her eyes moved in delight from the brass-and-crystal chandelier to the carved Chippendale sideboard and matching chairs with pierced backs and fine scrollwork. At the sight of the exquisite Sèvres china place settings, she squeezed David's arm and whispered, "I see a good deal of the Sèvres survived your childhood prank."

Perplexed by these words, he was glad for the distraction of helping her into her chair, for it gave him a chance to recollect her meaning. As he did, he was warmed by the thought that she held in her memory the incident of the escape of the garter snake.

He was not, however, warmed by the soup, which had arrived at a temperature that made him suspect it had just been recently removed from the icehouse instead of the hearthfire. Paige, who was rather surprised that the leek soup had been served cold, was reluctant to comment, for fear it was a Welsh custom—or, even worse, that it reflected badly on Mrs. Jones. She had just caught the look of consternation on Lady Susan's and Kit's faces when David flung down his spoon and spluttered, to the nearest footman, "The temperature of this soup is unsatisfactory. Take it away at once and bring us the first course!"

Paige was certain that Mrs. Jones's reputation would be redeemed by the next course. All approved the delicacy of the baked salmon, and Paige fully relaxed when she tasted the first morsel of the honeyed lamb and found it delicious. Her ease was short-lived, however, as her husband complained to his mother that something was not right about the dish.

"I fear what you are missing is the rosemary," Lady Susan observed unhappily.

David was about to deliver a scathing denunciation of the new cook's skills when he glanced at Miss Roche, who had begun to pale at his vehement criticisms. Conciliatorily, he commented, "Well, it is obvious that Mrs. Jones is a local, for at least she knows how to prepare *bara lawr* and morels."

With trepidation, the dinner party awaited the arrival of the second course.

David commented positively on all the dishes except the buttered cabbage, which he found an unworthy companion for the green goose, trout cooked with bacon, and cockle cakes. Laughingly he suggested that Mrs. Jones needed to be educated in vegetables suitable to the aristocracy.

Paige herself was less disturbed with Mrs. Jones than she was with her husband's breech of etiquette in casting aspersions upon a member of the household staff in the presence of other servants, for she was acutely aware of the two footmen, listening impassively by the sideboard.

As the sweetmeats were passed around, Paige made up her mind to speak to David about his arrogance, even though her tenure as wife and mistress of the household was only temporary.

Her first opportunity to do so was the following morning at breakfast. As she entered the room, she observed David ordering the footman to remove the eggs at once, for they were as dry as a bone.

Taking advantage of this exchange, and the fact that they were the only two who had risen early, she confronted him (after heaping her plate with potato cakes, sausages, and toast). Between bites she pointed out that he was behaving as though he were still captain of his regiment instead of lord of his manor. "Since Wales, to my knowledge, is not threatened with foreign invasion, you need not bark out commands to the servants as if they were Johnny Raws preparing for their first engagement."

Perplexed at these harsh words, David wondered aloud, "Are you referring to my sending back the eggs?"

"That, and the soup and the lamb and the cabbage at dinner."

"You suggest that I should put up with cold soup, unseasoned lamb, and peasants' fare in my own home—to coddle the servants' feelings?" he said incredulously.

"If you do not take my meaning, I must take you in hand and teach you alternative methods of wielding authority."

Much as he wished to remain in her good graces, he bristled at the officiousness of her tone and found himself remonstrating, "I am sure the curriculum will not include lessons on humility, for it is a concept with which you are unfamiliar."

Stifling a retort, which she instantly recognized as likely to prove his point, she forced her lips into a tight smile and decided to respond only to the first part of his statement. "You are right. Humility will not be included, for it is not at all a suitable attribute for an earl's dealings with his servants."

"Just so! That's why I behave the way I do. I've learned

it's better to show them where they're wrong right off, lest they develop bad habits which take forever to correct.''

"And I, too, believe that bad habits should be nipped in the bud. That's why I'm speaking to you about yours,'' she counterattacked. "However, you will notice that I have timed our discussion so that we have no observers. That is lesson one. I hope you'll keep this in mind, as well as the points that follow, next time you're displeased with cook's offerings. And lesson two is, try to put yourself in the place of the person receiving the criticism. That way you'll be more inclined to speak in such a way that the other person will hear you without feeling attacked. My last point is that criticism should be delivered directly, rather than through a third party like the footman. I considered all three points while planning how to discuss this with you this morning,'' she concluded proudly.

"You need not have concerned yourself about *my* feelings. I can take criticism from anyone, at any time, about anything,'' David said angrily, never at his best in the early hours.

Skeptically, Paige inquired, "How many times have you been rebuked by a subaltern carrying a message from your superior?''

"Never!'' he said exasperatedly, for the first time in his life wishing a conversation with Paige would come to an end. His wish was granted, as the footman returned just then with a platter of moist-looking eggs. Paige, having eaten her fill, excused herself to accompany Mrs. Rhys on a tour of the house.

She was enchanted by the ballroom. At either end, over the doorways, hung beautifully detailed seventeenth-century Brussels tapestries. And from the exquisitely plastered and gilded ceiling were suspended massive cut-glass chandeliers, which caught the sunlight streaming through the French doors and flashed colorful patterns around the room. Visions of gaily attired men and women whirling about in this elegant setting momentarily made her forget the housekeeper's presence.

As though reading Paige's mind, Mrs. Rhys disclosed that it had been two years since there had been dancing in this room. Thinking that such a perfect setting should not remain unutilized, Paige declared, "As soon as this house is out of mourning, we shall give the finest ball in Wales."

At this, Paige's first acknowledgment that the house was in mourning, Mrs. Rhys sniffed and allowed herself her first positive reaction to the new mistress. This inflexibly proper retainer had immediately disapproved of both Paige's brightly colored clothes and her commanding ways. Before the countess's arrival, Mrs. Rhys had hoped to be able to maintain the independent control of the household she'd come to enjoy under Lady Susan and Lady Louisa. But she doubted this strong-willed creature would rely on her judgment.

Paige had no inkling of the housekeeper's lack of regard for her, so she was able to spend some moments of reverie without minding what Mrs. Rhys might think. Strolling farther into the room, picturing the ideal location for the musicians, Paige suddenly halted as she took in the implications of planning a ball six months hence. Was she imagining she would still be David's wife? Surely, if all went according to the plans she and David had made before leaving London, their annulment would be effectuated in half that time. Did her impetuous statement mean that she no longer wanted to go through with the original agreement? No definite answer came to mind, and as the time was not right to sort it out, she stored it away to contemplate later.

Her first opportunity came sooner than she expected when Mrs. Rhys was called away to clarify some instructions she'd given to the chambermaids. Paige decided to take advantage of her solitude and stepped outside to investigate the grounds. The French doors opened onto a large stone terrace, which she imagined would be a highly romantic setting in the moonlight, with strains of music drifting on the night air. Behind a large formal garden was planted a stand of thick pine trees. Ridiculously, she thought of the flag of England as she stared at rows of red roses marching alongside ageratum and sweet alyssum. Paige much preferred wild gardens and soon, tiring of the regularity of the layout, wandered down the hill and through the screen of trees to see what lay beyond.

As she broke out into the open, she gasped in recognition. Below her lay the magical tarn she had seen the day before. Wheeling around, she studied the warm red limestone exterior of the house perched above her. *Why, it was Penllyn we saw yesterday! How odious of him to conceal the identity of his home and rob me of the joyous anticipation of daily savoring this scene. Just another example of his arrogance,* she thought, then reconsidered, *or of his ludicrous sense of humor.*

So, did she or did she not wish to remain married to this man? she inquired of herself, reviving the issue she had raised in the ballroom. David was certainly one of the few men she'd met who didn't bore her after fifteen minutes of conversation; and though his sense of humor sometimes irritated her, it primarily amused her. Then there were his kisses, which she found herself quiveringly reliving whenever her eyes strayed to his full, sensual mouth. Several times she'd even shamelessly found herself yearning for the touch of his lips on hers again. Shaking her head at the inappropriateness of this line of thought, she began thinking of other aspects of her situation.

Being honest with herself, she was also thoroughly enjoying her position as the Countess of Penllyn. After all, she was mistress of this magnificent estate, she celebrated, throwing out her arms in sheer pleasure. It would definitely be difficult to give all this up. Plus, she couldn't conceive of a better mother-in-law than Lady Susan; and it frightened her to think that if she married someone else, she might be saddled with a dragon like Lady Bragdon.

Amazingly, she found herself wondering what Jerry's mother was like . . . and this led her to contemplate a life as Lady Hadley. Though she had never seen Hadley's estates, she knew he was a wealthy man and suspected they'd be quite grand (but she doubted there could be another view in all Britain to rival this one). He, too, was entertaining and, next to Richard, was the finest dance partner she'd encountered. Best of all, she'd come to realize since the masquerade that he was in love with her—an emotion not evidenced by her husband. Just prior to his return to the army, she *had* wondered if David were beginning to develop a *tendre* for her, but his behavior since had been more distant. She supposed that was because he had given his heart to "Maria." The name conjured up flashing dark eyes and olive skin set off by brightly colored ruffles—all in all, a mysteriously exotic beauty.

Not wanting to pursue this surprisingly discouraging line of thought, Paige turned her attention back to Jerry but could not avoid continued comparisons with David. Life with Jerry would be filled with fun—or would it be frivolity? Paige realized she'd never seen Jerry's serious side and found herself wondering if it existed. Whenever she wanted to discuss some meaningful topic, he would accuse her of being a bluestocking. Statements such as these led her to believe that, though he was enamored of her as she was now, he would want her to pretend she had more hair than wit were she to become his wife. David, on the other hand, had a deeper nature, and though he might often disagree with her viewpoints, she felt that he valued them as an integral part of herself. . . .

As she realized these thoughts were getting her nowhere nearer to answering her original question, she turned back to the house, laughing at her present predicament. Five months ago she'd been virtually on the shelf, wondering if she would ever be capable of caring for a man. And here she was, a married woman torn between two men who stirred her heart. It was absurd!

As Paige climbed the slope to the terrace, she heard

herself being hailed and identified Kit's musical voice. Her friend was standing in the doorway waving her handkerchief, in case Paige's eyes were better than her ears.

Paige waved in return but did not quicken her steps, as the sight of Kit had sparked a new and troublesome thought. Paige herself had more than fulfilled the desire for adventure that had taken her to London, but Kit was no closer to becoming a wife and mother than she'd been at Waverly. Though she had to admit that Kit evidenced no dissatisfaction with her lot, Paige remembered her vow to devote herself to good works and decided to ask David for the names of any eligible males in the neighborhood.

"I told Lady Susan I'd find you outside, for you always get restless when cooped up too long," Kit greeted her triumphantly. "We were just discussing the sleeping arrangements for the party from London, but neither of us could remember exactly when they are to arrive."

"It is complicated," Paige owned, "as they are all arriving on different days. Lord Hadley will be the first. I expect *him* on Monday." Recalling the identity of the next visitor, she grimaced momentarily and continued, "Sylvester on Wednesday; Dorcas and Richard on Thursday; and Sir Walter on Friday." Kit looked overwhelmed with this information, so Paige suggested that they both join Lady Susan for a fuller discussion of the arrangements.

Current events in London, however, were to prove upsetting to this trio's carefully prepared plans. Of the five invited guests, only Lord Hadley was not to deviate from his scheduled arrival.

Richard and Dorcas's plans were upset by information from Waverly that the steward had fallen seriously ill. Richard was obliged to return there at once for an indefinite period of time. Reluctant to leave Dorcas to her own devices in London, her husband insisted that she accompany him into Surrey. Dorcas, however, had other ideas. She'd been looking forward to spending the rest of the summer in Sylvester's company at Penllyn and made an impassioned and convincing argument that being with "dear Paige" without Richard's presence might bring the two women closer together. Since this was a goal Richard aspired to, he acquiesced, with the condition that she not travel without suitable male escort. Not quite believing her good fortune, Dorcas pointed out that David's cousin, Sylvester, was to set out for Penllyn two days hence and perhaps could be prevailed upon to render this service. Richard could find no fault with this scheme and was relieved to have matters so fortuitously resolved.

Dorcas and Sylvester had scarcely finished congratulating themselves on duping Richard into giving them unwitting permission to spend three nights together on the road when Sir Walter Townsend coincidentally called on Sir Richard to suggest making a threesome with the Undershaws for the trip into Wales. Informed of their change in plans, he volunteered to help escort Lady Undershaw.

So it was that Jerry arrived on Monday, and Sylvester, Dorcas, and Sir Walter on Thursday.

Jerry had scarcely had time to change out of his traveling clothes when David took him on an extensive tour of the estate, pointing out in meticulous detail every change that had been made since Jerry's last visit two years ago. Consequently, his guest was in an irritable frame of mind at dinner and in Paige's eyes did not acquit himself well. But, whereas David and Paige saw only rudeness in his sarcastic comments about Wales, Kit saw biting humor delivered by a weary traveler.

David would have been pleased had he known that Paige was keeping a mental scorecard on Jerry and himself, and that after the first evening the points were in his own favor. By the time their remaining guests arrived on Thursday, however, the score was even—for Jerry had made a special effort to regain his sunny disposition, and David's mood had soured proportionately.

Sir Walter was still priding himself on his role as chaperone, for he was not ignorant of the rumors that amorously linked his two fellow travelers. His frequent pronouncements that he was an extraordinarily light sleeper and his strategy of always obtaining "the middle room" had succeeded in thwarting any nocturnal rendezvous.

Sylvester and Dorcas's remaining hopes for nights of shared bliss at Penllyn were dashed when they discovered their rooms were in different wings. However, Sylvester's mind was ever fertile, and that evening, when conversation in the drawing room waned, he offered to show Dorcas the family portrait gallery, knowing full well that the rest of the party would rather be drawn and quartered than to gaze upon the visages of the Owens ancestors. Sir Walter was not taken in by Sylvester's ploy but was too comfortably settled in his coze with Lady Susan to intervene. He watched them depart with a wary eye but was soon distracted when Lord Hadley suggested that Paige entertain them with a song.

This request was followed by peals of laughter from the rest of the company, all of whom had previously been exposed to Paige's musical talents. Jerry didn't mind being deliberately funny but was embarrassed at having provoked laughter unwittingly. Sensing his discomfort, Kit hastily explained that Paige was not "musically inclined" and volunteered to sing a few songs herself.

Jerry scarcely acknowledged Kit's offer, for he was preoccupied by the discovery that his paragon, the countess, lacked a requisite female accomplishment. But his disappointment was soon swept away by Miss Roche's clear, lyrical voice. As one used to having his ears assaulted by the Miss Coateses and Miss Singletons of the world, he was delightfully surprised by Miss Roche's obvious gift. Unconsciously, he began bobbing his head to the beat of the lively ditty she had selected as her first number. He was not alone in his appreciation of the entertainment, for the others soon started to clap their hands rhythmically, and Sir Walter gave in to the impulse to harmonize with her in his deep baritone.

Kit's face was flushed and her eyes sparkled as she gave herself over to the music and the exhilaration of being a success. Jerry could scarcely believe his eyes. Could this be the same reserved woman he had known in London?

Later, after the others had retired and he and David were alone, he asked Penllyn if he knew of Miss Roche's family. Paige had given David a brief sketch of her friend's background, which he now recounted. Her father, Lord Desmond, had been an impecunious Irish peer who had also possessed a small estate in Surrey. He had left his only daughter penniless upon his death more than two years ago, and, as there were no sons, the title and holdings (such as they were) passed to a distant relative in Ireland. Miss Roche was now dependent on Penllyn's own wife for a home.

Jerry's eyes grew stormy at the thought of any father leaving his daughter dependent on others. No wonder Miss Roche had found his own dissolute habits reprehensible! With this on his mind, Jerry soon retired, for he was weary and sore after another day of "country activities."

David was not sorry to bid his friend good night, as he had been looking forward all evening to blowing a cloud but had been reluctant to inflict this barbarous indulgence on his family and guests. He had just lit his cheroot when he felt a slight draft and turned to see who had entered the room.

Expecting that Jerry had returned, he was startled by the appearance of his wife, in a state closely resembling the one she'd been in when he had first met her at the Cock 'N' Hen. She wore a frilly red dressing gown, and her hair tumbled about her shoulders in disarray.

Wondering if this apparition were the result of too much brandy, David blinked, but still he beheld the object of his heart's desire.

"Is Snow in here?" Paige asked, an edge of concern in her voice. "I find I cannot sleep without him curled beside me."

"No, I haven't seen him since breakfast, but I will be happy to take his place," he responded, taking advantage of an irresistible opening.

"Rogue! I doubt if you'd stay curled up long enough for me to get much sleep."

Overwhelmed by the quantity of possible responses to this observation, he poured her a large brandy and recommended it as a sleep-inducer, since Snow had undoubtedly decided to bed down in the barn.

Accepting both his assessment of Snow's whereabouts and the glass of brandy, Paige made herself comfortable in a chair by the small fire he'd lit to ward off the nighttime chill.

As she tucked her feet under her, she asked, "Well, now that you've met my sister-in-law, what do you think of her? Is she not all I said?"

"Her personality seems as shallow as you'd described, but I can understand how her physical attributes could cause men to overlook her deficiencies."

Paige was annoyed that David was reacting as most men did to Dorcas. She'd expected his tastes to be more discriminating. "I suppose her dark looks remind you of . . . someone," she said huffily.

Pleased at the jealousy implied in this accusation, but perplexed as to its origins, he replied, "Someone?"

"Yes! You were most vocal during your feverish deliriums—and frequently spoke one name with great feeling."

Not having formed a passion since his salad days, when he'd offered his heart to Gwyneth Roberts and had been resoundingly rejected, he could not imagine what name he had called out. However, thoroughly reveling in the novelty of Paige's interest in his love life, he decided to bait her by making up a name. "Was it Lucia?"

"No!" she exclaimed, horrified by the introduction of a new player.

"Alicia?" he proposed, barely able to control his enjoyment of his wife's reaction.

Thoroughly disgusted, she shouted, "Maria!"

Looking at her blankly, he searched his memory for a woman with that moniker, but the only face that came to mind was not a human one.

"What did I say about her?" he wondered aloud.

"Well, you said that she was a 'good, loyal girl' and had 'never failed' you."

Instantly David recognized the words of praise he frequently bestowed on his favorite mounts, "Maria" being one of them. In fact, she was the one that had carried him from Paris to Brussels on that fateful day in June. Wishing to prolong Paige's jealous interest in him (which was better than no interest at all), he decided not to enlighten her about Maria's identity. Instead, he began to rhapsodize about her soulful brown eyes and strong, gentle nature.

This was too much for Paige. The acknowledged existence of a rival pricked her competitive instincts, which now prompted her to consider using feminine charms to make David forget his Latin beauty. The problem was that Paige was not well versed in these artifices and so resorted to batting her eyelashes, as she had frequently observed Dorcas doing.

Performing this unnatural act, she looked so much like a child trying to cajole sweets from the governess that David was forced to bite his lower lip to keep from laughing out loud. Delighted by her ingenuous attempt to appear seductive, he decided to reward her efforts by scooping her into his arms and forcefully kissing her tantalizing mouth. Surprised by the immediate success of her ploy, Paige offered little resistance and was soon experiencing a sensation she'd never imagined existed. . . .

Inspired by his wife's response, he let his lips drift to the hollow of her neck, which proved to be a mistake, for Paige tensed and drew away.

Sensing that he had frightened her, David quickly apologized and huskily blamed his want of conduct on the brandy and length of her lashes.

Knowing full well that she had provoked the incident, Paige remonstrated, "You need only apologize for the brandy; I must apologize for the lashes."

Steadied by her aplomb, he suggested dispassionately, "We are both tired. It's been a long day. Let me just dampen the fire and I'll escort you to your room."

As they arrived at her chamber, he raised her hand to his lips and bade her sleep well.

Paige scrambled into bed, planning to mull over the significance of this disturbing encounter with her husband, but had scarcely begun to relive the kiss when she dropped off to sleep.

Chapter XII

DAVID found her the next morning in the breakfast parlor, her plate heaped with a sampling of every item on the sideboard. As her greeting consisted of her customary wave of the left hand (so as not to interrupt the flow of food to her mouth), he realized with relief that his precipitous behavior the previous evening had not made him repugnant to her.

Noting that the eggs were again too dry for his liking, he bit back the criticism that leapt to mind and resolved to handle the matter later in a way guaranteed to meet with Paige's approval. He then outlined his plan for the day's pleasure. "Are you up for a ride to the haunted castle at Mawrgaer? Supposedly Merlin cast a spell on the place when its owner refused to join Arthur."

By the anticipatory gleam in Paige's expressive eyes, he knew he'd made the right suggestion. Jerry, entering at that moment and overhearing the proposal, asked with the hint of a groan how far away this relic was—and was it all uphill?

Observing the care with which Jerry eased himself into his chair, David replied cheerfully, "It's only a two-hour ride, but I'll see if I can locate a pillow small enough to fit on your saddle."

Before Jerry had time to contrive a face-saving response

to this suggestion, Dorcas sashayed into the room and demanded to know what was planned for the day. She made it clear that she certainly hoped they weren't going to sit around sipping tea and discussing domestic affairs.

Hearing other footsteps outside the door, David delayed his explanation until the full party was present. Once the plan was elucidated, everyone was enthusiastic about it, and only Lady Susan (and subsequently Sir Walter) begged off.

The entire household was soon involved in preparations for the excursion. Servants were sent ahead with hampers containing a picnic luncheon, while the ladies and gentlemen readied themselves for departure.

When Sally had finished dressing Paige, her mistress asked her to see to Kit, who frequently had difficulty pulling on her boots. The maid found Miss Roche in a highly agitated state. "What's got you so riled up, miss? You look as though you were bound for the tooth-drawer, instead of to one of the most famous attractions in Wales."

"It's the getting there," Kit moaned. "I've pretended to Lord Hadley that I'm a neck-or-nothing rider, and now he'll find out that I can scarcely keep my seat at a gallop. Whatever will he think of me?!"

"Is *that* all?!" Sally scoffed, rolling her eyes. "He'll likely think how happy he is to have an excuse not to ride hell-bent over the mountainside. I've seen 'im hanging on for dear life as the master led him over the fences. He didn't have the face of one enjoying himself."

"You mean Lord Hadley is not an out-and-outer?"

"Not hardly," Sally sniffed, remembering Lord Hadley's cautious descent of the stairway that morning.

Much relieved, Kit set her hat on her head at a jaunty angle and walked confidently toward the stables.

Once under way, the riders seemed to form up as pairs. David and Paige were in the lead, closely followed by Dorcas and Sylvester; Jerry and Kit ambled comfortably in their wake.

No one was disappointed as they came upon their destination. Dorcas and Sylvester conveniently lost themselves in the dark, winding passages, while the remaining foursome walked about the more open space.

Paige was taken by the contradictory nature of the ruins. From one vantage point, broken battlements cast shadows on the exposed dungeons, producing such a menacing atmosphere that she shivered and instinctively moved closer to David. From the safety of his nearness, she stole a second glance and discerned more details that altered her original impression. Sunlight filtered through the trees that were encroaching on the abandoned site and caressed the delicate ferns undulating in the soft summer breeze.

"Oh, how entrancing this is! I expect to see Merlin appear at any moment now. Surely you, with your considerable influence, could have arranged that treat for your guests' entertainment," Paige quizzed half-seriously, longing to immerse herself further in the romance of the legendary past.

The demands of the present soon dispelled this mood, as the others began clamoring to satisfy the appetites they'd worked up on their ride. The variety of pickings left everyone replete; and to keep the entourage from sliding into lethargy, Kit suggested that they gather bilberries from the bushes that grew in abundance in the woods. Paige leapt to her feet in enthusiastic endorsement of this diversion, only to confront apathy on the others' faces.

Dorcas, whose heart was set on an interlude with Sylvester in a secluded copse they'd discovered while reconnoitering, alternately proposed collecting pine cones, certain that this scheme would have no appeal to anyone but Sylvester. And she was right, for David and Jerry voiced a preference for napping in the warm sun, neither admitting that he'd consumed slightly too much wine with luncheon.

Seemingly reluctant, Sylvester agreed, sighing, to act as protector to Lady Undershaw in case she should encounter a polecat on her peregrinations.

Jerry's skeptical eyes followed Sylvester and Dorcas into the woods. David, picking up the unspoken message, commented, "I agree. There's something smokish about those two. My usually inquisitive cousin has been distracted since his arrival, and based on experience, this usually means he is preoccupied with women or money. Since, with my recovery, he has none of the latter, it must be the former."

Jerry chuckled and said, "And it isn't Miss Roche or your wife's company he craves, for I've never seen him make a special effort to gain *their* regard. And he's not very subtle, is he? A tour of the Owens portrait gallery? Even your brother refused to acknowledge its existence. If it weren't so execrably boring, I would have gone along with them just to foil their plans."

David sighed philosophically and admitted, "I know I ought to do all in my power to thwart his ambitions, but I think they're two of a kind—and if they were to run off together, Sir Richard would have no choice but to obtain a divorce." Then, sensing his friend's discomfiture with this prosaic evaluation, he added, "I know that sounds heartless, but Richard Undershaw is too fine a fellow to be saddled with a termagant such as she—but let us not keep Morpheus at bay with this chatter; I fear the others will appear all too soon."

An hour later, Paige and Kit returned, their skirts stained and full of juicy blueberries. Happening upon the recumbent forms of the two men, they reacted similarly: their expressions softened and their hearts filled with tenderness. Turning to each other, they withdrew to where the servants waited and spilled their caches into a proffered hamper. Then they silently seated themselves on the grass not far from the men.

The sight of Jerry lying there so vulnerably reactivated feelings Kit had thought well buried. Perhaps—just perhaps—he could prefer *her* to Paige. He did seem to be paying more attention to her here than he had in Town. . . . Chastising herself for reopening this doomed scenario, she directed her gaze at Penllyn.

According to Lady Susan, he, too, was suffering the pangs of unrequited love—or so it seemed, as Paige treated him more like a brother than a sweetheart. Kit cast a sidelong look at Paige in hopes of catching a revealing expression on her face. To Kit's horror, her friend was staring at Jerry, a speculative look in her eye.

Seeing the two men side by side prompted Paige to continue her comparison of them. Jerry's artless pose belied his reputation as a rake; with his hand tucked under his cheek and a curl falling across his forehead, he resembled an innocent child. She had a sudden urge to kiss his cheek. That thought recalled David's hungry embrace last evening. *What would a kiss from Jerry be like? Would it be as unsettling? Probably more so,* she concluded reasonably, for if the stories were true, he was an expert in that line.

A kernel of a plan to settle once and for all her feelings for these two men began to form in her ever-resourceful mind. She would contrive a set of circumstances that would cause Jerry to discard his scruples about making love to his best friend's wife. In short, she would get him to kiss her. She could then compare her responses. If she felt the same as when David kissed her, she would know that neither man was necessarily "the one," and that she just liked kissing. However, if Jerry's kiss, given all his skill, did not produce the breathlessness of David's, she could feel sure that the sensation she experienced with David was love.

The third alternative was, of course, that she would find Jerry's kiss preferable to David's. The thought of this outcome left her somewhat depressed, so she decided to see if she could find the grove where Dorcas was gathering pine cones.

Before she'd gone very far, she encountered Dorcas and Sylvester hastening toward her, big with news that they'd spotted two polecats and had dropped their pine cones as they took flight. As no polecat appeared on the path behind them, Paige suggested that they were out of danger and could slacken their pace. She noted that Dorcas must have taken quite a fright, for her clothes were more rumpled than usual and her hair was in disarray.

As they approached the clearing where she'd left Kit, shouts from the rest of the party indicated that David and Jerry had awakened. When they heard the news of the marauding polecats, they proposed an imminent departure.

On the trip back, once again Kit and Jerry lagged behind, enjoying a companionable respite from conversation. Relieved to discover that Miss Roche was not the sort of woman who was constantly trying to show off her equestrian ability by riding fast and furiously, he began to see her as an individual apart from "Paige's friend."

They had lost sight of the other four, trusting their mounts to know the way home, when a fierce, wild cry startled the horses. Miss Roche was unseated before Jerry could come to her aid. Dismounting in alarm, he found that her head had struck a rock and she was unconscious.

Ordinarily he would not have moved her, but, recognizing the howl that had caused the upset as belonging to the often ferocious polecat, he gathered her into his arms and hoisted her onto his saddle, allowing her head to rest on the horse's mane. Mounting behind her, he pulled her inanimate form against his chest, encircling her waist with his arm, and gingerly threaded his way over the rocky terrain.

As Jerry was fully occupied with holding Miss Roche in position, he was relieved to find that his steed really did know his way back to Penllyn.

Midway back, rising out of a deep, dark mist, Kit was shocked to find Jerry's arms wrapped tightly around her person. As she started in confusion, Jerry's deep voice crooned in her ear, "Be still. You are all right. Your horse bolted and you were knocked senseless when you fell. We are nearly at our destination. Just lean against me and all will be well." Kit willingly acquiesced and, despite an agonizing headache, was disappointed when the remaining party, having doubled back, came upon them.

Jerry became the hero of the day, a role he relished and decided to prolong by cosseting the beneficiary of his gallantry. He danced attendance on Kit all evening, ordering restoring cordials and offering to "keep Miss Roche company" while the others entertained themselves with whist and piquet.

While David was relieved that Jerry had shifted his attention from Paige, Lady Susan smiled to herself in recognition of the possibilities inherent in this incipient pairing.

Kit was so much restored the following day that Paige felt no compunction about going off with Lady Susan to pay a call on their nearest neighbor, Lord Cardington, whom David had suggested as a possible catch for Kit. The purpose of this visit, from Paige's point of view, was to ascertain his suitability for her friend, but for Lady Susan it was an essential courtesy call from the new Countess of Penllyn.

The visit fell far below Paige's expectations, as Lord Cardington proved to be a poorly preserved septuagenarian. Moreover, he was so hard of hearing that his guests (whom he apparently thought were his wife, dead these past five years, and his daughter, who was married and living in Edinburgh) were soon hoarse from their attempts to correct these misapprehensions.

On the return to Penllyn, Lady Susan apologized for dragging Paige such a long distance to no purpose. "I had no idea he had failed so. It's been over a year since I last saw him."

Paige did not blame Lady Susan but found her ire rising against David. How could he have supposed that Kit could be happy lost in the Welsh mountains with only a senile old man for company?!

Therefore, Paige was not in the best of moods when she

arrived home, only to find the household in an uproar. It
seemed that David had had words with Mrs. Jones in his
study, which had resulted in that poor lady's collapse upon
her return to the kitchen. After being carried to her room
by Williams, she had bolted her door and refused to speak
with anyone.

Weary after her wasted journey, Paige refused to become
embroiled immediately in the turmoil. With all the dignity
she could muster, she ascended the stairs to her room,
changed out of her dusty apparel, and drank a leisurely cup
of tea before confronting her husband.

Paige's entrance into David's study was greeted with a
look of pleasurable anticipation. "And how did you get on
with Lord Cardington? A handsome man for his age!
Perhaps a bit old for Kit, but she seems to have an
adaptable personality."

In icy tones she replied, "A bit old? Methinks your
humor goes too far, my lord! You have wasted my time on
a fool's errand, and I have much to say on the subject
later, but for the moment we must discuss dinner."

Perplexed at this abrupt change in subject and her
overall agitated manner, he inquired solicitously, "If the
fare at Lord Cardington's was too light for your voracious
appetite, I have no objection to moving up the dinner
hour."

"My dear lord and master, there is no question of
moving *up* a dinner that will never be prepared! It seems
you have so offended Mrs. Jones that she has locked
herself in her room and refuses to come out even to attend
to her duties."

"But how can that be? We had a most cordial chat, and
she promised that my eggs would be just as I desire them.
In fact, I must commend you on your lessons for dealing
with the servants. I did just as you suggested: I talked with
her directly and unobserved; and I put myself in her place.
That is, *I* imagined how I would want criticism, and gave
it to her as forcefully and honestly as can be done. I was

quite pleased with myself, and was sure you'd commend me for my actions." Pausing, he said in a less confident tone, "But you look as if you are about to give me a tongue-lashing."

Paige had been planning to, but, not liking to be so predictable, she said in measured accents, "As your temporary wife, I have not the right to ring a peal over your head about your conduct; all I wish to know is what you said to Mrs. Jones, so I can counteract it and entice her back into the kitchen."

Annoyed at her superciliousness, David raised his voice and announced, "I-told-her-she-was-cooking-the-eggs-too-long—and didn't use enough spice with the lamb—and things along those lines."

Raising the volume of her voice to match his, she summarized hoarsely, "You informed the cook that you knew more about cooking than *she* did."

"No!" he shouted. "I only told her what I wanted!"

As this observation produced a contemptuous look, David, goaded into trying to deflate her pretensions, fulminated, "That always worked with Maria!"

Between clenched teeth his wife scoffed, "I'm sure it did. But then, Mrs. Jones is a sensitive, well-bred British woman."

Sylvester, who had been passing the study on his way to the drawing room, was cheered by the sounds of dissension between the countess and earl and reflected that harsh words by day usually meant separate beds by night. If this kept up, perhaps his position as heir would be secure. Almost before he had a chance to remove his ear from the keyhole, the door was flung open by the countess, who was so intent on her mission that she stalked right past him without noticing his presence.

Paige cajoled Mrs. Jones into resuming her duties, then returned to her husband in a more conciliatory spirit. She found him in a brown study. He had spent the intervening time damning himself for losing his temper and damning his wife for provoking it. Her request for a glass of sherry gave him a chance to compose himself, and he found himself asking in a calm voice, "How did I go wrong with Mrs. Jones?"

Accepting the proffered glass, she replied, "David, surely you know that for a female servant, a summons from the master is tantamount to dismissal. You should have given *me* your complaints to deliver."

Exasperated, he said, "Women! I'll never understand them. *Yesterday* you told me I shouldn't deliver my concerns through a third party; today you tell me it was wrong to deliver them directly. What will you want tomorrow?!"

Paige was struck by the logic of this and took a sip of sherry to conceal her dismay. Unable to keep her nose in the glass indefinitely, she smiled beguilingly at her husband and conceded, "Touché."

Momentarily struck dumb by her unexpected concession, he narrowed his eyes as comprehension dawned on him. "Oh, no, you don't! I am on to your wiles; your smile may be bewitching, but it will take more than that to make me forget that you have attacked me for doing exactly what you asked me to do: I spoke to Mrs. Jones along the lines that *you* suggested, and I gave you Lord Cardington's name because *you* begged me to name the most eligible bachelor in these parts. Both things you now fling back in my face; and when I make some valid points in my own defense, you opt out of the fight. Explain yourself, madam!"

Though cornered, Paige found herself admiring David's willingness to see an argument through to understanding, if not agreement. Mentally she gave him a point on her scorecard. Out loud she replied, "Yes, I understand your confusion about the lecture I gave you on how to handle the servants. It was prompted by your criticism of the cooking, but it was meant to apply to your dealings with nondomestic matters. I thought you understood *that.* . . ." she concluded. Then, seeing the spark of anger flare once again in his eyes, she hastily added, "But I see I was wrong. However, in the case of Lord Cardington, it was *you* who were definitely in the wrong. I told you quite clearly that motherhood is one of Kit's reasons for wanting to marry; and how you could imagine that doddering old man could find his way to her bed, let alone remember what to do once he got there, surpasses everything!''

"Oh, surely you exaggerate. Jason is only eight years my senior, and last I saw him he was taking fences at a reckless pace," David protested.

"Eight years your senior?! Have I gone to the wrong house? The Lord Cardington *I* saw was five and seventy if a day."

"Gracious! You mean that old coot is still alive? After his stroke last year, I naturally assumed he had stuck his spoon in the wall, and the title had passed to Jason." No sooner had he pronounced these words than he began laughing uproariously at the thought of Paige's reaction when she'd been introduced to this old man, thinking he was Kit's potential suitor.

His laughter was so infectious that Paige soon joined in and regaled him with an imitation of Lady Susan's fending off His Lordship's attempts to embrace his "long lost wife." When she had exhausted her anecdotes, however, she remembered that her anger at David had been justified in this case, for he should have verified his facts before subjecting her to the most uncomfortable hour she'd spent in years. "So when do I get *my* apology?" she demanded, abruptly shifting the mood.

Hard put to be serious once again, David fixed his face so as to appear grave and accorded handsomely, "Sorry, my dear, for inadvertently ruining your afternoon."

As he watched her lips curl into a self-satisfied smile, he yielded to the temptation to wipe it off her face in the most agreeable way he knew. He'd gotten as far as grasping her shoulders when a discreet knock heralded the arrival of Williams, who reminded them of the approaching dinner hour. Paige didn't know whether to feel relieved or deprived of what David's actions seemed to foretell. She rather thought, as she dressed for dinner, that it was the latter.

Paige's fear that the quality of the food at dinner would suffer from Mrs. Jones's upset at this afternoon's *contretemps* proved groundless; and she retired to her chamber with the sense that the problem with the cook had finally been solved.

Snow was once again absent, and as the view from Paige's window presaged a storm, she began to worry about him. A massive oak was bending in the wind as if it were a sapling, and cracks of thunder echoed through the mountains.

In the grip of an unreasonable fear that Snow might somehow come to harm, Paige decided to search for him. Throwing a shawl around her dressing gown in case she needed to venture out-of-doors, she tiptoed downstairs.

Candles were flickering in the drawing room. As she pushed the door open, hoping to enlist David in the search, she was taken aback at the sight of Lord Hadley, asleep in a chair.

She started to back out, but an especially loud crack of thunder roused Jerry, who turned to discover his anxious-looking hostess.

"Were you looking for me?" he inquired hopefully.

"No; I did not know you were still about. I am seeking Snow, who I fear is out in this storm."

Rising to his feet with alacrity, he said, "Two can cover more ground than one. Allow me to join you in the search."

Finding no sign of Snow in the downstairs rooms, Paige insisted she would feel better if she knew he were sheltered in the barn. "Could we not try there? As the storm has not yet broken, surely we have time for a quick inspection."

Jerry was not convinced of the wisdom of this undertaking,

but wanting to prolong these rare moments alone with Paige, he agreed.

As they traversed the expanse between the house and outbuildings, the wind's fury whipped Paige's dressing gown around her legs, and she had to cling to Lord Hadley's arm to keep her balance.

This action was seen and duly noted by Sylvester, who was watching the approaching tempest from his window. He wondered how David would react to learning of this tryst and determined to be the one to tell him.

Oblivious to this malicious observation, the couple reached the shelter of the barn just as the storm broke. Getting no response from her shouts of "Snow! Snow!" Paige began walking around the huge interior of the building, thrusting the lantern into every corner in hopes of seeing the light reflect off his green eyes. She was assisted by Jerry and by the flashes of lightning that rended the sky. Just as they were about to despair, Snow announced his presence with a loud meow and clambered down the ladder from the hayloft.

"You scoundrel, you, waiting till the last possible moment to make an entrance," she scolded, releasing the anxiety that she'd accumulated during the search. Then, picking him up tenderly, she murmured, "Come, I will take you home at once, for you will be far safer there."

Jerry, who had moved to the doorway, intervened in this one-sided dialogue, observing, "He may be safer in the house than here, but his life—as well as ours—may be in jeopardy getting there." He gestured toward the water cascading over the door frame and the bolts of lightning plummeting toward the earth.

It took only one glance for Paige to see the truth in this. Practical as ever, she suggested that they find a place to sit until the worst of the storm had abated. Jerry rummaged around and finally located two buckets, onto which he and Paige gingerly lowered themselves. After what seemed an eternity on these hard, makeshift stools, Jerry climbed up to the loft and began pitching down forkfuls of hay while Paige arranged the fallen clumps into a small mound on which she hoped they could comfortably settle themselves.

As they sat beside each other, watching Snow chase his tail in play, Paige realized that this was the perfect opportunity to put into action her test for determining her feelings for Jerry. Remembering her success with David, she decided to again make use of her long lashes. Grasping his arm, she inquired as to how long he thought the storm would last. When he turned toward her to reply, she fluttered her eyelashes in much the same manner she'd used in the drawing room two nights ago. The results, however, were markedly dissimilar. Jerry, a look of concern on his face, asked, "Has a speck of dust invaded your luscious green orbs?"

Reacting to this ambiguous question in the only face-saving way possible, Paige admitted to this predicament and asked his assistance in resolving it. She guessed shrewdly that he might not be able to resist the proximity of her lips as he assisted in the removal of this nonexistent speck.

She soon discovered that she'd overestimated either her shrewdness or Jerry's susceptibility to her charms, for he applied himself vigorously to the task and withdrew immediately after ascertaining that the offending particle either was gone on its own or defied detection.

Paige was still racking her considerable brain to find another way to provoke the kiss when Nature's ferocity died down and Jerry proclaimed, "Let's make a run for it now, before it resumes." He abruptly jumped to his feet and pulled her to hers. The self-control he'd been exerting over the past hour deserted him as the force of his assist brought her body against his. With one arm around her waist, he tilted her chin with his free hand and covered her mouth with his.

The result of this first intimacy was not what either had expected. Paige had not anticipated, as one of the "outcomes" of her experiment, that she might actually dislike Jerry's kiss. But the force with which he assaulted her lips left her with only a feeling of distaste. She thought with longing of David's passionate embraces. . . .

On his part, Jerry was surprisingly disappointed. He'd never had so stiff and unyielding a response to his lovemaking from a married (and therefore experienced) woman. He was now exceedingly sorry he'd compromised his friendship with David to no purpose. Full of remorse, he stepped back and offered his apologies for having taken advantage of the situation, assuring her she need never fear it happening again.

Paige needed no such assurances, for she'd concluded her experiment. . . . It was David she loved!

Chapter XIII

THEIR dash through the muddy yard to the house did not go unobserved. Sylvester had remained patiently at his station by the window, hoping their absence would be lengthy enough to support the insinuations he was planning to make when he confided the incident to his cousin. A glance at his watch as Paige and Jerry emerged from the barn revealed that his diligence had been rewarded.

A taller figure watched from another window. David had followed his usual custom of enjoying one last cheroot in his chamber before retiring and was just opening the window to disperse the smoke when he noticed a light moving inside the barn. While puzzling out the meaning of this illumination, he was surprised to see Paige step out, carrying Snow. Behind her was a male figure whose stride David recognized as Hadley's. Involuntarily his stomach lurched as the worst of explanations came to mind. Unable to draw his eyes away from the tableau before him, he began to be reassured by what he saw. There was nothing furtive or loverlike about their movements. Indeed, Paige's attentions seemed fully focused on the cat in her arms. And Jerry, whose expression became visible as he leaned closer to the lantern, appeared to be concerned with the state of his boots. David felt fairly sure there must be a logical explanation for this midnight outing but fervently hoped that one or the other of the parties would confirm this feeling by talking openly about it on the morrow.

He need not have lost any sleep worrying over this, for, in between mouthfuls, Paige regaled her companions at breakfast with a vivid portrayal of the hardships and terror she and Hadley had overcome to rescue their feline friend. Sylvester was the only one who did not find himself amused by Paige's hyperbole, for her version of the story rendered his own valueless as a means of turning David against his wife. However, later in the day, when he confessed the failure of his plan to Dorcas during a stroll through the gardens, she proposed another way to use the story.

"Why do you not cut short your stay here and leave at once for London? There you will be free to put your own tale into the rumor mill, and let the tabbies do the rest. By the time my self-righteous sister-in-law and her family return there, David will be forced to defend his wife's reputation—perhaps to the death. The only person who would care enough to interfere with the spread of the gossip is Richard, and he is safely tucked away at Waverly. Of course, you must be careful that this is not traced back to you," she cautioned.

Smiling wickedly, Sylvester commended her. "It is no wonder I love you. Our thoughts are so deviously similar." Oblivious to their exposed position in the garden, he slipped his arm about her waist and murmured, "It will be hard to leave you, but I must do something fast to end their marriage, else I'll lose my position as heir—and likely spend the rest of my life pursued by creditors. This afternoon I'll announce that I've had a letter from a friend in need and that I must leave to go to him early tomorrow."

Sylvester would have set off less optimistically if he'd known that Sir Richard had, in fact, spent only a few days at Waverly and was now back in London. His steward had been nearly recovered by the time Richard had arrived in

Surrey and was able to resume his duties within the week—leaving little for his master to do.

Free now to join the party at Penllyn, Richard started back to Grosvenor Square in a light mood. He was curious to see the beautiful Welsh countryside and looked forward to the company of his sister and her husband. However, his smile of anticipation faded abruptly as he recalled that a visit there would mean a reunion with Dorcas. For the first time, Richard fully confronted his dissatisfaction with his marriage. Since he'd wed, his life had been far from peaceful. His wife antagonized his much loved sister, was rude to the servants, and engaged in unladylike pastimes.

He began to imagine life without her. . . . Perhaps it would be best for both of them to have a few weeks apart. If she could endure a month in the country, he could sacrifice a few more weeks getting better acquainted with the attractions of the city life she so loved. He might even come to share her enthusiasm for activities he now eschewed. By the time his coach pulled up in Grosvenor Square, he had decided to remain in London and sample its delights.

He found, however, that the city was bare of suitable company in August, and he soon yearned for sympathetic companionship. He called on Cornelia several times, only to find her from home. Finally he yielded to the impulse to visit Mme. Lisette, using as his excuse the purchase of a welcome-home gift for Dorcas.

This would be the first time he'd seen her since the masquerade (if indeed she were the Lilac Lady). When he reached her shop he thought at first that it was closed, for as he peered through the window he could see no sign of human occupation. The door, however, yielded to his touch and set off a tinkle of bells which called forth Mme. Lisette herself from the workroom.

"Monsieur!" she caroled, delighted to see her Black Domino once again.

His heart leapt at the genuine joy she exhibited on seeing him, and he found himself stammering an explanation for his call. She seemed not to notice his awkwardness and invited him to join her for sherry in her cozy parlor.

Settled in their chairs, clasping delicate glasses of the rich amber liquid, Mme. Lisette expressed her surprise at "Monsieur's presence in London." Twirling the stem of his glass thoughtfully in his fingers, he realized that he did not have a plausible explanation ready. Lacking one, he found himself, to his horror, blurting out, "I am writing a book, and I need the solitude that London in the off-season offers."

"But this is famous! It is a novel?"

Unable to think fast enough to contradict this hypothesis, he affirmed it, then briskly inquired about the success of her business.

Not to be diverted from Richard's incredible disclosure, Mme. Lisette ignored his question and asked one of her own. "What is the subject of your novel?"

Scanning his beleaguered mind for inspiration, he remembered the plots of several books Dorcas had gushed over. "Well, I'm embarrassed to admit it, but it is a romantic mystery—something like Mrs. Radcliffe's." Then, seeing the incredulity on her face, he added, "But of course I'll use a pseudonym."

Feeling more like Cornelia than like Mme. Lisette, she exclaimed, losing her accent in the process, "You surprise me, sir. I had not taken you for a romantic. What is Lady Undershaw's opinion of your venture?"

In spite of himself, Richard burst out laughing at the thought of Dorcas's face were he to announce his intention to become a popular novelist. "I fear my wife knows nothing of my plans, and I hope I can count on your discretion."

Mme. Lisette dared not probe further into Sir Richard's secret, so she turned the subject to the debate over the Corn Laws and the disastrous implications for the poor. Another half hour passed in animated discussion of the pros and cons of this controversial legislation. Though reluctant to draw the conversation to a close, Richard was acutely aware that he was enjoying, only too much, the company of this surprisingly well-informed female shopkeeper.

Remembering that he had not yet completed the stated purpose of his visit, he requested Madame to show him her designs for the Fall Little Season, so that he might select suitable ensembles for his beloved sister and wife. Madame found herself cheered by Richard's positioning his sister before his wife and had to resist the impulse to show him the least attractive design for Dorcas.

Overwhelmed by the choices presented to him, Richard deferred to the modiste's superior knowledge of fashion and requested that she make the selections herself. Since Cornelia had already given considerable thought to Paige's fall wardrobe, she quickly suggested a simple cambric morning dress in a rich chocolate brown, trimmed at the throat and wrists with ecru Venetian lace. Putting aside her personal feelings about Dorcas, she recommended a garnet-and-silver-striped dimity walking dress, guaranteed to enhance Dorcas's dark beauty. His mission completed, Richard had no other reason to stay, so reluctantly took himself off.

Upon his return home he found a note from Cornelia requesting his presence at a small dinner party the following evening. It was small, indeed, for Richard found he was the only guest. They spent the first several minutes commiserating on the sparseness of company in London during the summer. As this topic was exhausted, Cornelia recalled that she had not evidenced surprise at his lengthy sojourn in Town or inquired as to its reason—which she surely would have done if she'd not recently conversed with him as Mme. Lisette. Playfully she asked, "Tell me, Richard, whatever is a confirmed country bumpkin like you doing away from his estates at this time of year?"

Expecting to hear about his novel, she was amazed when he replied, "I can be frank with you, dear friend." Trouble darkening his clear blue eyes, he admitted, "I fear that I have not been a proper husband to Dorcas. Instead of trying to understand her view of life, I have demanded that she conform to mine. So I've decided to make use of the time she's in Wales to explore the amusements that divert her."

At this speech Cornelia found herself clenching her fists and grinding her teeth in irritation at Dorcas's hold over Richard. Unable to control her tongue, she blurted out, "What gaming hell shall be first on your list?"

Undaunted, Richard replied evenly, "I suppose I could start at Crockford's. I understand the play is deep there." Then, laughing, he added, "Also, I'm curious to find out if the premises smell of fish."

"Fish?" echoed Cornelia.

"Yes; seems the fellow was a fishmonger before he set up his gaming house."

Appalled at this intelligence, Cornelia chided, "Next, I suppose you'll tell me you're going to Astley's Royal Amphitheatre!"

"Well, as a matter of fact, that *is* on my agenda. I don't suppose you'd care to accompany me, Corny?" he suggested, using his childhood nickname for her.

Hard though it was to decline this invitation, Cornelia heeded Paige's warning not to be too much in her brother's company as Cornelia, for fear of his uncovering her secret identity. Thinking quickly, she announced that she was leaving on the morrow for several weeks with her aunt in Brighton. Richard was truly disappointed at this news, for he had also hoped she would accompany him to Madame Tussaud's Wax Museum and to see the Elgin marbles.

Imagining how much fun it would be to see these sights with him, the seed of a plan for doing this began to germinate. If she could not go as Lady Bragdon, perhaps she could as Mme. Lisette. . . .

"Oh, Richard, if it's company you want on these excursions, you'd do best to find someone recently arrived from the country or, better yet, from abroad. Most city dwellers have already seen these marvels." She was grati-

fied with the result of this advice, as she observed the
dawning of an idea flit over his face. Afraid, however, that
his solution and hers diverged, she inquired, "Have you
someone in mind?"

"A few names come to mind, but I suppose if I'm really
to understand it from Dorcas's perspective, it should be
someone of her own sex."

Not fully satisfied with this answer, Cornelia probed
further. "You don't mean to say that you are thinking of
taking a lady of the Quality to a gaming hall?!"

"Well, not precisely a *lady*," Richard elucidated.

Pleased with this response, Cornelia pretended to misin-
terpret his words. "Ho, ho! Say no more, Richard, you sly
dog, you."

"No, it's not at all what you're thinking, Corny."

Enjoying his embarrassment, she continued to tease
him. "And what is it I am thinking, little Dickie-dimples?"
she taunted, reactivating a cruel moniker she and Paige
had tormented him with when he was a somewhat overfed
adolescent.

"For *that*, I'm not going to tell you."

Richard was sorry when the evening came to a close. He
and Cornelia got on famously, and he felt he could confide
anything to her and she would understand. Cornelia felt
similarly, and she fell asleep anticipating the fun they
would have investigating the more common *divertissements*.

On the other side of Town, Sylvester had arrived at his
lodgings with a plan for disseminating his story. He would
call on Dorcas's cousin, Lottie Morrow, and permit her to
drag the sordid details of the countess's perfidy from his
reluctant lips.

It worked like a charm, and soon he was hearing the
rumor from several different sources, with nary a mention
of his own name in connection with it. Since the rumor
seemed to be spreading of its own accord, he was free to
pursue his customary pleasures.

A visit to a Covent Garden green room led to a brief liaison with a minor actress, and continued play at Devonshire House left him three hundred pounds to the good. For the first time in his checkered life, Sylvester felt confident about the future.

Mme. Lisette was in a similar frame of mind as she awaited Richard's arrival at her shop to escort her to view the Elgin marbles. She had been appropriately demure when he had suggested a series of outings designed to relieve the tedium of the off-season, but she eventually allowed herself to be persuaded.

They'd already visited Astley's, and Cornelia had been glad of Richard's protective presence, for the crowds were rougher and louder than she'd ever imagined. She found it necessary several times to press closely against him to avoid a surge of drunken sailors. His nearness and the uninhibited pleasure-seeking atmosphere heightened her formerly denied sensual longing for Richard.

As she scanned the street for the first sign of his dappled grays, the scandalous thought of seducing him entered her mind. As soon as she permitted this notion into her consciousness, she was able to find several arguments to justify it. Both she and Richard were unfulfilled in love, and neither was naive about its expression physically. She could conceive of no greater happiness than to lie in the arms of the man she loved. Visualizing this scene, she was immediately recalled to reality by the thought of the possible displacement of her wig, for of course it would be as Mme. Lisette that she would conduct this *affaire*. After all, she was aware that Richard's attraction was to the blond and foreign beauty of Lisette, not to her own classic English looks. And even if he had found Cornelia to his taste, he wouldn't think of compromising her virtue. But try as she might to think of herself as a French shopkeeper capable of seducing another woman's husband (and her best friend's brother), Cornelia could not in reality discard her own moral principles.

Sighing in a reluctant giving-up of her fantasy, she peered once again out the window and this time was rewarded with the sight of Richard driving his phaeton and team through the tangle of tradesmen's carts on Bond Street.

As he skillfully wended his way toward the shop, Richard anticipated another agreeable afternoon. Mme. Lisette was the perfect companion: she was intrigued by all she saw; sought his opinions; and greeted each new experience positively, no matter how discommoding. He was in a way to losing his heart to her, which would not do at all. He had taken his marriage vows and would stand by them, even if it meant a bleak and discordant future. However, drawing up to the shop, he put aside these melancholy ruminations and prepared to enjoy the time they had to spend together.

The rest of the month passed pleasantly and all too quickly for Cornelia and Richard. They were so absorbed in each other that they were oblivious to the hints their friends began dropping about Paige and Hadley.

Before they knew it, their idyll was at an end—as members of the Penllyn party arrived in Town.

It was several days before the returning protagonists got wind of the rumors about Paige's supposed infidelity.

Jerry heard it first at White's (where he was much congratulated) and rushed immediately to Berkeley Square to set things aright. Brushing past Capper, he located David in the library and launched into a vehement denial of the gossip. David was understandably perplexed at Jerry's disjointed narrative and, pouring him a strong whiskey from the nearby decanter, asked him to explain his "explanation."

Taking a huge swallow of the contents of his glass, Jerry began, "Let me be frank. Word is about that the countess—

that is, your wife—and I were, I mean, *are,* more than just friends—in fact, that we are, that is, *were,* intimate. I guess one might say that we *were,* in fact, intimate, in that we got to know each other famously well in your absence—and, um . . ." He paused, sticking his finger beneath his shirtpoints. "And I did kiss her once. But she did not like it above half and I'm sure wished me at Jericho, but I swear there was nothing in it."

Before he had a chance to leap from his chair and grovel at David's feet (which he had worked himself up to do, despite the loss of dignity involved in this act), the earl quelled him with a gesture of impatience. "Do get ahold of yourself, man. I collect you have been dallying with my wife, and that has gotten about."

Overcome with agitation at the earl's darkling stare and his use of the term *dallying,* Jerry finally did leap from his chair, protesting, "It wasn't that way at all! I will admit that I flirted with her and that I kissed her once—but it went no further than that." As David's features settled themselves into a look of mild disbelief, Jerry felt even more wretched than he had under the earl's previous malevolent gaze. On the defensive, he accused, "It's all *your* fault, anyway: hinting at a mystery about your marriage, and leading me to believe your feelings were not engaged. How could you think your best friend would have designs on your wife if he thought it were a love match?!"

"Oh, so you admit you had designs on her, then," David drawled, beginning to feel amused by Jerry's uncharacteristic awkwardness and not wanting to let him off the hook too easily.

"Darn right I had designs on her! She is the most taking woman in London, and you don't seem to appreciate her worth."

Before Jerry could elaborate on this theme, David interrupted, saying sharply, "I'll thank you not to tell me what's in my own heart. You've made enough dangerous suppositions already, and see where *they* have led: my wife's reputation is in shreds, and it is left to me to patch it up.''

Jerry was instantly contrite. "I'm sorry, David. I will do whatever you ask to make amends.''

David was of two minds about how to respond to Jerry. On the one hand, he was aware of how difficult it would be to salvage Paige's reputation; but, on the other, he was convinced of the innocence of the relationship between Paige and Jerry, and conscious of his own role in throwing them together.

The latter emotion won out, and he released his friend from the tenterhooks on which he'd been dangling by saying, "I accept your apology and I would like to make use of your offer to help. I have an idea that I think you may even find pleasurable: if you are constantly seen in our company, and with another woman, people must surely begin to realize that the gossip is false. And I think I know the ideal lady for you to squire around, that being Miss Roche. Since she is usually in my wife's company, my hope is that society will conclude that rumor has linked you with the wrong member of the household.''

Relief flooded Jerry's face as he realized that the chances of being knocked down by his friend were now close to nil. This out of the way, he became caught up in David's imaginatively simple solution and promptly agreed to his part in it. Their pact was sealed by a handshake.

After Jerry departed, David went in search of his wife. Paige, in her chamber, had just heard about her unsought notoriety from Sally, who had heard it from the second footman at Lady Sefton's. After a few moments of guilty self-recrimination, followed by worried speculation of David's reaction, she rallied her wits to devise both an explanation to give her husband and a scheme to extract the Owens name from disgrace. Discarding several hastily contrived falsehoods, she decided she owed him the truth. After all, she knew David to be an honorable man, who would not divorce her in the midst of a scandal—thus ruining her character forever. So she would tell him of her flirtation with Jerry, and the kiss, and apologize.

The next part was more difficult. How could she get them out of it? Pacing about the room, trailed by a waddling Snow (who'd apparently found country fare to his liking), Paige halted at the window overlooking the garden. Kit was below, filling a basket with flowers, an act that led to a skeleton of an idea: why not convince people it was *Kit* Lord Hadley was pursuing, not herself? This would explain his constant presence at Berkeley Square and perhaps even his trip to Wales. And the servants could confirm that lately he'd been spending as much time with Kit as he had been with her. Yes! That was it. David and she would appear in public with Kit and Hadley, and the rumors would soon die of their own accord.

As Paige rushed from the room to confront her husband, she discovered him poised in the act of knocking on her door. While his hand was still upraised, she launched into her tale, blurting, "Oh, David, the most terrible thing has happened—and it's all my fault—but I have contrived a way out."

"Yes, my dear, and unless you wish the entire household to know of it, I suggest you invite me in at once."

Impatient to unburden herself, she unceremoniously pulled him into the room and slammed the door.

Guessing that they both had the same topic to discuss, David settled back in his chair, prepared to be entertained by her animated version of it. He was not disappointed, for her green eyes flashed in indignation that anyone could magnify a mere kiss into a full-blown *affaire*. Any lingering doubts about the veracity of Jerry's story were dispelled by Paige's account.

He sat up straight in his chair as she began to unfold her stratagem for extricating them from this imbroglio. Had the minx been listening at the library door? No; she seemed too anxious about his approval of her scheme to be already sure of it. Her nervous fingers repeatedly crushed the grosgrain ribbons hanging from the high waist of her primrose gown, causing David to pity the poor maid who would have to press them flat once again. And her eyes stared unblinkingly into his, as though the force of her look could will him to approve both her past conduct and her well-intentioned approach to disentangle them from the disagreeable aftermath.

"So, although it means we will have to be much in Jerry's company—which you may not like, after all I've told you—you must see that it is the only solution that will answer," Paige finished pleadingly.

Pretending to mull it over for a moment or two, David responded drolly, "Well, since you and I and Jerry all agree it's a good plan, we have only Kit to convince."

"Jerry? But I have not discussed it with *him,* though I do think he will go along with it."

"Yes, as I have already told you, he will."

"You confuse me, sir. How can you have told him of a plan I have only just concocted?" Paige wondered, wide-eyed with astonishment.

"I hope you will not be too much chastened to learn that I have already originated this scheme, and have in fact set it in motion. Jerry is willing to squire Miss Roche to any event we feel is appropriate."

"You let me spend the last ten minutes crawling on my hands and knees, petitioning you for understanding, and you all the while were reveling in my discomfort?!" The pitch in her voice rose as she discovered a fresh grievance. "And you had the nerve to confide it to Jerry before consulting with *me!*"

Snow, who had been snuggled on David's lap, began hissing and spitting at his mistress, as though to ward off this unfair assault. Stroking Snow's ruffled fur, David soothed, "Pay no mind to her. She is merely miffed that the obvious solution occurred first to *me.*"

Addressing her remarks to their feline intermediary, Paige objected, "How like a man to presume that I would care one jot which of us originally devised the plot. Such pettiness! It is a waste of time to be competing on inventiveness when there is a serious problem to be remedied.''

"Rowrr," Snow replied, apparently quite taken with the logic of this statement.

"Traitor," David muttered, nevertheless continuing to stroke the object of this epithet. "Speaking of wasting time, Paige, you'd better speak to Kit at once, for Princess Lieven's musical evening is this Friday, and I think it would be a good place to make our debut as a foursome.''

"Good point," Paige conceded. "I'll go down to her directly."

"Well, Snow," David said, hoisting the cat to his shoulder as he rose, "I see you were right. She's much more reasonable than I first gave her credit for. But I think she overfeeds you. Soon we shall need to be borrowing Prinny's corset to keep your stomach from dragging on the ground.''

"Prrtt?" was Snow's only response.

Paige caught up with Kit snipping yellow tea roses. "In what room can I expect to find these beauties tonight?"

"I thought the central hallway needed brightening up. Would you like a few for your own room?"

"Only if you'll arrange them for me. You know how ham-fisted I am," Paige acknowledged.

Kit was obviously in such a happy and contented mood that Paige was loath to upset her with the gossip that was circulating. However, never one to postpone unpleasant tasks, she started right in, describing both the unfounded rumors and the plan that she, David, and Jerry had agreed to.

Kit was aghast. "Paige, that is horrible! How could anyone believe such a story, when you and David have so lately been going around smelling of April and May?"

"What?!" Paige exclaimed, a montage of surprise, denial, and delight playing about her features.

Nonplussed, Kit retreated, explaining, "Well, what I meant is, you've been spending much more time with David than with Lord Hadley, and you both seem so agreeable in each other's company . . . so it must mean that whoever started this rumor has not recently been much in your presence. Do you have any idea who the culprit is?"

Paige was so struck by this previously ignored aspect of the situation that she was diverted from exploring Kit's enigmatic observation about her relationship with David. Who could possibly dislike her enough to spread such lies? Dorcas's name immediately leapt to mind, but Paige quickly dismissed it when she realized that the scandal would reflect on her sister-in-law as well. Sylvester was another possibility, but his recent behavior had been less antagonistic than previously. Of course, that might be a ruse. As Paige could think of no one else who bore *her* a grudge, her thoughts turned to Lord Hadley's circle. Perhaps a spurned lover was seeking revenge, or, more likely, the husband of one. Her curiosity piqued, she vowed to pursue this further with David and Jerry.

Breaking from this brief reverie, she admitted to Kit that she was stumped about the source and turned the conversation back to Kit's acceptance of her role in setting things to right.

Kit would do anything to help her friend, but her heart had reservations about being so much in Hadley's company. She had schooled herself into controlling her feelings when he was about, which was easy enough to do, given the informal nature of their intercourse. However, to be on his arm night after night, as he forced himself to act the part of her courter, seemed more than she'd be able to cope with. But cope she would, for there was no alternative. Drawing herself up with an air of resolution, she declared, "I'll do whatever you ask, though I doubt if we'll be convincing as an enamored couple."

"Nonsense! Lord Hadley has had much practice pretending

to be in love, and I can coach you in the appropriate ways to respond.''

Kit blanched at Paige's blasé assessment of Jerry's ways with women. She was sure Paige misjudged him, for she herself had seen the *real* Jerry at Penllyn when she'd fallen from her horse. He was a man of gentleness and sincerity. With this in mind, Kit now realized that the next few weeks could provide an opportunity to bring out Jerry's best traits. Constantly at his side, she would be able to observe his conduct and intervene immediately to correct it if necessary. Having designed a role for herself with which she'd be comfortable, she was able to accept Paige's offer of instruction with a degree of enthusiasm.

Her schooling was soon put to the test at Princess Lieven's musicale. As the foursome entered the crowded rooms, the noise level dropped ominously. Kit's knees began to give way, and it was only the reassuring pressure of Jerry's hand on her elbow that kept her upright. Grateful for this support, she flashed him a shy smile, which (had she but known it) was precisely what Paige would have suggested.

Paige herself was nervous, but her demeanor was one of confidence. On David's arm, she moved without hesitation toward the nearest cluster of acquaintances and enthusiastically greeted them. Watching his wife's poise disconcert those who had planned to snub them, David was impressed anew with her style. As he gazed at her, a warm glow invaded his eyes and a half smile touched his lips. These signs of love were not missed by their detractors and supporters alike. Mrs. Drummond-Burrell took this opportunity to jab Lady Jersey in the side and hissed, "See, I told you it was a love match."

Not to be bested, Sally Jersey retorted, "At least on *his* side," and continued to scrutinize the pair.

As if overhearing this challenge, Paige reached up and smoothed down David's cowlick, which had been disturbed by the breeze that had greeted them as they'd stepped from the carriage. This tender act called forth a smug chuckle from Mrs. Drummond-Burrell and a groan from Lady Jersey, who could not deny that this intimate gesture did not appear to be feigned.

Kit had found the earlier part of the evening much less onerous than she'd expected. Jerry had been on his best behavior and very attentive. She was just feeling complacent about both their credibility as a couple and Jerry's conduct when Viscount Spencer approached.

"Jerry, you rogue. What's this I hear that you've been rusticating in Wales? We missed your dashing figure in Brighton. Dull party, isn't it? Wouldn't catch me here if my long-toothed sister hadn't needed an escort. Is this your latest?" he loudly whispered, gesturing toward Kit.

"Miss Roche, allow me to introduce Viscount Spencer. He's a particular friend of mine, and not usually this rude."

Kit, who had begun frowning when the viscount had uttered his first speech, politely but stiffly acknowledged the introduction. She thought to herself: *No wonder Jerry's gotten such a reprehensible reputation, if this is an example of the company he keeps.* Her hopes that the viscount would take himself off at once were quickly dispelled as he cozied up to Jerry and reported in graphic detail the pleasures to be found at Brighton.

Disliking the turn of the conversation, Kit excused herself and joined some acquaintances across the room.

It was not long before Princess Lieven announced that the entertainment was about to begin. Cognizant of his obligation to appear fascinated by Miss Roche, Lord Hadley (with Viscount Spencer in his wake) hurried to her side to escort her to the music room. Drawing abreast of Kit, the viscount consulted his watch and proposed a wager to Jerry in a mischievously low voice. "Lay you a monkey that no later than thirty minutes from now half the gentlemen will have escaped from their seats. Can't stand this caterwauling they call 'opera.' "

"Only a half? I'll bet three-quarters will be gone in that time. It's a wager, then?"

Nodding, the viscount stuck out his hand. "And Miss Roche will be our witness."

Scowling, Kit could hold her tongue no longer. "I'll be no party to such puerile transactions! Besides, since we will be sitting in front, and it is rude to be turning around in one's chair, *you*, sir"—glaring at Jerry—"will be unable to count how many of your fellow uncultured boors have slipped out."

The spectacle of Miss Roche flushed with indignation brought a glint of amusement to Jerry's eyes. Turning to the viscount, he shrugged his shoulders and said, "Well, Percy, I'm afraid we must call our wager off if I am to redeem myself with *ma petite chou*."

Mouth agape, Percy commented incredulously, "Sorry, old boy; I didn't realize you were under this lady's thumb," and withdrew to seek more diverting company.

"Well done, my dear! He will be off to spread rumors that you and I are about to tie the knot, and that should put to rest the speculation about the countess and me," Jerry declared with a satisfied air.

This compliment rang in Kit's ears for the remainder of the evening, so that she was able to overlook his too frequent refilling of his wineglass.

On the trip home, everyone agreed that their debut had been a success. Congratulating his wife on her theatrical skills, David noted, "When you reached over and took my hand during the Beethoven piano sonata, I saw Mrs. Drummond-Burrell register it approvingly."

Paige was glad it was dark, for she flushed with embarrassment at the memory of finding her fingers entwined with David's, seemingly of their own volition. Feeling the need to respond, she remarked, "Edmund Kean is not the only great actor in London these days. Your timing was precise to a pin when you kissed my wrist in the hallway. I had wondered what you were about until I saw Sally

Jersey round the corner. The tale of our grand passion will be on everyone's lips by noon tomorrow, thanks to Silence Jersey!''

As it had, in fact, been passion rather than Lady Jersey's presence that had prompted the kiss, David grinned sheepishly at his wife.

Silent observers, Kit and Jerry independently picked up the underlying currents that flowed between their companions. When Kit glanced at her ersatz suitor, he winked at her significantly. It looked as though Paige and David would soon be the only ones in Town unaware of the mutuality of their love.

Chapter XIV

As might be expected, Dorcas was among the first to hear inklings that the plot she and Sylvester had concocted was in danger of being overset. The Blandish sisters, whom Dorcas had encountered at Lottie Morrow's that morning, were replete with anecdotes from the night before which, they said, proved the rumor about Hadley and the Countess Penllyn was all a hum.

"And there the earl and countess were, holding hands and gazing dreamily into each other's eyes, oblivious to their audience," rhapsodized the romantic elder sister.

Dorcas had to suppress an exclamation of disbelief, for she knew full well that Paige and David must be putting on an act. There had certainly been no evidence of hand-holding between them at Penllyn. *That Paige is just too clever by half!*

Anxious to discuss this new turn of events with Sylvester, she sent him a note asking him to meet her at five o'clock in Hyde Park, where it would look as though their encounter were by chance.

Obeying the summons, Sylvester maneuvered his rig through the crush of other vehicles toward the appointed place. Dorcas ordered her maid to wait for her, then climbed up beside him. Sylvester's mood had been almost

sunny when he'd received Dorcas's message. It soured
immediately as she imparted her news.

"So they've decided to brazen it out, playing the lovebirds,
eh, and have enlisted the aid of Hadley and Miss Roche.
Well, one evening's work cannot undo a well-entrenched
rumor, m'dear. I will not be so smug in future. I must
attend as many events as possible so as to use all opportuni-
ties to make mischief."

His air of confidence relieved Dorcas's anxieties. She
squeezed his knee reassuringly and offered to help, if he
thought it necessary.

Suddenly she pulled her hand back as though scalded,
for she had heard someone hailing Sylvester. They both
looked up to see a ridiculous figure shaped much like
Humpty Dumpty riding toward them.

"Wolcott!" moaned Sylvester. "Probably in the basket
again. Can't hang on to a groat for more than a minute.
His father gambled away his inheritance and left the estate
heavily mortgaged. Poor Cedric hasn't the wit or character
to turn things around," finished Sylvester loftily.

"Nor the looks to snare even the most mutton-faced
heiress," Dorcas noted dryly, scanning the person of Lord
Wolcott.

"Thought that was you, Owens. Servant, ma'am,"
Lord Wolcott addressed Dorcas, tipping his hat and expos-
ing five lonely strands of hair stretched across his naked
pate.

"Cedric, didn't realize you were in town. I haven't seen
you lately at Crockford's."

"Not too plump in the pocket. Had to retire to Thorngate
for a bit. Back yesterday. Off to try my luck tonight. See
you there?"

"Of course," Sylvester responded, whipping up his
team in response to urgings from the carriage behind him.

True to his word, Sylvester joined Wolcott at the faro
table at midnight. It was obvious that Cedric was losing
badly but refusing to call it quits; Sylvester's run of luck

was just the opposite. As they left together, Wolcott swallowed his pride and implored, "Badly dipped. Need a few pounds to tide me over."

Feeling magnanimous with his own winnings safe in his pocket, Sylvester chose not to ignore this hint. "Come 'round to see me tomorrow. I think I can help you out. Been there m'self, you know."

Calling at Owens's rooms the following morning, Cedric was rewarded with a loan that exceeded his expectations. "Thank you. Very generous. Don't know how long it will be before I can pay you back. If there's any service I can perform for you, I'd be more than pleased."

Sylvester, smiling devilishly, experienced the headiness of power that often comes with having someone indebted to one. . . .

It was to be a temporary sensation, overshadowed by the continuing success of David and Paige's attempts to squelch the gossip. Bets were already being placed on the date of Lord Hadley's marriage to Miss Roche. By his own observation, Sylvester had to admit that his cousin's wife's performance was masterful; her show of tenderness to her husband was obvious, but not ostentatious. If this continued, he'd have to take more drastic measures.

Within a week, that seemed necessary. The original rumor had all but evaporated, and Sylvester was on a losing streak at the tables as well.

An opportunity to do damage presented itself at a rout party given by the Undershaws in honor of Lady Undershaw's natal day. Sylvester spied Hadley lighting a cigarillo on the deserted terrace and thought what a scandalous scene it would be if Paige were to be seen joining him there. Frantically scanning the room, Sylvester caught Dorcas's eye and signaled her to meet him at once in the hallway.

Minutes after doing so, Dorcas approached Paige with a message. "Oh, there you are! Someone just told me Lord Hadley is on the terrace looking for you. I believe it has to do with Miss Roche."

Alarmed, Paige hurried toward the door.

At the same moment, Kit espied Jerry engaging in the nasty habit of smoking. Unmindful of the consequences of her actions, she rushed out to ring a peal over his head.

So, what the observers Sylvester had hastily positioned at the open French doors actually saw was an innocuous gathering of three friends, instead of a lovers' tryst.

Paige was surprised and relieved to see Kit with Hadley, for Dorcas's message had implied something amiss.

"What has happened?" she asked quizzically, glancing from one to the other. "I feared Kit might be faint."

Jerry looked down at Miss Roche with a raised eyebrow and inquired, "Don't tell me you've called in reinforcements to wrench the offending stick of tobacco from my lips?!"

Puzzled, Paige replied, "But it was you yourself, sir, who summoned me."

"I? I did not summon you, beg pardon. It must have indeed been Miss Roche."

"I scarcely have seen Paige all evening. I only saw *you* alone out here, smoking that filthy weed," Kit countered defensively, chagrined at his supposition that she could not handle his bad habits by herself.

"Well, then why would Dorcas tell me that you were looking for me?"

"What exactly were her words?" Jerry interrogated, a frown darkening his handsome brow.

"Near as I can recall, she said that someone told her you were out on the terrace looking for me, and that it had something to do with Miss Roche." Noting his suspicious expression, she added, "What are you thinking of, Jerry?"

Not wanting to reveal his growing misgivings about Dorcas, Jerry remained silent.

Light dawning in Paige's eyes, she exclaimed, "You don't believe that Dorcas would seek to further damage my reputation by tricking me into a compromising situation? My own sister-in-law?!" she protested, forgetting that only recently she herself had considered Dorcas as the source of the rumor.

"But that's how she snared your brother," Kit cried out, clapping her hand over her mouth at her own audacity.

Paige admitted that Dorcas was capable of such deviousness in order to benefit herself but could not see how, in this instance, any advantage would accrue to her. Paige remarked on this to Hadley, whose enigmatic response was, "Perhaps your sister-in-law has motivations we don't comprehend."

Perplexed, Paige laid the tale before David and sought his view of the matter later. Piecing together this anecdote with what he and Jerry had concluded about his cousin and Dorcas at Penllyn, David thought he might have the answer to the question of the originator of the rumor. Without evidence, he was loath to reveal his suspicions to his wife, so he merely agreed that this incident was mystifying and reminded her that, in any case, it had proved harmless.

If his hunch were true, they could expect more such episodes; but he would not confront Sylvester without proof. Pondering this as he finished his last brandy before retiring, David decided to enlist the aid of the ever-resourceful and discreet Sir Walter Townsend to track the original rumor to its source.

The next morning David pounced on Sir Walter before he could join Lady Susan in the drawing room and dragged him into his study. Having heard the entire story, Sir Walter agreed with David's identification of Sylvester as the probable culprit and promised to do whatever he could to uncover the facts. David hoped the investigation would be swift, so he could warn off Sylvester before the mischief became more serious. On the other hand, he was ironically grateful to his cousin for providing the excuse for David's loverlike advances to his wife, and for effectively dousing any remaining embers of romance between Jerry and Paige.

Reflecting on the past few weeks, David now felt more

certain that the annulment would not occur. The instincts
he'd always trusted to keep him alive on the battlefield told
him his wife was not always playacting in her attentions to
him. He wasn't positive, though, that she knew her own
heart and worried about scaring her off by declaring
himself. He would bide his time and enjoy their public
lovemaking.

The sight of these two billing and cooing was increasingly
alarming to Sylvester, who feared they were as active in
their private lovemaking as well. He determined to do
something quickly to ensure that he would become the
next Earl of Penllyn. For several days he pondered how to
achieve this end and discarded several schemes as
unworkable. When he once again encountered Lord Wolcott
at Crockford's and remembered that Wolcott owed him
several hundred pounds, he hit upon a way to have this
debt repaid and secure his own future.

A week later at Watier's David and Sir Walter were
deeply engrossed in sharing their discoveries about the
source of the gossip over Paige and Jerry. The evidence
seemed to indicate that it had originated from the drawing
room of Lottie Morrow, Dorcas's cousin. Sir Walter had
just asked the earl how he intended to make use of this
information when a crowd of drunken young bucks staggered
into the room.

David turned around in annoyance at the rowdiness of
the group, glared at them, and turned back to Sir Walter.

Lord Wolcott, who was of the party, slurred loudly,
"Look who's staring down his nose at us—the high and
mighty Earl of Penllyn."

"Shh!" giggled one of his inebriated friends, as he tried
to draw Cedric across the room toward a card table.

"I won't be quiet!" Lord Wolcott declared petulantly,
shrugging off Robert Eddington's arm. "What right has he
to look askance at us when his wife's carrying on behind
his back with his best friend?"

At these words all heads turned toward David, who

slowly rose from his chair to face his detractor. Young Lord Wilberforce hissed to Wolcott to apologize, but instead Wolcott compounded his insult by placing two fingers behind his head in imitation of horns and laughed at the earl's stormy countenance. Hoping to prevent further unpleasantness, Wolcott's friends forcibly escorted him to their table. David would have followed, but the agile Sir Walter grabbed his arm and calmly pronounced, "Don't do anything foolish. He's obviously foxed."

Recognizing the sense in this advice, David sat back down and finished his drink. As the hour was now quite late, David and Sir Walter rose to leave, whereupon Wolcott shouted, "Better not hurry home, for you're liable to find your place in bed already occupied."

Pulling out of Sir Walter's restraining grip, David crossed the room in two strides and struck Wolcott across the face so forcibly that the younger man fell back in his chair.

"Name your second, sir," David growled. Then, turning to Sir Walter, he asked, "Will you act for me?"

Reluctantly Townsend agreed, as did Eddington for Wolcott. Sir Walter was surprised to note a smirk of satisfaction on Wolcott's face and vowed to do everything possible to avoid the duel.

In this effort he was seriously handicapped, for David not only insisted that no one learn of the impending duel but refused to accept any apology that might have been extracted from Wolcott (this refusal did not signify, as Wolcott refused to entertain the notion of begging the earl's pardon for the offensive conduct at Watier's). Sir Walter had to console himself with the knowledge that David was by far the better shot.

Paige was surprised when, the next afternoon, David suggested that they cancel their plans to attend a small dinner party at the Atleys' in favor of spending a quiet evening at home. Feeling a bit fagged from having been so much in society, Paige was agreeable.

After a quiet dinner with Lady Susan, Paige and David

sat down at the chessboard. The evening passed quickly, as they each concentrated their full efforts on defeating the other. At midnight, the game having stalemated, David announced his intention of retiring. Paige accompanied him to his door and was totally dumbfounded when he clasped her face between his hands, whispered, "My love!" kissed her on the tip of her nose, and withdrew into his room. Paige stood riveted to the spot for several seconds before walking unsteadily toward her own chamber.

My love? she repeated to herself. *Could I have heard him right? He did not have to say it; there was no one around to observe.* Her heart beat more rapidly. Perhaps he really meant it. Perhaps he'd forgotten Maria. She'd been wondering for a while if his public caresses and endearments were really feigned—some of them had seemed so spontaneous and genuine, as her own to him had come to be.

But how could she be sure? She dared not risk professing her love for him, for fear of ruining what seemed to be developing naturally between them. Perhaps Lady Susan would have some advice. She might even be privy to David's confidences about his own feelings.

Having decided on a course of action, Paige undressed and snuggled under the covers. Touching her nose, where he'd kissed her, with her fingertips, she drifted off to sleep thinking how lovely it would be if David were beside her.

In the adjoining chamber, David spent a restless night. Though he was confident he was a better shot than Wolcott, there was always the possibility that his opponent would get off a lucky shot. With this thought, David was struck by a pang of guilt: he had not said good-bye to the two people he loved best—his wife and his mother.

Lighting a candle, he located writing impedimenta and penned two notes, addressing one "Paige" and the other "Mother." He propped them up on his dresser, hoping they'd never have to be delivered. Then, on an impulse, he unlocked the door that connected Paige's chamber to his and softly tiptoed into her room. The light from the full moon illuminated her peaceful countenance. Drinking in this heart-stirring scene, he promised, *It won't be long, my love,* and silently returned to his own bed, where he fell instantly asleep.

Three short hours later he was shaken awake by Dickson, who informed him that Sir Walter Townsend was waiting for him below.

Dawn was just breaking when they arrived at Wimbledon Common. There was as yet no sign of Wolcott and his party, so David and Sir Walter had ample time to mark out the ground. They had finished executing this prerogative when two post chaises careened onto the common. Wolcott and Eddington jumped out of one, and several of Wolcott's friends tumbled out of the other, dragging a somewhat frightened-looking man carrying the case of a surgeon. David felt fairly certain that the medical man had not agreed of his own free will to be a party to this illegal encounter. Sir Walter had had to part with five guineas to obtain the services of their own sawbones, who remained discreetly hidden in the Penllyn carriage.

Greeting Eddington, Sir Walter made a final inquiry: "Your man still does not relent or apologize?"

His features reflecting his dismay, Eddington confessed, "No. I have done my best, but he is adamant. I cannot credit it. Look at him! He is not a skilled marksman, and he offers a broad target, yet he's strutting about as though he were Manton himself."

Sir Walter had known Eddington since he'd been in short pants and trusted his integrity, so he admitted to some concern. "Something havey-cavey about this. I've thought so since Wolcott deliberately provoked Penllyn. Have you checked his pistols carefully?"

"I've had similar suspicions, but could find no fault with them. You, of course, will want to examine them yourself."

The two men exchanged pistol cases and solemnly

inspected their contents. Sir Walter, a firearms expert, began his inspection by hefting Wolcott's weapon. Frowning, he balanced its partner in his other hand. He began to wish he'd brought another knowledgeable person to consult with, for the balance seemed imperceptibly off. Scrutinizing each part individually, he could find no anomaly—yet he was convinced that the pistols had been tampered with. Playing a hunch, he inserted a twig into the barrel and was rewarded with the discovery of rifling at the breech end. Calling Eddington over, he told him of his findings and requested that he verify them.

As Eddington's probing had the same result, he called over lords Wilberforce and Steele to confirm the illegal alteration of the weapon. After doing so, the three men moved *en masse* toward their principal, while Sir Walter rejoined a very curious David.

Moments later Wolcott was thrust toward David by his party. Casting frightened glances at his outraged entourage, he launched into a graceless apology for dishonoring Penllyn's wife's reputation.

Frigidly, a confused David accepted the apology, then turned his back and walked directly to his waiting carriage.

On the way to Berkeley Square, Sir Walter revealed what had instigated the apology. "I don't think Wolcott had the motive or knowledge to have effected the alteration of the pistols," David mused. "Someone else is behind this."

"Sylvester?" interjected Sir Walter.

"Well, he has the best motive of all for wanting me dead before I produce a son. In addition, he's a gambling buddy of Wolcott's."

"What will you do, man? You cannot accuse him without proof."

"If it's proof I need, it's proof I will get," David resolved ominously.

Chapter XV

In Grosvenor Square, his brother-in-law had also come to a decision after a sleepless night. Sir Richard Undershaw could no longer deny that he'd lost his heart to Mme. Lisette. She was always at the forefront of his mind: at parties he would imagine her on his arm, and her laughing blue eyes haunted his dreams. He'd completely run out of excuses for frequenting her shop, but he still stopped by for sherry—and she seemed to need no explanation.

What a coil! Here he was, bound for life to one woman and madly in love with another. Unbidden, the word "divorce" came to his mind. To dissolve his marriage (for a shopkeeper!) would certainly cause a scandal, but to offer Lisette a *carte blanche* was reprehensible to him personally. So, for the first time, the noble gentleman from Surrey permitted himself to entertain seriously the notion of divorcing Dorcas. Seemingly he had no grounds, but perhaps if he offered her a generous settlement, she would not contest it. And, if she were agreeable, he felt sure they could weather the societal repercussions. Richard did not mind if he were ostracized from the *haut ton*, for he cared not much for their opinion or their way of life. And Dorcas, who thrived on Town life, would be "the wronged party" and therefore the object of sympathetic attention.

No doubt she'd have a bevy of suitors and would remarry in no time at all.

This thought triggered a new line of speculation. In the past few weeks, Dorcas's behavior had been such that he'd fleetingly wondered if she'd not already found a lover. She'd taken to shunning his husbandly advances; and twice he'd caught her out in untruths. Last Thursday, as he'd strolled toward his club, he'd spied her familiar form getting into a carriage driven by a gentleman whose face Richard could not see. This would not have been exceptional, for Dorcas had many admirers; however, she had just moments before announced that she was going shopping with her cousin Lottie. And on another occasion, recently, she said she'd been to a rout at Lady Cathcart's—but Edward Cathcart, whom Richard had run into a few days after this event, had said how much he'd missed seeing Richard and his lovely wife at the party.

Instead of feeling either jealousy or anger, Richard found himself hoping there *were* someone else in Dorcas's life, for that would make it easier to take the action he was contemplating. Two incidents, however, were not enough to draw such a conclusion. He'd certainly need more evidence, but he had no idea how one went about uncovering clandestine liaisons. Mulling this over for a moment, he thought of his clever sister. Perhaps she would know how to go about it. Besides, it was high time he revealed all to her and got her advice. She could always put problems in their proper perspective.

Knowing Paige was an early riser, he consumed a light breakfast and set out for Berkeley Square. He was surprised to encounter David also entering the house—and not in riding clothes. Richard hoped for his sister's sake that the earl had not been out all night.

David, who had been anxious to speak to his wife, was annoyed to find Richard paying a call but greeted him warmly. "You're up with the rooster this morning, Richard. I'm sure Paige will be happy to see you. Might I expect to have the honor of going a few rounds with you at Jackson's tomorrow?'' This agreed to, David went upstairs to destroy the two letters he'd written in anticipation of the duel.

Paige was in the breakfast parlor, looking fetching as usual and attacking her meal like a trencherman. Kissing her food-filled cheek, Richard remarked, ''After twenty-six years, your appetite still amazes me. Why you are not as round as Prinny I do not know.''

Noticing his abstracted air, she countered, ''I work it all off contriving original solutions to other people's problems. What is *yours* this time?''

Chuckling at her smugness, he retorted, ''You mean Miss Know-It-All is not already in possession of that information?''

Unexpectedly turning serious, Paige gazed at him thoughtfully and mused, ''I do not know the specific dilemma, but I suspect it has something to do with your attraction to Madame Lisette.''

Aghast at her perspicacity, Richard stood stock still and stared incredulously at her. ''How did you know?'' he finally gasped weakly.

''As it involves another's reputation, I must needs hear what you have to say before revealing that.''

Paige had become privy to the extent of Mme. Lisette and Richard's involvement from Cornelia herself only yesterday. She could vividly recall that unsettling conversation, which had begun with a morning call from Lady Bragdon.

''Good heavens!'' Paige exclaimed upon seeing her friend. ''How can you be in two places at once? Should not Madame Lisette be in her shop?''

''I am sick to death of Madame Lisette and her shop!'' Cornelia replied heatedly.

Paige, alarmed at her friend's unusual vehemence and negativism, chided, ''I told you six days a week would become too much for you. Your staff is capable; why not take a holiday?''

Cornelia's eyes slipped away from Paige's gaze as she responded, ''But that will not solve my most pressing problem. . . .''

''Which *is* . . .'' Paige prompted.

''That your brother is in love with Madame Lisette,'' Cornelia blurted, glad to get it out at last.

''And how does Lisette feel about that?'' came the unexpectedly calm reply.

Paige's reaction caught Cornelia off guard. She'd anticipated that the focus would be on the inappropriateness of Richard's feelings, not on her own, so she countered defensively, ''That is irrelevant. Your brother is a married man and should not be enamored of a shopkeeper.''

''And what would the shopkeeper do if he were not a married man?'' Paige persevered, eyeing her friend sagaciously.

Flustered by this line of inquiry, the usually unflappable Cornelia began moving around the room, randomly picking up objects and setting them back down without regarding them. Suddenly she whirled around and with tears in her eyes snapped, ''Oh, God, Babette, how should *I* know?! Why don't you ask Madame Lisette?''

Paige, recognizing that strong emotion must be afoot for Cornelia to have called her by her childhood name, rolled her eyes and patiently intoned, ''But you are Lisette, and if Richard is in love with *her*, he is also in love with you.''

Cornelia stopped her aimless meandering, an arrested expression on her face, which then crumpled as she burst out, ''He does not love *me*. He loves Lisette. He never comes to call on *me* anymore; he's always with Madame Lisette.''

Trying to get to the heart of the matter, Paige bluntly challenged, ''Cornelia, are you or are you not in love with my brother?''

''Oh, yes!'' Cornelia moaned miserably. ''These last ten

years. I waited five Seasons for him to come up to scratch before I accepted Tracy. And now he's finally fallen for a character I created from my imagination, not for the real me.''

Concealing her amazement at her own ignorance of Cornelia's long-standing *tendre* for Richard, Paige sensibly pointed out that although Lisette was in fact a character Cornelia had created, ''she'' had, nevertheless, aspects of Cornelia's own personality—aspects that she'd had to suppress because of society's dictates about the behavior acceptable for a properly-brought-up young lady.

Since this logic was in the vein Cornelia wanted to hear, her face became instantly wreathed in smiles. ''You're right! I hadn't thought of that. Madame Lisette is more like the little girl Richard used to play with, and the one who first fell in love with him. . . . Thank you, Paige; I'm sure now that he does love me,'' Cornelia concluded, throwing her arms around her friend.

Paige returned the embrace warmly but felt compelled to recall her friend to reality. ''I'm usually happy to hear about people in love; however, in this case it saddens me, for we cannot forget that Richard is already wed to Dorcas—and therefore I can see no future happiness in it. I know you both too well to believe that you could settle for an illicit liaison, and I suspect divorce is out of the question.'' But, as divorce offered the only chance for them to get together, Paige decided to pursue this possibility. *''Is* it out of the question, Cornelia? Would you be willing to go through a scandal to become my brother's wife?''

Without hesitation, Cornelia responded, ''Yes!''

It's worse than I thought, Paige mused. Attempting to garner the facts, she queried, ''Have you and Richard discussed this step?''

''You mean, I presume, as 'Lisette,' for Richard does not know that I am she.'' Paige nodded, and Cornelia proceeded to answer her question. ''No, and I doubt he

will, for he is too honorable a man to desert his wife. So
what am I to do?''

Her heart heavy with concern for her friend's plight,
Paige confessed that no solution came to mind, but—ever
optimistic—was hopeful that upon reflection an answer
would present itself.

It hadn't, however, in the ensuing twenty-four hours,
and now here was the other of the protagonists, standing
before her. Perhaps his revelations would offer a clue to a
way out of this morass.

As Richard was still gaping at her in wonder, Paige
gently urged him to unburden himself. Taking a sip of the
coffee she'd poured him, he realized it was senseless to
postpone his confession any longer. ''Babs, what I have to
say may shock you. I can only hope for a measure of your
understanding.''

Distressed that Richard would feel a need to plead for
her understanding, Paige put her arms about his neck and
kissed him on the cheek, saying, ''Richard, I know you
are a decent and kindhearted man. If you have done
something improper, I am sure you had a good reason.''

Encouraged by these words of support, Richard poured
out his story. After giving Paige the background on his
relationship with Madame Lisette, he concluded with his
suspicions about Dorcas and his consideration of divorce.

Only a flicker of an eyelid betrayed his sister's surprise
at the news of Dorcas's possible infidelity. Though Paige
could believe that Dorcas was capable of such perfidy, she
thought Richard's evidence was not substantial enough to
support divorce proceedings. As though reading her mind,
Richard said with a sigh, ''I know I need more than that to
substantiate my hunch, but I am at a loss as to how to go
about it. Do you have any ideas, Babs?''

Thinking to herself how much in love Richard must be
with Lisette to be sitting there, calmly discussing (and
even attempting to prove) his own wife's betrayal of him,

she replied out loud, "I know naught of these matters, but David might. If you do not object, I will put the matter to him."

As Richard had a high regard for his brother-in-law's integrity and judgment, he agreed at once.

Seeing Richard push back his chair as though readying himself for departure, Paige laid a forestalling hand on his arm and begged, "Oh, do not go yet. I have more to ask you."

Richard, who had been relieved at disclosing his most heinous secret without alienating his sister, now became uncomfortable and waited uneasily for her to continue.

His worst expectations were realized when Paige asked with no roundaboutation, "Am I to understand that you love this woman so much that you are prepared to go through with the divorce even if you cannot prove Dorcas's unfaithfulness?"

"I do love her that much," he declared with passion, "but I am unsure of *her* feelings. Naturally, I have restrained from declaring myself until I am able to make her an honorable offer. And I cannot do *that* until I commit myself to ending my marriage," he continued, his voice quavering with emotion. "Oh, God, Paige, what a mull I've made of things!"

In her need to comfort him, Paige lost control of her tongue and said consolingly, "I know it looks like that now, but I am determined to find a way out for you and Cornelia."

Jerking his head up, Richard exclaimed, "Cornelia? What has she to do with this matter?"

Stalling for time, Paige temporized, "Oh, dear, did I say 'Cornelia'? I can't imagine why her name came to mind." Sensing that she was not going to get out of this easily, she resorted to a half-truth and admitted that Cornelia had been the one to enlighten her about his relationship with Lisette.

Raising his eyebrows at his sister in disbelief, Richard

objected, "How can she know of my relationship with Lisette?"

"She can and she does," was the enigmatic reply.

"But how? Why?"

Paige felt, illogically, that if Richard could by himself recognize that Lisette was Cornelia in disguise, it would be conclusive proof that he was in love with Cornelia. So she prompted, "I'm sure that if you'll take a moment to reflect you'll discover the connection between Lisette and Cornelia."

Annoyed at not getting a direct answer to his question, Richard protested that he was not in the mood for parlor games.

"Nor am I. I am in deadly earnest."

Recognizing that the obstinate set of her countenance brooked no further argument, he began to search his memory for clues of a relationship between his childhood friend and his newfound love.

His first thought, which he voiced aloud, was, "Well, I suppose that Corny could have her dresses made up by Lisette. But I doubt if Madame would confide to one of her patrons the name of her suitors. . . ."

Impatiently Paige interrupted and urged, "That's not it. Try again."

"Well, they're not related, as Corny has no French connections on either side of the family. . . . Odd, though, now that I think of it—they do rather have a look of each other. . . . Is that it? Is Lisette a by-blow of Sir Reginald, and therefore Cornelia's half sister?"

Paige laughed outright at the thought of Sir Reginald interrupting his preoccupation with horses and hounds to dally with, say, a serving girl. She had often wondered, in fact, how he'd spared the time to father Cornelia.

Watching the genuine amusement in his sister's face, Richard muttered, "Well, I guess that's not it—but damn it, they do look alike," he reasserted as he thought of two pairs of blue eyes set in heart-shaped faces.

"Indeed they do," Paige said encouragingly.

Feeling as though the answer were right at his fingertips, Richard frowned in concentration. As he conjured up images of both women, he began to see other similarities, not only in their looks but in their actions and interests. Both were ardent Whig supporters, and for the same reasons. And Cornelia *was* fluent in French. And they were of the same height and figure.... Suddenly he remembered that once before he had fleetingly suspected that Lisette, as the Lilac Lady, was actually Cornelia—and finally he began to entertain what was becoming the obvious answer to this conundrum.

Paige was heartened by his cry of, "Good God! It cannot be! Cornelia's much too proper to engage in such an outrageous hoax...."

"As *you* are much too proper to fall in love with a French shopkeeper," Paige noted in ironic tones.

Taken aback, Richard could not at first fathom her meaning. But the spark of mischief in her eyes got the message across: both he and Cornelia had broken with convention and done the unthinkable.

Haltingly he spoke the words that only minutes before would have seemed inconceivable. "Cornelia is Lisette? I am in love with Cornelia?"

Waiting to hear his feelings about his discovery, Paige merely nodded in confirmation.

"Oh, now I can understand why I was drawn to so unsuitable a person as a modiste. She possessed many of the qualities I'd always admired in Cornelia." Smiling ruefully, he continued, "You see, Babs, I have always thought of Cornelia as unattainable. She is so beautiful and could have any man she wanted. I could not hope she'd return my regard. In fact, I was actually relieved when she married Tracy, for that put her once and for all out of my reach. It's hard to believe that I've been unknowingly making up to her these last few months. My God! Whatever does she think of me?!" he cried, gazing imploringly at Paige.

"What she's always thought of you—that you are the only man in the world for her," Paige declared fervently, pleased with the dramatic ring of these words.

Richard could scarcely believe his ears. Cornelia, in love with him? He would go to her at once and profess his undying devotion!

But before he had a chance to act this out, prudence intervened. To involve Mme. Lisette in a divorce was one thing. She would not suffer so from the slings of society as would Lady Bragdon. To impugn Cornelia's reputation was insupportable. He could not ask her to throw away her respectability for him.

He was cast into gloom, which persisted despite Paige's reassurance that she would find a way to bring two such deserving people together. Laughing bitterly, Richard countered, "It cannot be done. Even your ingenuity is no match for this tangle. However, should a miracle occur, you will find me at Waverly, where I can count on the peacefulness and natural beauty to begin the healing process."

Sadly, Paige agreed with the sense of this course of action, hugged him fondly, and bade him, "Do not be too hard on yourself. You're only human, and Dorcas was never the wife for you."

No sooner had the door closed on Richard than it opened again to admit David. One look at Paige's troubled countenance and David put aside his own mission, inquiring, "Why so blue-deviled? Is it something I can help with?"

"I wish you could, but I am afraid the situation is beyond helping," she said dejectedly. "Unless you happen to have proof that Dorcas has been unfaithful to Richard."

Lowering his immaculately clad person into the chair just vacated by Richard, he drawled, "I am astonished that particulars of your sister-in-law's infidelity could serve to cheer you. I know you do not like Dorcas, but I had rather thought you had fond feelings for that brother of yours."

"I do! That is why I need evidence that she's been cuckolding him."

"And how, pray tell, would this be to Richard's advantage?" the earl wondered, beginning to be concerned for his wife's sanity.

Impatient at her husband's lack of understanding, Paige explained, "Because Richard is in love with Cornelia, and she with him . . . although she doesn't know that he knows that he's in love with her, because she thinks he loves Madame Lisette—which he does, of course. And she's willing to marry him if he gets a divorce, but he feels that he cannot subject her to the scandal, although it would not signify if it were Lisette. . . ."

As she ran out of breath, David placed one hand on her forehead and with the other groped for her pulse, clucking concernedly, "I collect that you are not well. All this racketing about we've been doing was bound to take its toll eventually. Oh, just as I thought. Your face is flushed and your pulse rapid."

Paige was well aware of these symptoms but had a different diagnosis of their origins. It was David's touch, and the genuine caring in his clear gray eyes as he caressed her wrist, that had produced her heightened color and agitation.

Reluctantly removing his strong fingers from her quivering arm, she retorted, "There is nothing physically the matter with me. I am merely upset that I cannot think of a way to alleviate Richard and Cornelia's unhappiness."

"I am afraid I must be really entering my dotage, for I cannot credit how someone like Richard can be married to one woman and apparently in love with two others."

Exasperated, Paige elucidated, "No, no, not with *two* others—just Cornelia and Lisette," and proceeded to relate the story in more understandable terms.

When she'd finished, David remained silent, staring thoughtfully out the window.

"So, do you know how we can get some evidence?" Paige prompted.

"Divorce in our circles is almost unheard of. Are you

sure, my love, that Richard and Cornelia care enough, that their regard for each other is strong enough to withstand the ostracism that's bound to be the result?''

Paige needed no time to consider this question before replying in the affirmative, then added, ''I collect that this line of inquiry means that you are in possession of some information about Dorcas.''

''I have nothing that would hold up under close examination, but ever since our visit to Penllyn, I've felt almost sure that she's been playing Richard false with Sylvester.''

''Sylvester?! They deserve each other! If only it were so. . . . How shall we discover the truth and make use of it?'' Paige implored.

David's brain began to work rapidly. ''I am not at all certain that that will be necessary. There may be another way to resolve this,'' he speculated enigmatically. ''As a matter of fact, it is Sylvester I came to you to discuss. I believe he tried to have me killed this morning,'' David announced dispassionately.

At these words the color drained so rapidly from Paige's face that David feared she would faint. This reaction in an instant cleared up any remaining doubts he'd had about his wife's love for him. He would have taken her in his arms there and then and declared himself, but if his plan were to succeed he must confront Wolcott at once, before Sylvester did. There was just no time for lovemaking.

To reassure her he hastily added, ''As you can see, the attempt did not prosper,'' and went on to outline the circumstances of the duel.

''That blackguard!'' Paige summarized heatedly. ''What will you do to be sure he won't try again?''

''First I must call on Lord Wolcott to substantiate my suspicions. Then I will suggest to Sylvester that he take an extended holiday. Do you think, dear, that it's worth the sum of ten thousand pounds to be rid of my scoundrel of a cousin?''

Deducing from this speech that David was planning to give Sylvester that sum to leave the country, she produced what to her seemed a much more attractive alternative: "Why not have him thrown into jail?"

"I'd love to see him there, but that is tantamount to a public announcement that we've got a loose screw in the family. Mother would suffer greatly."

Paige could see the wisdom in this and agreed with his original scheme, adding as a caveat, "But you will not go alone, will you? It occurs to me that Sylvester might already be with Wolcott, and together they might succeed where one failed this morning."

"Thank you for thinking of that—I had not—though I don't anticipate that will happen. I'll take Johnson along, with orders that should I not come out in a half hour he should force his way in. Now I must be off. I expect I won't be back before noon."

Paige accompanied him to the door, where she clutched his sleeve and whispered, "Do be careful, David."

To her surprise he gave her his half smile, and said, "Have no fear. I now have too much to live for to be taking unnecessary risks," and was gone.

Chapter XVI

AFTER she closed the door softly behind him, Paige remained standing with her hand on the knob and reflected on her recently revised ideas about marriage. Had she known that it was possible to be seen as an equal by one's husband, she would have given matrimony more serious consideration previously. But then she might have accepted a prior offer and would have never met David. . . .

Returning to the table, she refilled her coffee cup and, in so doing, came to a decision. She loved him; she wanted to remain his wife; and she would tell him so at the earliest opportunity. Certainly it was a risk to expose her feelings, for he might not return her regard. But it was a risk she needed to take, for she could no longer live with this longing and uncertainty: she wanted to be his wife in more than name only.

Her mind was just returning to the problem of Richard and Cornelia when her mother-in-law entered the breakfast parlor, looking radiant in a lilac sarcenet morning dress.

Peering behind her, Paige said, "Oh, is not Sir Walter with you? I thought I heard his voice in the drawing room."

"He has just this minute left. I was hoping to find David here with you, for I have some news which I wanted to relate to you together."

"I can see by your face that, whatever it is, it must needs be pleasant. You have a decided sparkle in your eye and a bloom about your cheeks, madam!"

As this observation was greeted with an uncharacteristically girlish giggle, Paige played a hunch and guessed, "Has the esteemed Sir Walter been whispering endearments in your ear?"

Lady Susan giggled again and announced, "We are to wed."

At these words Paige leaped up, overturning her cup, and embraced Lady Susan crushingly. "Oh, I'm so happy for you! He is a dear, and you are perfect for each other. When does this great event occur?"

"Naturally, we must wait until I am out of mourning—which is just as well, for by then we should know how the future looks for *this* household," the older woman said, casting a meaningful look at the younger.

Paige did not pretend to misunderstand this innuendo. "I think I can assure you that matters here will be resolved soon. It all depends on whether David has been able to transfer his feelings for *Maria* to *me*."

Puzzled, Lady Susan exclaimed, "Maria? Whoever is Maria?"

Lady Susan's bewilderment was so obviously genuine that Paige realized she was not in her son's confidence about the matter.

"Apparently she's a Spanish beauty who captured David's heart," Paige confided forlornly.

Knowing full well that David had forgotten "Maria" —if indeed she had ever been important to him—Lady Susan toyed with the idea of confiding to Paige David's desire to make their union permanent. However, she was reluctant to do her son's work for him. So she drew an analogy with her own situation in an attempt to reassure her daughter-in-law. "While I know nothing of that, I do not think it signifies. My experience with men is that they can, more readily than women, forget past loves. I have no doubts that Walter loved Lavinia deeply during their thirty years of marriage (indeed, I am hoping he did, for it would have taught him how to love)—but now he loves *me*, and that is all that matters.''

''You are right, of course. That *is* all that matters—but I am not as sure of David's heart as you are of Sir Walter's. I am, however, resolved to find out. Do you think you could learn to accept me as your daughter-in-law—permanently?''

Lady Susan's effusive response left no room for doubt. . . . Overjoyed at learning that Paige truly loved her son, she vowed to let David know immediately that he need no longer worry about his wife's rejection.

When nuncheon had passed and there was no word from David, an anxious Paige ordered a carriage to take her to Lord Wolcott's. There she found Cedric slumped in a chair, looking chastened. Not even bothering with the usual social pleasantries, she briskly inquired if her husband had been there, and how long it had been since he'd left. Dispiritedly, Wolcott mumbled that Lord Penllyn had left some time ago to call on his cousin, so Paige set out for Sylvester's rooms.

It was with relief that she saw Johnson walking the earl's horses in front of Sylvester's lodgings. Almost before her own carriage had come to a stop, she leapt to the street to interrogate the groom. Johnson's news was reassuring; Penllyn appeared to be helping Sylvester pack for a trip abroad, and a message had been dispatched to Lady Undershaw. This last intelligence so intrigued Paige that it was with some difficulty that she restrained herself from entering the premises. Instead she returned to Berkeley Square to impatiently await her husband's arrival.

Restless and in need of distraction, Paige scanned the drawing room for something to occupy her. She ruled out embroidery, for though it would occupy her fingers, it would not divert her mind. As a last resort she picked up the three volumes Lady Susan had brought home from

Hookham's and was surprised to find among them Maria Edgeworth's *Tales from Fashionable Life*.

Paige was deeply engrossed in "The Absentee" when there was a gentle tap on the door. Annoyed, she ran through a mental list of people whose knocks were that timid and concluded with hope that it was Kit: she hadn't seen her all day, and she particularly wanted to advise her that she and David would not be attending Princess Esterhazy's soirée that evening.

It was not, however, Kit who entered at her bidding. Instead of the small form Paige expected, she found herself confronted with the tall, slender person of her maid, Sally—who seemed unnaturally subdued.

"Yes, Sally?" inquired Paige, mystified by her maid's seeking her out in the drawing room. Her puzzlement grew as Sally shuffled from one foot to the other and cleared her throat as if about to deliver a rehearsed speech.

"Is something amiss?"

This second question loosened Sally's tongue. "That I'm not sure of, ma'am. I hope you won't think me forward, but I was straightening the master's chamber when I discovered this envelope addressed to you. . . ."

Paige put her hand up to receive it, saying, "Oh, not forward at all. Quite proper of you to have brought it to me at once."

It had taken an hour of soul-searching for Sally to decide what action to take about the letter. She loved her mistress dearly and wanted her to be happy, but she could not help but be aware that there was something amiss with her marriage to the earl. Though they seemed companionable enough, it was apparent that they never shared the same bed.

Sally had found the letter quite by accident when emptying the master's dustbin and, as it had a crumpled appearance, was sure he had meant to destroy it. There had been another discarded envelope, but it was so torn that the addressee was unidentifiable. This made Sally wonder if the earl had not tried, several times, to compose a letter to his wife—with no success. Being of a romantic nature, she imagined that the earl was trying to reconcile in writing whatever differences had kept them in separate beds, and while *he* may not have been satisfied with his literary efforts, perhaps his wife would feel differently. . . .

Now actually standing before her mistress, she wondered if her fantasies had not gotten away from her and confessed, abashed, "Actually, to be honest, I found it in his dustbin," adding, "I hope I did right, ma'am."

Paige was so eager to get at the letter that she didn't consider giving even a token reprimand to her maid for her presumption. Instead she thanked her, broke open the seal, then remembered to dismiss her. In increasing agitation, she began to read:

Dearest Love,

If you are reading this, it means I will never see you again—a thought that shrivels my heart to contemplate. I had expected to be able to tell you this while gazing at your adorably revealing countenance, for I cannot know how you will receive this declaration—and wanted to know as soon as possible whether I could look forward to a lifetime of happiness or of gloom.

For you see, my dear wife, I have known these past several months that you are the love I've been seeking, and want to spend the rest of my life with. (Life? I am preoccupied with living, which will seem all too understandable to you, considering the circumstances under which you receive this.)

I suspect you already know of the deep joy I take in your company. It's wonderful to think that a chance meeting at a second-rate inn has led to my finding an enchanting sprite who stimulates me in so many ways: chess, political debates, riding, *communicating with the servants*—I do all these things better, just to keep up with you.

There are some other things, Paige, that I suspect I could do better with you than with anyone else, and it's taken a lot of restraint to not make use of the connecting door. But I won't bring a blush to your cheeks by elaborating on this theme. I can only regret (very much!) that the delivery of this note to you means I can never find out. . . .

You may be wondering why I waited till now to declare my feelings. Though I may be brave on the battlefield, I am a coward in love. Until recently I've felt Jerry possessed your heart, and I loved you enough to not wish to interfere in your happiness. But I can see now that Kit is a more likely wife for Jerry than you, and I hope you can forgive my saying so. My wish is that you may someday find someone you can love as much as I do you.

> With all my heart,
> David

P.S. "Maria" was my favourite *horse* on the Continent. I am sorry I deliberately misled you, but it gladdened my heart to think you might be jealous.

Sniffling her way through a second reading, Paige finally credited that her fondest desire had been fulfilled. Any activity was now futile, and she paced the room, periodically opening the door to the hallway at the slightest sound, hoping to find David striding toward her.

Eventually her vigilance was rewarded, for she heard the front door open and David's voice calling for her. Checking that her appearance was suitably enticing, she rushed into the hallway, prepared to fling herself into her husband's arms.

Her steps slowed and her smile faded as she took in the superfluous (but undeniably real) presence of Jerry and Kit, attired in riding habits. They had obviously just returned from the park and must have encountered David on the steps.

"Oh, there you are!" David greeted his wife cheerfully. "All is well—but let us all retire to the drawing room to discuss the particulars."

Though Paige wished Jerry and Kit at Jericho, she assumed the role of gracious hostess and rang for tea as the others settled into their chairs with an air of expectancy. David had just given a hint of the news he was about to impart to their two friends, and this was enough to whet their appetites.

Since David's tale could not be commenced until the servants had set out tea, Paige took the opportunity to report Lady Susan's joyous news. Kit gave a squeal of excitement, and David beamed broadly, saying, "But that's famous news indeed! I can't think of a better husband for my mother than Sir Walter."

Jerry interjected, "Or a better father-in-law for yourself. He is a great gun."

"So I know. He saved my life this morning. I guess he's decided the entire Owens family requires his protection." As Capper had withdrawn, after depositing the refreshments before Paige, David was immediately able to amplify this intriguing statement.

Paige was horrified to learn, during David's narrative, that the duel had been provoked by Wolcott's casting aspersions on her reputation. Wringing her hands, she cried huskily, "Oh, do not tell me that you almost lost your life over me! You are too good—I am not worthy of it."

David met her gaze, and for a moment it was as though there were only the two of them present. "On the contrary, it is only for *you* I would risk my life."

A sigh escaped Kit as she realized that the romantic fantasy she'd conjured up for Paige and the earl on the way to London was being played out before her eyes.

Her audible exhalation roused Paige and David from their trance. David then continued his story by describing his visits to Wolcott and Sylvester. David had had to force his way in to see his first quarry, who had left instructions that should the earl call he was not to be admitted. However, when confronted in his study, Wolcott had readily crumbled and confessed the entire scheme. Sylvester had promised to cancel Wolcott's debt if he provoked a duel with Penllyn. Cedric had been reluctant because he was a poor shot, but Sylvester had assured him with a wink that there was no way he could miss if he used the pistols that would be supplied. When David had pressed the point, Wolcott had admitted that he' had guessed the pistols had been tampered with and pleaded for the earl's understanding and forgiveness. Seizing the advantage, David had proposed a way Wolcott could make amends for his ignoble act: he would write a confession, implicating Sylvester, and sign it. This had been done with despatch, and the earl had left with the document in his pocket to pay a visit on Sylvester.

David had not anticipated that he would achieve his goal as easily with his cousin, who was skilled at wriggling out of tight corners, and had been surprised and a little wary at having been admitted at once.

Sylvester greeted him affably, inquiring about his health and the well-being of his family. David had to admire the man's audacity but was eager to get to the point.

"We're all well, no thanks to you, dear cousin," was David's reply.

Sylvester affected a puzzled expression and remarked blandly, "I do not take your meaning."

"Let us not fence with each other. I know all, and I have come with a proposition that I think will be satisfactory to all concerned. . . ."

Although Sylvester's eyes shifted at these words, he continued to pretend ignorance of his cousin's meaning. "I did not know, David, that your wound had affected your reasoning, but this conversation leads me to believe it is so."

"Then you may think Lord Wolcott similarly addled

when you read this document, though I doubt a magistrate
would agree with you,'' David countered. A line of worry
furrowed Sylvester's brow, and he reached for the proffered
document—which David pulled back at the last minute,
saying, ''I'm afraid I cannot trust it in your hands. Let us
read it together.''

Upon hearing the first paragraph, Sylvester was smart
enough to know that the game was up. Resignedly, he
asked what the ''proposition'' was. David quickly outlined
his terms. If Sylvester left the country this very day to
reside abroad permanently, taking with him Lady Undershaw,
David would pay him the sum of ten thousand pounds and
settle any outstanding debts. Wolcott's letter would be put
in a safe place, and if Sylvester ever returned to England,
it would be presented to a magistrate.

To his surprise, Sylvester found the plan appealing but
was concerned about one point. ''I am not sure that the
lady will accompany me. What of her marriage?''

''Her husband is contemplating divorce for reasons of
his own. Why not send a message 'round to Dorcas
proposing this flight?''

This was done. The messenger, having been instructed
to wait for an answer, returned within the hour with an
affirmative response written in an excited feminine hand.

David spent the remainder of the afternoon assisting in
the reconciling of accounts and left only after seeing
Sylvester and Dorcas on their way to the coast.

As David concluded his narrative to his three rapt
listeners, Paige jumped to her feet and exclaimed, ''Richard
must be informed at once, if it is not already too late—he
is about to leave for Waverly!''

As though on cue, Capper flung open the door and
announced, ''Sir Richard Undershaw.'' Entering the room
in great perturbation, Richard was oblivious to everyone
but Paige.

Upon seeing Sir Richard, David gestured to Capper to

bring some brandy and glasses. While David poured him a large drink, Richard explained in distress, "She's gone. I returned from White's to find the house in an uproar. Dorcas has packed her belongings and left—I know not why or where, for she left no message."

As Richard took a swallow from his glass, Paige began to make all known to her brother.

As the story unfolded, Richard was assailed by two opposing emotions. On the one hand he was humiliated that his wife had run off with another man; and on the other he was exhilarated that the way was now clear to pay his addresses to Cornelia. After he had vacillated between the two for several moments, the latter eventually won out. Cautiously, he sounded out the group as to the suitability of his seeking out Cornelia at once to declare himself. As the reaction was unanimously in favor of his doing so (with Miss Roche the most vociferous advocate), Richard left to visit his love.

Before the remaining foursome had an opportunity to comment on Richard's situation, Capper reappeared to announce with obvious pleasure, "It wants but an hour till dinner, and as it's to be a special one in honor of Lady Susan's betrothal, I thought an early reminder would not be taken amiss."

"Good God!" Jerry vociferated. "Is it that late? I'll scarcely have time to change into my finery (must look my best for Princess Esterhazy's tonight), order some posies for the blushing bride-to-be, and get back in time for the preprandial sherry. I'm off, then," he added unnecessarily, brushing a curl from Kit's forehead as he passed her chair.

The others decided to follow his example and headed upstairs. Paige was hoping to at last steal a few moments alone with her husband, but as Kit's chamber was just beyond theirs, they were accompanied right to their doors.

Likewise, David had been wanting to find some private time with his wife. Dressing hurriedly, but with results that Brummell himself could not have faulted, he knocked on their connecting door. Paige's seemingly delighted, *"Entres, mon cher!"* was encouraging, but his subsequent sally into her room was stopped short by the sight of Lady Susan ensconced in a comfortable chair.

"Mother!" he choked, trying to hide his dismay. "You look lovely! No wonder Sir Walter popped the question." Changing the direction of his steps, he crossed the room and dropped a kiss atop her snowy head. "I didn't think he'd be able to resist those violet eyes for long. They certainly always brought *me* to heel."

"Oh, you silver-tongued flatterer! Let us carry on this flirtation out of the hearing distance of your wife. I have much to tell you."

Paige stared longingly after her husband as the pair exited from the room and allowed a very unladylike expletive of frustration to escape her lips. She knew that no other occasion for intimate conversation with David would present itself again until long after dinner.

And indeed this proved to be true, as champagne toasts to the newly betrothed couple before, during, and after dinner extended the celebration late into the night. She might as well have gone to Princess Esterhazy's soiree (as Jerry and Kit had done), for all the privacy this evening at home held. Sir Walter had no sooner taken his leave, and Lady Susan retired to her chamber, than Richard and Cornelia arrived to share their bliss with their closest friends.

Though the secret of their love for each other would have to be kept for many months (until the divorce proceedings could be completed), David had his doubts that they'd be able to keep it quiet for long. They couldn't stop gazing into each other's eyes and touching each other, as though to reassure themselves of their good fortune. Their joy was worthy of another round of champagne toasts, and Paige found that her head was beginning to swim. Ringing the bell, she asked Capper to provide some coffee.

After two cups, she started to feel more the thing and brightened as Cornelia and Richard announced their departure. Promising Cornelia that she would pay a morning call on the following day, Paige hustled her brother and future sister-in-law unceremoniously to the door, then turned to face her husband.

As though in slow motion, they moved toward one another, and just as David's arms reached out to encircle his wife, the door burst open and Hadley appeared with Kit in tow. One look at their faces and David pulled the bell for more champagne.

Kit sat on the settee, glowing, while Jerry disjointedly extolled, "Just what I need to keep me in line . . . musical voice . . . lovely red hair . . . wonderful with children."

"Jerry!" chastised an embarrassed Kit. This prompted her fiancé of several minutes to snuggle down on the settee next to her and plant a kiss on her ear. Another weak protest escaped her but was silenced immediately by her intended, who firmly covered her lips with his own.

Though happy for her friend, Paige viewed this scene with a jaundiced eye. She had had her fill of other peoples' romances and now longed only for her own. But it would be bad form to refuse champagne in their honor, so she resignedly hoisted her glass, said all that was appropriate, and swallowed several sips. As Jerry loosened his collar and casually flung his leg over the arm of the settee as though settling in for a long stay, Paige gave up any hope of seeing her evening's plans realized. Pleading fatigue, which was all too true due to the quantity of champagne she'd consumed, Paige retired to her chamber, where she had every intention of collapsing, fully clothed, onto her bed. Sally, however, would not allow it, and Paige soon found herself attired in a scarlet satin nightdress with her freshly brushed hair about her shoulders. Tucking her mistress comfortably under the counterpane, Sally blew out the candle and quietly departed.

Below, and equally disappointed, David managed to rid

himself of the ebullient Jerry without seeming inhospitable. Vowing to invade Paige's chamber at first light to resolve once and for all their future as a couple, David entered his room wearily, wanting now only the solace of his bed. Even this was to be denied him, for, pulling aside the hangings, he was faced with the realization that his evening was not yet at an end. There on the quilt was Snow and, amazingly, a miniature version of "him" suckling.

David could not help chuckling. Leaning down to stroke the new mother's head, he whispered, "So much for *my* powers of observation. I have severely misjudged your gender! Perhaps your mistress was more discerning." Without a second thought, he went to rouse his wife.

Hearing Penllyn's voice, Paige at first thought she was dreaming—until she felt him shake her shoulders. "What is it?" she exclaimed, startled at his presence at her bedside in the middle of the night.

"Come quickly. Snow is in need of a midwife."

Although these words made no sense, Paige allowed herself to be led into her husband's chamber, where in the firelight she could discern Snow cleaning a second kitten. Softly she smiled at David and whispered, "He's doing fine by himself—I mean *her*self."

Silently, in awe, they watched the birth of the third kitten. Sometime during this event Paige discovered that David's arm was about her shoulders. When no more kittens appeared and Snow seemed comfortably settled, Paige, now more awake than at any time in her life, cast a wicked glance at the tall figure by her side. Saucily she said (forgetting to bat her eyelashes, though she'd intended to when this moment came), "Your bed appears to be undeniably occupied. We must find you other accommodations. Alas, I am afraid the guest rooms have no fresh linens. But, as we are legally wed, I don't suppose there could be any harm in our sharing my bed for the night."

In a flash, David scooped her up in his arms, kicked open the connecting door as if it were made of paper (resolving to have it removed from its hinges the next day), and proposed, ''How about sharing it for the rest of our lives?'' But he gave her no opportunity to answer, for his mouth closed over hers. Her response left no need for words.